M000086386

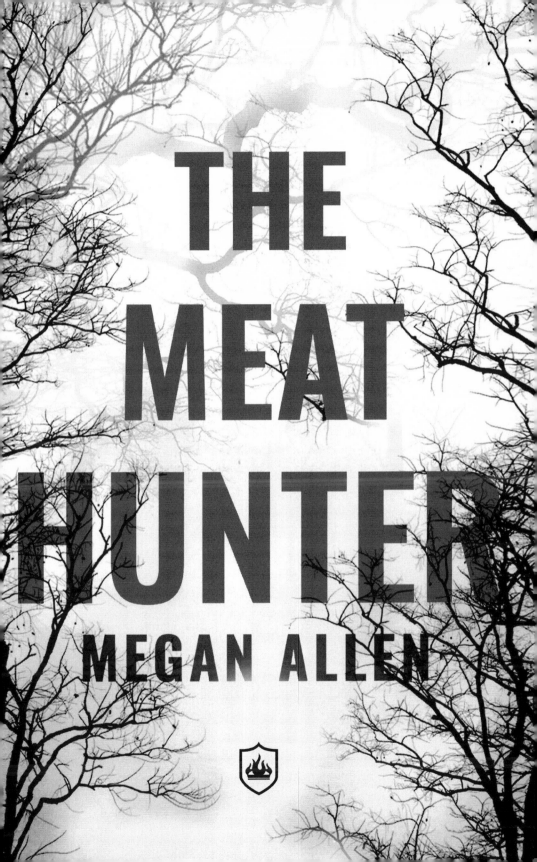

THE MEAT HUNTER

MEGAN ALLEN

This is a work of fiction. Names, characters, businesses, places, events and incidents are either the products of the author's imagination or used in a fictitious manner. Any resemblance to actual persons, living or dead, or actual events is purely coincidental.

Published in the United States by

BURN HOUSE PUBLISHING
ATLANTA GEORGIA

1050 Crown Pointe Parkway, Atlanta, Ga. 30338
www.burnhousepublishing.com

Copyright © 2019 Megan Allen

Jacket and book design by Chelsea Jewell

Names: Allen, Megan, author.
Title: The Meat Hunter/ by Megan Allen
Description: First hardcover edition. | Georgia : Burn House Publishing, 2019.
Identifiers: ISBN-13: 978-0-9990548-4-0 | ISBN-10: 0-9990548-4-8
Subjects: BISAC: FICTION / Action & Adventure. | FICTION / Thrillers / Crime. | FICTION / Mystery / Detective.

If you'd like to contact the author with comments, or find out about her life or future projects, she'd love to hear from you at meganallen012@yahoo.com.

If you'd like to contact the author or publisher with comments, we'd love to hear from you at asklucy@burnhousepublising.com.

MANUFACTURED IN THE UNITED STATES OF AMERICA

First Edition

Dedicated to the second pig in line. The one who must watch, and wait, and know.

BOOMER'S PORK'N PIGS

AMERICA'S PREMIER PRODUCER OF BELLIES AND WHOLE HOGS

HOME
OF THE
HAPPY HOG

Fresh as it Gets

100%
NATURAL

Ol'Fashion Meat

ESTD.1956

Bacon

Sausages

Porkchops

Hogs Delivered Daily, Live or Processed

www.boomersporknpigs.com

AN ACTUAL RECORDED TRANSCRIPT
Two men inside a barn on an Iowa pig farm

One man points at a wall some distance away. "I'll bet I can bank this little runt bastard off that wall and into the barrel."

"No way," says another man. "That's over thirty feet."

"Bet you ten bucks." The first man reaches down and extracts a tiny newborn pig from a bucket. The pig squeals, its head twisting as its new eyes try to focus in on the man who holds it.

"You're on. Ten bucks." The second man nods his head thoughtfully. "But if you make it, I get a chance to tie."

The first man grins wickedly as he takes a slight step backwards to gain leverage for the toss, then leaps forward and flings the runt mightily across the barn. The pig screams as the wall rushes at it, but then comes the squishing sound of impact, followed by a second, solid thump as the runt smashes into the bottom of the barrel. "Yes!" calls out the first man triumphantly. "Top that, you sunovabitch."

The second man walks over and peers inside the barrel. "It's still alive, I think," he says, as he reaches down to poke at the baby pig.

"Well you better hurry the hell up then. If he's dead it don't count."

CHAPTER ONE

TWENTY YEARS AGO

The little girl lay sprawled out in the very last pen on the very last row of the stock yard. She lay half on hardened ground— with a few bits of straw scattered here and there to make it appear less hard— and half on a giant boar hog. She clutched tightly to the boar's neck, great rivulets of tears pouring down her cheeks where they splashed onto the side of the hog's face, and then down its cheeks as well.

"I know, Daddy. I know." She cried out at a big, rough looking man who stood close by.

The man's face also showed pain, as he remembered a lost day from his own youth, but just beyond the pain was a stiff wall of resolution. "We've talked about this, Molly," the man said as firmly as he could. "We've talked about it. You knew this day was coming."

"I know, Daddy, I know." Her face brightened suddenly as an idea came to her. One hand left the hog, with tiny fingers reaching out to tug at the man's jeans. "Hey," she said, her voice a quivering but hopeful thing, "I have an idea. We can bring him back next week. Next week, Daddy. Let's do it next week."

"No, Molly." The man reached down to pull her away. His hand found her arm and began to tug at it, while her other arm tried desperately to wrap itself around the neck of the boar. "Enough!" said the man sternly. He yanked harshly then, causing her to lose grip, and her contact with the boar was broken. As he carried her away, she turned her head, burying it deeply into his shoulder. But her eyes stayed high, fighting for one last glimpse of her friend.

"No," she moaned softly, "no." Then they turned a corner and were gone.

PRESENT DAY

It was the first day of hunting season. Molly Bishop's favorite day. She lay flattened to the ground, stretched out on a slight rise, a small mound of tumbled rock and earth which time had thought to place there. The early morning air was cold, and very still. A clump of scrub oak grew from the top of the rise, overlooking a clearing, and it was behind this cluster of stunted trees she concealed herself. And waited. Across the clearing, and not too distant, stood another rise, another mound of rock, and beyond that, another. It was a valley of intense geology, with mounds and boulders strewn about so thickly that one could walk in a straight line only a few paces before slamming into one. In between the rises and the boulders were small patches of grass, tiny meadows. It was upon one of these open places she now concentrated her gaze. And continued her wait. Finally there was a movement, ever so slight, as a few wisps of tall grass at the edge of the meadow began to bend outward, away from one another. Molly stiffened. Her index finger slid inside the trigger guard, pressing lightly, while a thumb extended upward, finding the safety and clicking it to the off position. She had barely finished when a doe, eyes wide with caution, took a few tentative steps into the open. It stood there, body frozen while its head swung slowly around, scanning the surrounding area. Finally, after a long pause, its ears pushed forward, its tail lifted, and it snorted, a wheezing, sneezing sound which shot out from its nostrils a visible blast of steam. Molly softened. Her body relaxed, her finger moving away from the trigger, but her eyes held steady, focusing in first on the doe, then on the area of tall grass from which it had just emerged. She didn't have long to wait. Soon there was more rustling, more bending grass, and a magnificent buck rose up. The male deer studied his female, a few steps out in front of him. Sensing she was in no danger, he also moved cautiously into the meadow. They stood side by side, the doe looking off to the right, while the buck studied the terrain to the left.

Molly's sensory system was now fully awakened. Adrenaline raced through her body. Her mouth went dry, the moisture sucked away in anticipation of the moment. The rifle came up, not too quickly, but purposefully, an eye clamped against the aperture of the scope as the crosshairs found their target. They centered on the buck's head, or more precisely a portion of the head just below the point where the base of the antlers enter the skull. She breathed in and out, slowly and evenly, willing her body into a deep state of relaxation despite the raging level of excitement her physiology was demanding of her. The scope never wavered. Years of training and years of putting that training into use had turned her into a highly competent hunter. Shifting slightly, the crosshairs moved away from the buck's head, edging gently down its neck, caressing their way across a shoulder until they paused again at a place where the shoulder rippled inward, meeting the ribcage. This marked the soft tissue entry point directly into the heart. She smiled then, a warm smile, and the scope moved on. It swept its way across the midsection of the animal, then past the hind-quarters, finally leaving the deer entirely and beginning a slow arc across the meadow and along the sides of a narrow gorge which cascaded down from a low hill off to one side. The crosshairs moved faster now, almost frantically so. Suddenly her eye caught an anomaly. The scope paused, and retraced slightly. And there it was. A man, laying out among the rocks of the gorge, blending in almost perfectly. This man also had a rifle, and it pointed directly at the deer in the meadow. Molly smiled again, but this time not as warmly, the crosshairs moving in to focus on the man's face. There was nothing distinctive about him. He was just a man. His lips curled upwards slightly and began to twitch, and there was something eager and evil about them. As she watched, the man's eyes widened and filled with a bloodlust as he visualized the kill. Her finger again found the trigger and began a slow, steady compression. One second later the valley reverberated with the sound of a blast and the man's face imploded, his nose crushed inward by the force of a bullet smashing its way deeply into his brain. The body lay there quivering for a moment, then slipped into a niche among the rocks where it disappeared from sight. Molly rose, and stood there for a time. She glanced back at the meadow where the two deer had been. They were gone. "Run, my babies," she whispered. Then she slung the rifle over her shoulder, climbed down from the rise, and lost herself among the tall grass, boulders and trees.

CHAPTER TWO

Some hours later, Molly drove steadily east, away from the boulder strewn canyons of Colorado and onto the lower plains of Kansas. She'd been signal free and phone free for the past few days, sneaking away to the mountains for some relaxation and rejuvenation. It was a journey she cherished and managed to work into her schedule every month or so. A soft blue light began to flash from the dashboard, and she tapped a button on the steering wheel.

"Molly here," she said, then brightened as a familiar voice came back at her.

"What the hell, Mol?" It was her employer and best friend, Carl Monroe. His voice trembled slightly, filled with both irritation and concern. "I hate it when you run away like this."

Molly laughed lightly. "I'm not running away, silly. I just checked into a spa for a few days. There's nothing like a good massage and an avocado wash to brighten one's outlook on life. You should try it. Might make you a bit more hospitable, and a bit less of an ass."

Carl cleared his throat, trying to chase away his growing frustration. "Look, I've just made a great contact, and we've got a chance at a really big client here. I need you on this." He paused. "Where the hell are you anyway?"

Molly also paused, calculating some math and considering some options. Finally she replied, "Where do you want me to be?"

"Dammit, Molly, where are you?"

"Saint Louis?" Her lie was a question, one laid out quickly and efficiently. "Or somewhere really close to there."

"What does that even mean? God, you're frustrating."

Reaching into her purse, Molly extracted a lip gloss, strawberry colored and strawberry flavored. Elevating her head, she leaned over and pursed her lips, pouting them as they pouted back prominently from the rear view mirror. She had this driving and applying makeup down to a science. As she applied the gloss her voice became muffled.

"Look, just tell me where you need me to be."

"Gallant, Kansas. Way the hell out on Highway 70." Carl paused, listening, then said, "What are you doing? Sounds like you're playing with a male stripper."

Molly smacked her lips together, licking them lightly. "I'm not sure," she said, laughing delightedly. "But it tastes like strawberries."

"You're a slut."

"And you're a man whore. But in the morning when you wake up, I'll still be a slut."

"What?"

"I don't know." She continued to laugh. "It worked for Churchill. Something like that anyway. But hey, send me all the juicy details and I can be in Gallant in an hour."

"An hour? How the hell can you get from Saint Louis to the middle of Kansas in an hour?"

"Good genetics, I'm thinkin'. Now text me the address and whatever else I need to know, and let me get back to my stripper."

An hour later she pulled her Camry off the main highway onto a side road, passing through a gate and under an arch with a sign that read, *Boomer's Pork and Pigs*. Tucked beneath that sign was another that proclaimed, *America's Premier Producer of Bellies and Whole Hogs*. Boomer's had a reputation, quite infamously, of being one of the most inhumane breeders and suppliers of pork products in the country. They were always on the radar, closely watched by activists and moralists alike, but they made up for their seeming lack of morality with sheer enthusiasm. More than thirty thousand hogs were raised here annually, housed in a group of long metal buildings that served as holding, breeding and slaughtering units. Molly drove past the buildings, which clung closely to the roadside and turned into a lot at the very end of the row. A small trailer sat there, parked beneath what appeared to be the only tree on the farm. A tall, not bad looking young man moved out from the trailer to greet her as she stepped from the car. The stench of pig and pig waste filled her nostrils. She nodded at the man. "Molly Bishop," she said, extending her hand. "McMillan Pharmaceuticals. I have an appointment with Mister Tignor."

The young man's eyes began an appraisal of her body, starting at ground level and working their way up until they stopped abruptly at around her breasts. It did not displease her. It was part of his programming to appraise her, and part of hers to revel in it, so her smile broadened at this moment of compatibility as the two shook hands. "You sure are pretty, ma'am," said the young man. "And yes, we've been expecting you."

"You're Mister Tignor?" There was a touch of surprise in her voice.

"Well, yes ma'am. I mean, sort of. But it's my father you want to speak to. I'm just Danny." The young man stepped back and turned, pointing at the nearest in the long row of buildings across the road. "He's waitin' for us."

Molly reached out, taking the man's arm as he began to lead her away. Her touch was tender and meaningful. "I don't think you're just Danny," she said, her eyes playing with his.

The building they soon arrived at, the one where the senior Mister Tignor waited, was the slaughtering unit. Even before Danny opened the door to escort her inside the stench of blood and meat began to flood the air around them. "I hope you don't mind the stink, ma'am," said Danny, showing a touch of embarrassment. "After you been around here as long as I have you don't notice it much, but I know it's bad."

Molly continued her grip on Danny's arm, even tightening it a little. "No, it's fine," she said. "I was raised on a farm like this. I like it."

Reaching her free hand up to his face, she swept a wisp of hair from his forehead, her eyes now piercing into his. "It's very… manly." The young man blushed openly, and escorted her inside. They entered from the west end of the building, often referred to as the *fresh end*, as it was where the live hogs sat and waited before being shuffled down the line. There were several large ventilation holes cut into the walls at this end, allowing the afternoon west winds to blow freely through, reducing the stench of butchered pigs being processed just to the east. And being here, with a breeze always blowing away from them, the live hogs were never able to fully grasp the significance of what this particular day had in store. So they stayed fairly calm, tricked into a state of complacency. Several dozen of the animals now milled around them nervously. One, a young boar, moved over quite close, reaching out its snout to sniff at Molly's feet. She kicked at it aggressively. "Filthy pig," she called out. She looked at Danny who glanced back at her, his face showing surprise, then delight at her reaction.

He kicked savagely at another nearby pig and began to march forward through the hogs, clearing a path for them. He moved clumsily, but purposefully, from one to the next, delivering blow after blow as the animals scattered. Molly followed along, laughing joyously, her hand clinging to his shoulder. They came to a gated wall, designed to block the view of the actual slaughtering from the still live pigs. Danny swung open the gate and they moved into a new chamber, this one comprised of two narrow chutes. One chute lay empty, but the other had a line of shoats, just weaned young pigs, crammed into it. Molly stopped and pointed. "You're killing babies here. Where's the profit in that?"

The comment amused the young man, and he reached up to scratch his head. "Special order. Some of my dad's friends. They like the young ones for roastin' whole. You just stick'em in a broiler and pop'em on the table. Tender little buggers." They moved closer to the chute, where another man stood on an elevated platform against a far wall, and just above the hogs. He turned to face them as they approached, holding out a long, metal tipped rod in Molly's direction.

"You wanna zap one, ma'am?" the man asked, grinning widely. "I've got them all lined up here for you."

"Don't be a wiseass, Smitty," said Danny. "She's a lady." As he spoke Molly stepped forward, relieved the man of the rod and leaned out over a low railing. One of the shoats, the smallest and the one nearest, looked up at her and backed away. Molly thrust the rod at the pig like a man staving off a snake with a spear. A short, powerful jab. As the tip of the rod made contact an electric charge ignited, and the young piglet was knocked quickly off its feet to the ground. It lay there for a moment on its side, with legs twitching and a wash of drool beginning to flow from its mouth. The man called Smitty jumped down from the platform, grabbed a grappling hook hanging just overhead, and sank two points of the hook deeply into the pig's hindquarters. The animal struggled briefly, crying out as Smitty yanked on a line of cordage attached to the hook, and the shoat was hoisted aloft. It hung there, upside down and still twitching, so Molly stepped forward and jabbed at it again. The pig screamed once and went limp. It hung there lifeless, a small splatter of blood and drool dripping from its mouth. Danny looked over at Molly in amazement. "Damn, girl. You got balls. You can work for me anytime."

A voice sounded from behind. "You kids got nuthin' better to do than play games?" Molly turned, and was confronted by a giant of a man. He stood in the doorway of an adjoining chamber, a gnarled, weathered hulk, his face bearded and grizzled, like that of a mountain man about to ascend his final mountain. The man spoke again. "You Miss Bishop?"

Molly glanced at Danny, young, handsome, vibrant, standing close by. There was no resemblance between the two she could see. She smiled, stepping forward to greet the man.

"Yes, sir. Molly Bishop. From McMillan." She bit down on her lip and flashed a challenge at the old man. "I've come to make your life a whole lot more profitable, Mister Tignor."

The man stared hard at her for a moment, then glanced at his son, who was also staring. "You're pretty," he said finally, echoing Danny's words. "But that don't mean a damn to me. It's been my experience that workin' with a woman is a helluva lot less profitable than workin' with a good sow. So state your business."

"Wow," thought Molly, her mind sweeping back to a more primitive time. "How pleasantly Neanderthal." She stepped closer to Tignor, and then even closer, until she was near enough to touch the big man. She smiled at him. "That's exactly what my daddy used to say. Except he would always add a sow puts money on the table while a woman just fritters it away." Reaching out, she ran a hand across his sleeve, high up near his shoulder, picking at a loose straw. "My father was very close to his pigs."

Tignor squinted, trying to reason with her words. "Well I ain't that close," he said. "But I do like a profit. What's this big deal your boss is tellin' me about?"

Molly turned and moved back over to where the shoat hung, still dripping a mixture of blood and saliva from its open mouth. She reached out and playfully poked at it, causing the dead hog to sway back and forth at a level even with her head. Tignor, his son, and the worker Smitty, all turned to stare. "This is a photo op," she said with a grin as the shoat brushed against her face. "A girl and her pig."

"That's some sick shit," said Smitty in a voice so low no one heard him.

Molly then asked to be shown the breeding area, which turned out to be an indoor arena of sorts, placed off to one side in a building behind the others. There were a series of pens set down against each interior wall of the structure, with a narrow walkway running between them. Like a hallway running among enclosed cubicles. In each of the pens sat, stood or lay a huge boar, most of them contentedly chewing on small clusters of cob corn while they waited for the arrival of the females. The old man signaled Smitty, who retreated through a gate.

"Well this is it," said Tignor. "The fun room, where all my big boys come to play." He looked purposefully at Molly. "Now I have no idea what your intentions are, but I certainly hope you haven't come here to waste my time. Just how in the hell do you propose to make me money?"

Molly reached into a clutch dangling from her waist. She retrieved a small vial that appeared to be filled with a clear fluid. Shaking the bottle in her hand, she held it up to eye level. "This," she said. "Our new miracle. What's your insemination rate here at Boomer's, Mister Tignor? Seventy-five, eighty percent?"

The old man shook his head. "I don't know exactly. Probably closer to eighty. I'm not all about the science here, lady. We breed'em and birth'em, raise'em and slaughter'em. Science is a young man's game." He glanced at his son. "Unless you're raisin' an idiot." Danny winced as his father continued. "If you've come here to sell me some kind of new breedin' concoction you're wastin' your time. It's been tried before." Tignor waved his hands around expansively. "I've got boars and I've got sows. We put'em together and they screw when they're ready, and we butcher'em when we're ready. Not meanin' any disrespect, but we been doin' it this way for thirty years. I got no time for science." Molly lowered her hand, the vial now dangling between her fingers. Her lips twisted, but just for a moment.

"I want to show you something," she said, her voice boring into the old man. "I think even you'll get it. Unless you just like throwing money away. I wonder if you have any sows ready for breeding now. Right now."

Tignor's face stiffened as he tried to be offended. But when he considered it, he wasn't certain he was supposed to be, so he became somewhat subdued instead. He ordered Danny to bring in some sows, and while they waited he reappraised the young lady standing before him. She was more than just pretty, having a quality that allowed her to put a man in his place without him feeling too badly about it.

Soon, a dozen sows were ushered into the chamber and further pushed into the farthest pen, the largest, which as of yet had no boar. Smitty had also returned with Tignor's son, and the two went to one of the near pens, both carrying batons which they used to convince a large boar hog to leave its corn and enter the breezeway. The boar was reluctant at first, ignoring most of the blows while it waddled slowly forward. Then it caught sight of the sows. The giant hog rushed forward, nearly knocking Smitty down as it moved in to cover the females. As most of them scattered screaming around the edges of the pen, the boar trapped one against a metal railing, slamming into and mounting it at the same time. The sow squealed as she tried to escape, but the railing and the weight of the boar held her fast. Meanwhile, Molly pulled from her pocket a tiny metal spray can. With the three others looking on she entered the pen and began to roam among the pigs. She noticed one in particular that was intent on putting some of the other sows between it and the boar. She reached out, spraying a small orange patch on the sow's hindquarters, and turned to face the three men. "This one won't be bred," she stated confidently. She then moved along to each of the corners where more sows cowered. Her hand reached out again, and the spray misted out onto another of the females. In a very short time she sprayed two others, bringing the total of orange spotted females to four of the twelve. "Watch them, gentlemen. Watch them carefully. They won't be bred today." She moved away then, to a side of the enclosure where the men waited.

"You gotta be kiddin'," said old man Tignor. "He'll tear them apart. I don't know what you think you know, young lady, but my boar there is gonna bang the hell out of them girls in about thirty minutes flat. They may not all get impregnated, but they all get him. The twenty percent fail rate don't come from lack of tryin'. It comes from infertile females."

Molly stepped over closer to the big man. "Why don't we make it interesting," she said with a sly grin. "I'll bet you a hundred bucks that boar you're so proud of doesn't even get to mount one of the sows I've marked."

Old man Tignor looked smugly at Molly. He looked out at the boar, just now finishing up with its first conquest and moving on to another terrified sow. He glanced at his son, Danny, and the two exchanged their own grins, just as sly. "You're on missy. Like I said before, you're pretty, I'll give you that."

For the next forty-five minutes Molly and the three men sat transfixed as the boar mounted sow after sow. There was one brief moment, near the end, when one of the painted females appeared trapped, squished up against two others when the boar lunged at it. But at the last instant the sow managed to wriggle between the two, and merged its way into the mass. Finally, the boar staggered off into a corner and collapsed. It had done all it could to carry on the bloodline for the farm. At least for that day it had. "Well, I'll be goddamned," said the old man. "How is that even possible?" He looked at Molly, confusion and amusement playing at his face simultaneously. "Is it the paint?"

"No," Molly laughed aloud. "It has nothing to do with paint. It's simply a fact of nature that's been in front of you all along. Farm breeding isn't like natural breeding. The kind you find out in the wild. Out in nature, when a female is ready she signals a male and the sex is at least somewhat consensual. Here, the females are given no opportunity to suggest they'd like to play. They are thrown into a cage and some screw-happy hog-daddy comes along to tame them. In society, the bastard would get life. Here he's rewarded with corn and all the girls he can handle." Molly paused, noticing the men were all transfixed on her. "One other thing you need to understand. Pigs aren't dumb. In fact some of them have been outsmarting you for years. It takes only a bit of simple observation to pick out in any group of sows the few that are obstinate enough and crafty enough to outwit any boar you might throw at them. You can tell who they are right away. They're always on the fringes, a bit antisocial, but when danger or unpleasant circumstance arises they are the first to blend into the middle of the herd. The first to put others between them- selves and discomfort. Usually it's around three of twelve who have a strong enough *not today* mentality to avoid unpleasantness. Today it was four. Better for my demonstration, and better for you to under- stand the possibilities. You produce around thirty thousand bellies a year, I am told. It could be thirty-five, even forty. With no increase in breeding stock, and minimal extra expense, you're turning down over a half-million dollars in additional revenue. It's really quite staggering if you think about it."

"That's just crazy." Tignor scratched at his head. "You tellin' me

all the sows we been butcherin' up for failin' to produce have just
been avoidin' the boars? That's just crazy."

"No, sir. It's not crazy at all. As I'm about to demonstrate, it's
simply a fact." Molly looked at Danny. "Danny, would you do me a
favor and walk in with the sows and try to touch one of the ones I've
marked?" Danny looked at her, puzzled. "Please," she said.

The old man nodded at his son, and the young Tignor climbed
the low railing and entered the pen. All eyes focused on the sows with
the orange splotches. They made an immediate statement. As Danny
approached, the dozen sows began to mill around nervously, each
trying to establish some avenue of escape. When none was presented
to them, they continued to mill. The four painted ones, however, all
pushed deeply into the pile, quickly secluding themselves between the
railings and the other pigs, and safely out of reach. "Stop," hollered
out Molly as Danny froze in the middle of the pen. "Now obviously
Danny can force his way among the sows and get to the four. And
just as obviously they have nowhere to run. But a boar has no way
to know any of this. He has a whole pile of waiting ladies between
himself and the hiding sows, and that's good enough for him. So
for the whole breeding cycle those four simply move about, always
keeping a more tempting target between themselves and the male.
It's a game of hide and seek, and some of your sows are very good
at hiding. As I said before, they ain't dumb."

"Sunovabitch," said the old man, smacking his lips together
impressively. "So a lot of my sows aren't infertile at all, just crafty."

"That's right. It's very seldom a sow will fail to bear, especially
in the first five years. But we noticed in tests some time ago that
many of them are just too smart to be bred. Given the chance, I
believe we can revolutionize what you're doing here."

Tignor held up a hand. "But if they're so damn smart, just how
in the hell do you suppose we're gonna get the boars to them? We
ain't tyin'em down."

"I hear you." Molly moved up quite close to the old man, and
though he towered above her, they still managed to lock eyes. "That
wouldn't work anyway. That's why sedating them also doesn't work. A

sow needs to be upright, and if not quite willing, at least manageable. It's been a problem for years. Some producers have turned to inseminating artificially, but frankly, that requires a lot more work and the results, due to improper application, are going to be about the same as what you're seeing now." Molly produced from her pocket the clear liquid vial she'd shown them earlier. She held it out in front of her face. "That's why I've brought you this. Our little miracle."

"A drug?" The old man shook his head. "I told you we've tried all that stuff before. It just knocks the ladies out and they lie there on their sides, makin' it impossible for a boar to work'em over." Danny and Smitty exchanged a glance, nodding at one another as they shared a secret. Molly caught the exchange, her eyes flashing at them.

"It's not a knock-out drug. Or a rape drug." Smitty giggled as Molly continued. "It's more of an inducer, a relaxer. Once the sows have a taste of this they will still be fully capable of resisting, they just won't want to." She moved away from the men, to a bin located against a nearby wall. Reaching in, she extracted an ear of corn. "Watch this and learn," she said as she reentered the pen. She paused long enough to sprinkle a few drops of liquid from the vial onto the corn, then stooped low, until her eyes were at the same level as those of the sows. She moved easily among them, and whereas the pigs had scattered frantically at the approach of the men, Molly was allowed to not only merge with them, but to touch and stroke them, the whole while her voice calling out in a soothing chant. She approached the first of the marked pigs and offered it a taste of the corn. The sow's snout thrust forward and sniffed for a moment, as Molly continued to coo away at it. Finally reassured that her intrusion was a friendly one, the sow began to nibble away at the cob. "Watch this one closely," she said. She then rose gently and backed away to where the men waited.

All three watched intently, and the old man spoke out. "A couple bites of that corn isn't gonna mean anythin'. The last stuff we tried we had to inject into them. And at a helluva lot higher dosage."

Molly looked smugly at the old man. "I said watch and learn.

This has the potential to be a very profitable day for you. Or it might just turn out to be profitable for me. You already owe me a hundred bucks." She extended her hand. "You wanna go double or nothing?"

Tignor smiled wryly. "You've got a lotta mean in you, lady."

Molly turned to Danny, who was still intently watching the sow. "Why don't you go see how that pig responds to you now?" she asked. Danny shrugged, grinning at the others.

"What? You want me to go in there and screw her?" His grin widened as Smitty began to laugh.

"No," Molly looked back at him, her face expressionless. "Not unless that's your preference. What I want you to do is interact with her. A few minutes ago she was scared to death of you. They all were. Go in there now and see what she thinks of you."

The grin quickly left Danny's face. "I got no preference for pigs," he stated gruffly, while Smitty continued to laugh. He moved then, back in amongst the sows. Instantly they panicked, crashing into the railings, fighting to stay as far away from him as they could. Molly could only wonder at the sort of treatment they were used to in the confines of their cages. Only one pig failed to respond with the others. The marked one Molly had treated with corn. It stood there sedately while the other sows rushed madly about. As Danny approached, it turned its head to look at him, its tail twitching, but made no move to dash around with the others. He brought a baton out from a holster attached to his belt, whacking the sow solidly across its shoulders. It moved slightly, trembling, but stood its ground. He whacked it again, this time hard enough to cause the pig to stumble. It fell to its knees, sat there for a second, then rose and stood once again firmly in place, waiting for more punishment to be meted out.

Tignor's mouth fell open. "Well if that's not the damdest thing I've ever seen," he said, a hand reaching up to scratch his beard. "You could gang rape that bitch right here and she'd hang around for a second run." He shook his head. "Unbelievable."

Molly grimaced, but turned away to hide it. "Nice visual," she said. "I can come by next week and train your workers how to apply this stuff. It'll cost around twenty-grand a session, maybe three or four times a year. But the monetary rewards will be astounding. You'll be the first major player we'll be giving it to. That'll give you a nice edge." She then reached out her hand and held it there while Tignor did some calculations. Finally he reached his own out in an attempt to shake. Molly quickly knocked the hand aside. "I'm not looking to shake your hand," she said. "We both know the deal is too good to pass up." Her hand poked out again. "I'm waiting for my hundred bucks."

Later, as Danny walked her to the car, Molly once again took possession of his arm. She intertwined it with her own and spun around to kiss his cheek as he opened the door for her. "I like you, Danny," she said boldly. Her eyes bore into his. "I hope you don't think I'm being too forward."

"No, ma'am," said Danny, excitement beginning to rise in him. "I like you too. A lot." His face lowered and he stammered slightly, exposing a bit of shyness. "I've never met anyone like you before."

"Good." Molly smiled, her hands moving up to caress his chest. "Sometimes it's fun to just go for what you want." She pushed away then, and slid into the driver's seat. "I'm staying in town tonight, at the Stockman's." Her voice saddened. "All by myself. How sad is that?" Biting down on her lip, she swung the door closed, pouted sweetly at Danny, and drove away.

CHAPTER THREE

Gallant, Kansas was founded and named in the mid 1800's, or so the story goes, when a government wagon carrying goods for a small tribe of Kickapoo Indians lost a wheel and had to stop there for repairs. At that time it was just a small, dusty, unnamed outpost stuck up against a fork of the Kansas River. A party of fur traders headed east, out from the Rockies, stumbled upon the wagon and a fight broke out over the goods. The traders had just finished a rough year in the mountains and figured the government owed them the supplies for doing such a great job of trapping and mapping and carving out a trail that allowed for even deeper western expansion. Just about the time the fight grew ugly a lone Kickapoo warrior happened along and, of course, took the government's side in order to preserve the goods for his own people. He waded into the fray, his tomahawk flashing, and when he finished, several trappers lay badly bruised, and the whole lot of them were scattered out along the trail. It was then that a sergeant stepped out to thank and congratulate the warrior, but as he did so, a bullet ripped through the air, tearing into the Indian's skull. He fell instantly dead in the trail, and when they later buried him there, the sergeant and his men expressed what a *gallant* man he had been. Of course the incident was reported, and due to the violent nature of the attack, a proclamation came down from Washington that the Kickapoos were aggressive by nature and not to be trusted. The remaining members of the tribe were gathered up and relocated to a tiny swath of land to the north where they still suffer to this day. In a final irony, Gallant, founded on the very spot the warrior fell, went on to become a thriving trading post where trappers returning from the mountains could purchase goods at cost under the sanction and protection of a grateful government. It was a system that worked out splendidly for everyone but the Indians.

The Stockman's Inn in Gallant was typical of many small Midwestern town motels. There were twenty-eight units spread out in a long, single story line. Molly requested number twenty-eight because it sat at the very end of the row, and backed up against a wood-rail fence, with nothing beyond but wheat fields and oak trees for some distance. She also asked the young man at the desk if he would hold off on renting out room twenty-seven next door for as long as possible, as she needed the quiet to rest up after her long journey. As with most men, the clerk was taken enough by her that he nodded agreeably. He even removed the key for twenty-seven from the board behind the desk, stating that he just remembered there were some plumbing issues that needed to be tended to, and they probably wouldn't get to them until the next morning after Molly's departure. Molly reached out to caress the young man's hand as she winked at him in thanks.

Next door to the inn stood a diner, again typically Midwestern. A couple of pool tables lay off to the right of the entrance, and a juke box also sat off to the right, nestled up against a small, square, laminate-wood tiled floor suitable for one or two couples who felt the need to dance. To the left was a grouping of tables and chairs, some shelves displaying old western artifacts, and a pair of doors against a far wall, with signs atop each, one reading *Mustangs*, the other *Mares*.

As Molly entered the diner all eyes turned in her direction. She had changed from her business attire of white slacks and a collared blouse, and now wore a skirt, shortened enough to showcase her long legs, and a halter top knotted well above her navel. Overall, her clothing and skin were shown off in about equal portions. A group

of men at the pool tables stopped their game and stared appreciatively. Even the two waitresses roaming the room observed her, then
gave each other a knowing look that implied this was going to be a
rough night for the boys.

Molly paused long enough to give each of the men a glance,
then moved straight ahead to the counter where she sat herself down
on a stool. On the wall in front of her were the heads, a tradition and
inevitability in places like this. On one side a magnificent bull moose
hung in full battle array, its antlers spanning out defiantly. To the
other side was a mule deer and an elk, both in their prime, their faces
elevated proudly as they, too, appeared ready to challenge all comers.
Directly to the front, a boar hog crashed its way through the wall,
with perhaps half its torso hanging out into space. The boar's tusks
curled upwards, drawing its upper lip into a sort of friendly smile.
She studied the boar as she thought back in time to one of her first
memories as a child. Her father had taken her to a diner very much
like this one. On the wall as they entered was mounted the head of a
young boar. It wasn't nearly as imposing as the animal now displayed
before her, but in its own way it was trying hard to be impressive. She
had pulled away from her father and walked along the wall, seeking a
doorway. "Molly, what are you doing?" he had asked.

"Trying to find the rest of him, Daddy," she had replied. "Why
is he stuck in the wall?"

Her father had laughed, as had some other observers seated
nearby. "There is no rest of him, Molly." He reached up then, and
patted at the boar's face. It remained unmoved. "It's just a head."

"Oh," said Molly. She had stood there then, deep in thought,
and stared at the head for a long time. "Oh."

A voice called out. "Hey, darlin'. Saw you sittin' here all by yourself. Thought maybe you'd like some company." She turned to face a
rough looking young man of around twenty who seated himself on
the stool beside hers. He was unshaven and a bit unkempt, but still
not all that unattractive in his current rugged form.

"Hi," she said, reaching out to touch his arm. She glanced over his shoulder at the other men, his companions she supposed, who stood huddled together some distance away, broad smiles on their faces as they stared intently at the two of them. "I'm Molly."

"I'm Jim," said the man. "You're new here."

Molly laughed lightly. "I am. Came here to find myself a nice rancher I can fool around with." She studied the man. "You a rancher, Jim?"

Jim shuffled nervously. "Well no, not exactly. But I work on one of the biggest pig farms in the state."

"Oh," replied Molly, her voice showing obvious disappointment. "Well, good for you." She shook her head and waved a hand dismissively. "Actually, I'm just looking for a little privacy right now. I'm afraid I'm a bit of a broken woman."

"Well, darlin'." Jim's face grew eager. He smiled hungrily. "Let's you and me change all that."

Molly looked at the man for a long moment. "Not gonna happen, Jimmy boy." Again she waved her hand, shifting slightly in her stool as she turned away. "Bye now."

As the young man stumbled away, muttering to himself, a waitress moved over to her, hardly able to contain the thick grin that spread across her face. "You go girl," she said, tilting her head in the direction of the pool tables. "They're all a bunch of sick bastards if you ask me." She scratched her cheek with a pencil. "Especially that one. Thinks he's a ladies' man."

Sometime later as she was finishing her meal, Danny entered the diner. The men at the pool table nodded at him respectfully. Molly observed them through a small mirror set up over the register, and just beneath the half-boar. She smiled to herself as Danny removed his cap, shrugged at the other men, and approached. "Molly?" he said with a voice that implied he wasn't entirely certain it would be her.

She turned to him. "Danny. I've been waiting for you."

Danny looked over at the men gathered around the pool tables. Casually waving in their direction, he then dismissed them with a nod. "Figured you'd be dancin' it up with all these other guys."

Molly reached out, taking his hand in hers. "You're my guy," she said softly. "They're just boys. Let's get out of here."

As they left the diner and turned towards the motel, Molly squeezed his fingers. "Let's go around back," she said shyly. "I don't want anyone to see me sneaking you in." They walked across a lawn area, and then wove their way among a grove of oaks at the rear of the property until they were directly behind room twenty-eight. It was a moonless night, the sky filled with enough stars to make them gasp aloud. "It's so beautiful here," Molly sighed and turned to him. "I'm glad we met. I hope this is the start of a beautiful friendship."

Danny reached to pull her in close, reading the signs and deciding they were all pointed in his direction. "I hope it's a helluva lot more than a friendship." His lips tried for hers, but she turned her face at the last instant.

"Easy, boy. Wait till you get me inside. I like privacy." He grabbed her hand then, and practically dragged her along the side wall of the motel, in pitch blackness, until they emerged at the front, which was bathed in soft light and just feet from her door. Ripping the key from her hand, he fumbled with the lock until it clicked open, and pulled her aggressively into the room. Again he tried to kiss her as he slammed shut the door with his foot, and again she rebuffed him with her cheek. She leaned back away from him and touched his lips playfully with a finger. "Hey, slow down," she laughed out suggestively. "We've got all night. I want to make it special." Pushing away from him she moved to a dresser at the far side of the room. It was the only piece of furniture there, as the place was quite spartan. A bed, a dresser, a nightstand with a lamp. A standup armoire that served as a closet, and a shower, sink and toilet indented into a far wall with only a wisp of a curtain separating them from the room.

Danny stood there, hands on hips. "Gallant's best," he grinned as he looked around.

"Yeah." Molly reached the dresser, picked up a bottle of Crown Royal that waited there and poured a couple of fingers into each of two glasses. "I always go large." She turned, glasses in hand, and matched his grin. "This is the bridal suite." As she moved back over to him, she looked at the wall above the bed. Two paintings hung there. One, directly over the bed, was of a charging bull, nostrils flaring as it came at an unseen opponent, and the other, a bit smaller and off to one side, a cheap lithograph of a lady sipping wine. "But the art is good." She nodded idly at the wall as she handed Danny a glass. "I've seen a lot of places, but not many where the western flare mixes in so well with Matisse."

"Who?" He looked at her admiringly, his face taking on a sheen of blissful ignorance as he tilted back his head and downed the whiskey in a single gulp.

"Matisse." She sat down on the edge of the bed, patting the blanket beside her with her free hand, inviting him to sit. "A famous bullfighter from Madrid." Molly prided herself on creating the perfect story to match any circumstance. She was a master at it. "It is said he fought over a thousand bulls, each one falling before his sword. Until he met the last one, El Toro Grande, the bull of bulls."

"What happened?" Danny looked at her, marveled at her, like a boy thirsty for a story.

Molly turned her head, raising her glass to indicate the painting of the lady. "She happened." She turned back to Danny then, who now stared up at the lady with the wine. "She got ahold of him before the fight. Seduced him. Left him sated and drunk, so that when he entered the arena he staggered about. It is said perhaps she even drugged him, left him weak and helpless before the great bull. El Toro came at him like an avalanche, crushing him again and again as the crowd cried out helplessly." Molly's hand moved to Danny's thigh, caressing it gently. His eyes were glued to the painting.

"Goddammit," he said in a hoarse whisper. "Was he dead?"

"Almost." Molly's eyes joined his and they looked at the two paintings together. "But as the bull stood triumphantly over the fallen Matisse, the crowd caught a movement off to one side. All eyes turned, and a thousand voices gasped aloud. There, entering the ring and heading straight for the bull walked a lady— that one." Molly nodded toward the wall. "The other matadors screamed out at her to stay back, but on she moved. Then there was not a whisper to be heard. Not a sound. The crowd, the other bullfighters, everyone in attendance sat or stood in a silence so profound that it would be remembered as *The Holy Intervention*, and it would become legend with the people of Spain."

"Oh my god, what happened then?" Danny looked at Molly, again with a childlike innocence.

"She reached out to pet the bull," Molly continued, "who trembled before her. And Matisse, barely alive, looked up at her, his body torn and broken, his eyes pleading. She kneeled beside him, the great beast towering over them both, took his head in her hands and gently stroked it. 'I raised this bull,' she said to him, quite matter-of-factly. 'I held him when he was only a few hours old. I nursed him and held him and cared for him. And I loved him. Then my father sold him off to the ring, saying it's where he was meant to be. That's why he was born, my father said, to be a fighter, to face the sword and meet his destiny.'" Molly's eyes darkened as she finished the tale. "Then the lady let the head of Matisse slip away to the ground, and as the last of his lifeblood seeped away to mix with the clay of the arena, she stood defiantly, wrapping an arm around the neck of El Toro. She glanced back down one last time at the dying man who stared blankly back at her. 'No one fucks with my bull,' she said. Then, with her arm still wrapped around the bull's neck, she led it away, out of the arena, where they were never seen or heard from again."

"Holy shit," said Danny. "Holy shit. Is that shit true?"

Molly grinned devilishly, pushing Danny down on the bed with one hand. He went easily, and lay there, a broad smile etching its way across his face. His hand opened, the empty glass tumbling from it to land harmlessly on the floor. "It's just a legend, silly." She leaned her head down, kissing him fully on the lips. "Who could love a cow?"

Danny started to laugh then. He tried to raise his head, tried to kiss her back, but found he could only raise it a few inches before it collapsed back onto the bed. "Who could love a cow?" he sang out at her, still laughing.

Molly sat there with him for a moment, stroking his face with her hand. "How do you feel?" she asked him.

"Like a cow." He continued to laugh and couldn't stop. He chanted out, "I think I'm a cow." Patting his head, Molly rose and moved back to the dresser where the bottle of Crown Royal waited. She put her own glass down and carefully spun the cap back on the bottle, tightening it before leaning down to slip it into a side pouch in her suitcase. Then, from another pouch she extracted a syringe, removed the endcap and brought out a tiny vial of clear liquid, a duplicate of the one she had used earlier that day out at the ranch. She moved back over to the bed.

"How do you feel now?" she asked again. Her hand pressed firmly against his forehead, like a mother checking a child for fever.

"I can't move my head." He laughed merrily up at her, rolling his head from side to side, but unable to completely lift it.

Molly sat beside him, smiling warmly as she again stroked his face. "You've just been given a little dose of something to relax you," she said. "I've got something here that will make you feel even better." She removed her hand from his face then, and inserted the syringe into the vial, drawing back on the handle until a good portion of liquid was drawn into the glass chamber. She turned back to Danny, whose face shifted slightly as he looked up at her curiously.

"I love you," he said. His eyes were hazy and warm, his voice slurred. "I want you to know I'm not just here because of the sex. I mean it. I love you."

"Good boy." She patted his cheek with her free hand, while the hand holding the syringe moved in close to his neck. "I love you too," she murmured. As the needle sank into his flesh, he quivered slightly, the smile weakening somewhat, but still flickering across his lips. His eyes continued to press into hers. Molly sat there with him for more than a minute, waiting until his breathing slowed as his respiratory system moved him into a deep state of relaxation. "I've just given you a nice injection of the same stuff we gave the sow today, the one who stood there so willingly while you beat the shit out of her." Danny's face mutated then, his lower lip sagging downward toward his chin. A thin line of drool began to flow from his mouth, working its way across a portion of his cheek before falling onto the collar of his shirt. She lifted a finger, holding it out in front of his face. "Watch this," she said as her hand began to wave in a slow arc. "Follow it with your eyes if you can." Danny's face twitched slightly, but remained unmoved, while his eyes took on a strange, hollow intensity as they followed the finger swaying back and forth before him. "Good boy," she said again, her other hand reaching out to stroke his cheek.

Molly leaned over, resting her head on her elbows, her face now inches from his. "You know, I had a friend once, when I was a kid. She lived on the farm right across the road from us. She had this snake, a really quite remarkable corn snake that she kept in her room. Every week or so we would go outside to the barn where we would turn over bales of hay in search of mice to feed it. This snake had a voracious appetite, strangling and gulping down the mice as quickly as we threw them into the cage." Molly leaned in even closer until her hair brushed gently against his face. "Do you like this story?" she asked him as he stared blankly back at her. "Good. You just lie there and relax and I'll tell you what happened. One day I caught a young mouse, a baby actually, but instead of being all brown like the other mice, it had a small white patch on one side of its head. Somehow in my mind, that made it special. I even named it Patch." Molly giggled. "Anyway, we took it back up to the house to feed it to the snake. I remember holding it out over the cage, holding it there by its tail... but I couldn't drop it. My friend admonished me, laughed at me and said it was just a stupid mouse, but because I had found something special about it, I just couldn't do it." Her hand danced lightly across his face. "Have you ever felt that way about an animal? You know, made it different somehow, like it was privileged and had a right to live while everyone around it was sentenced to die?" Her eyes brightened suddenly, as a fire flashed across them, and her hand became rough as it clawed its way onto his chin, and then down his neck. "And then a funny thing happened," she continued. "While I held it there, high above the cage, the snake rose up and snatched it from my hand, crushing it in its jaws as it crashed back down again. My friend screamed out with delight, while I screamed out in agony, two entirely opposite reactions to the same circumstance." She looked at Danny, locked eyes with him, bonded with him, her hand once again moving up to caress his face. "Do you hear what I'm saying? To me it was devastating. But to her it was exhilarating.

"As I left her house I began to wonder why in the world the snake was more important than the mouse. It didn't really make any sense. It was only a natural progression for me to begin to wonder why a man— like you, for instance— is more important than, say, a pig... or a cow... or a lamb." She leaned down to kiss him on the forehead. "You're not, you know. I guess you would be if I allowed you to become special, but unfortunately I haven't, and you aren't. You're just a man who slaughters pigs and enjoys doing it. I'd like to defend you, but can find nothing endearing about that." Danny continued to stare up at her, and now she stared back. She patted him affectionately, again brushing her fingers across his cheek. "I wish we had one of those big boars in here right now," she said, a playful smile forming at her lips. "I'd let him fuck you all night long."

CHAPTER FOUR

It was after three in the morning when the steel door opened and Molly stepped into the darkened interior of the hog barn. The same barn she had entered earlier with Danny as they began to kick their way through the mob of pigs. It was eerily quiet now, but the stench of pig waste and pig death still enveloped her as she fumbled her way along the wall in search of a switch. She carried with her a large canvas bag, like a beach bag, only this one was a drab olive green, military looking, and not the brightly colored swatch one would expect to carry on a happy outing. The bag had a long, corded strap stitched into it, and appeared quite heavy. She slung the strap over her shoulder and withdrew from the bag a flashlight and a small-caliber automatic pistol. Molly was hunting again. With no switch on the wall near the door, which she found strange, she flicked on the flashlight and began to move across the empty holding area. She had gone only a step or two when a loud buzzing sound flew at her and lights flooded on. She froze, but quickly realized she was still alone. "Damn," she said aloud. "You gotta love technology." Moving swiftly across the room, she passed through the gate and entered the slaughtering area, where hours earlier she had killed the young shoat. She shuddered at the memory, with only the understanding that it had been a sacrifice, and not a murder, saving her from shame. It had been too strong an opportunity to pass up, one to bond with the men, gain their trust, their respect, even their adulation. The pig would have been dead moments later with or without her. It was an inescapable conclusion. The gift from the sacrifice was that it offered up Danny, and now the farm. Still, she bit down hard on her lip at the thought of the piglet screaming out at her, screaming and writhing as it died. Memories flooded in. Of holding pigs down while her father slashed away at their testicles, castrating the non-breeders. It lobotomized them in a way, eunuchized them, made them more docile and allowed massive amounts of feed to be poured into them for conversion into meat. Her entire youth consumed by the lessons of the farm. And it had always been about the meat.

"Daddy," she would call out. "I think that one just smiled at me."

"Pigs don't smile, Molly," her father would say. "They don't have emotions. Their job is to sit there and grow fat for us. They're just like any other product. So your daddy can make money and put bread on the table."

As she grew older Molly became amused that her father would often use the bread analogy as a profit partner for the meat. Once, when in her teens and feeling somewhat rebellious, she had asked him, "Why don't we raise wheat then, if it's bread you're after. That would do the trick. And just let the pigs be pigs." The question had not amused her father.

Molly moved on. As she entered each new chamber, more lights flooded on, illuminating the path ahead. Finally she reached the end, and a huge cathedral-like wall blocked the way, with no further egress. Off to the right, however, and punched through a side-wall, was one last doorway, this one open to the outside. She turned and walked through it and out into the night. She found herself in a fenced yard, lit by a series of soft night lights attached to posts that encircled the enclosure. The space was really quite large, a field that stretched perhaps fifty or sixty yards outward and to either side. As her eyes adjusted to the dim lighting she began to see the hogs. In large groups and bunches as many as a thousand hogs lay scattered across the yard, laying about as they slept through the night. Molly moved out, away from the building, and began to roam quietly among them. Occasionally one or two, more attentive than the others, would look up at her, but none reacted much, and within seconds their heads would drift back down and they would continue their slumber. Arriving finally at the outer edges of the enclosure, she began to walk its perimeter, looking for and finding several large gates. She opened each as she passed, swinging them wide in an invitation to the outside world. When finished, she moved to the middle of the yard, raising the hand that still held the pistol. In an instant the stillness of the night air crashed to life as Molly fired off round after round into the darkness.

Instant pandemonium erupted. A thousand pigs woke at once, clamored to their feet as one moving mass and began smashing amongst themselves. At first it was a great milling with no structure, no purpose other than blind panic. Then some, alone or in clusters, began to find the open gates. They streamed through into the night, while the masses of other pigs, still enclosed, quickly realized that something momentous was occurring. All they had ever known was a life of enslavement, beaten down and bloodied. A life of disappearing siblings whose screams could be heard just beyond the metal walls. A voice cried out to them. "Run!" Later, Molly would reflect on whether it was her voice they heeded, or another, stronger cry coming from within. It made little difference. Whatever its source, they heard it. And they ran.

Molly collapsed to her knees, trembling as the last of the hogs disappeared into the darkness. She knew the inevitabilities. Most would be hunted down, with many killed, and others returned to face the butcher. But some of them, like her ladies in orange, would outsmart all comers, slinking away into the wilderness, going feral and living free. "Run, my babies," she cried out again. "Run."

Old man Tignor, asleep in his home on a low hill just beyond the trailer, woke suddenly. A blast of sound had broken through his slumber. As he lay there, trying to grab onto his senses, another blast echoed away at him, then another. He rose and scrambled over to the window. The lights were on in the barns. Grabbing at a robe, he stumbled outside to his pickup. "What the hell," he said over and over. His mind raced as it grappled for substance. It would be his idiot son, he thought, and the other idiots who worked for him. Drunk probably, and setting off fireworks or shooting pigs. "Sunovabitch," he swore as he raced in the truck down the hill to the barns. Arriving there, he swung down from his seat, exited, and reached into the pickup's bed for a club he always kept at hand. The club was encrusted with dried blood, both on the thickened end used for smashing and small patches that had splattered their way up the handle. His *pigger* he called it. But now he thought it might serve just as well as a lesson for a bunch of drunken idiots. Swinging open the metal door of the barn, the same door Molly had entered, he worked his way inside and began a march purposefully down the long corridor which connected building to building. He found Molly in the very last of them, as she was heading back inside from the yard. "What the hell," he said to her as he stopped to stare.

"Mister Tignor." Molly smiled sweetly at the old man. "I was just coming to look for you. It seems like the pigs have gotten out. All of them."

"What?" he called out, his voice incredulous. "What do you mean they're out?" He shook his head, as if trying to clear a fog. "What the hell's goin' on? What are you doin' here? Where's my son?"

Molly laughed. "My, that's a lot of questions," she said. Then she raised the pistol and shot the old man in the leg.

"Shit," he screamed. He dropped to his knees, and as the pain struck at him, rolled further down until he lay on his side. The club clattered to the floor where it spun away. Blood trickled out through Tignor's robe, blackening a small patch of it. "Goddam it, woman, what do you want?"

"Shhhh." Molly raised the gun barrel to her lips. "It's time for you to listen."

"Where's Danny?" he asked again. The pain was obvious in his voice. "I don't understand."

"Dammit," said Molly, not angrily. "I warned you to be quiet." Tignor raised himself up until he was in an awkward sitting position. Molly shot him in the stomach.

"Sunovabitch," the old man screamed out at her. "Sunovabitch." He began to cry then, grasping at his belly, trying to hold back the blood and hold back the pain. "What did I do?" Tears began to pour down his cheeks. He tried desperately to beg her. "Just tell me what you want."

"Do you ever stop with the questions?" Molly kneeled down just a few feet away from the old man. She looked at him almost fondly. "Now stop being such a big baby," she said. "Contrary to all the movies and stuff, being shot in the stomach is rarely fatal. It's simply an inconvenience." She smiled as his face twisted in confusion. "Let's just face it. Your pigs are gone, your night is ruined, and you have a teensy-weensy hole in your belly. That's all chicken-shit stuff." She sat then, spreading herself out comfortably on the floor. She looked at the old man sitting across from her. He had stopped talking now, and sat there, blood seeping freely from both his wounds, a look of disbelief spread across his face. Molly waved the gun loosely in his direction. "You know, I remember when I was a kid." A story began to unfold, but unlike the ones she fondly created to confuse men and amuse herself, this one had a more sinister intent. Her eyes seemed to lose their focus for a moment as she gazed off into the distance. Then, in an instant, they returned to slice into the old man. "Back on the farm when I was growing up. The sows there would only be allowed to keep their babies for a short period of time, just long enough to bond and feel love for them, before they were stripped away. Some of them would try to stick their heads through the narrow slats in the pen, fighting for a last glimpse before their babies disappeared forever. Their eyes would mist up. Did you know pigs can cry? And their faces would droop desperately down until their snouts just touched the floor. Then, right in the middle of this agony, a gate would crash open and a huge boar would rush in to mount them, slamming them hard against the railing. The sows would scream out in pain and fear as they were forceably impregnated to start the whole cycle over again. And again." Molly tapped the barrel of the pistol against the side of her face. "Sometimes I try to feel what they must have felt, their babies stripped away while they were simultaneously raped and battered. I'll bet it felt something like being shot in the stomach... twice." Molly raised the pistol then, firing another round into Tignor's midsection as he screamed and rolled further onto the floor. "But I don't know," she continued. "I'm just guessing. Hey, you're the expert here. From both sides. You know what it's like to be shot, and you know what it's like to rape a pig." She laughed. "Hell, I should have thought of asking you sooner. Then we wouldn't have had to go through all this suffering."

Clutching his stomach, but still filled with enough life to want to live, the old man struggled to speak. "Look, I have money. Lots and lots of money. Just tell me what you want."

Molly set the pistol down and reached into her canvas bag. She pulled out another bag, this one of clear plastic. It was grossly bloodied, and appeared to contain meat of some kind. Opening the bag, she extracted the contents, and the kind of meat became immediately apparent. She held in her hand a hand, bloody, but easily recognizable, and with enough wrist and lower arm attached to give it a sort of handle. She held it up in front of her like a claw.

"What the hell is that?" Tignor cried out.

Molly raised the hand to her face. It looked something like a macabre back-scratcher. She brushed it against her cheek. "Why, it's Danny," she said, her voice showing surprise. "Don't you recognize your own son?"

"No," Tignor screamed. "No, it can't be. What did you do?" He broke down then, great sobs pouring out between the gasps of pain. "What did you do?" he cried out again.

"Damn," Molly said, putting the hand down and once again

picking up the pistol. "You're not taking this very well. I'm a little disappointed." She frowned. "You know, the last thing I said to your son was I wished he would get fucked by a hog. I want you to know I regret saying that. It wasn't professional, and it wasn't lady-like." Her eyes blackened, her face twisting for the first time away from frivolity and into darkness. "I want you to tell him that for me when you see him. That I'm sorry. Mostly, I guess, I'm sorry for the hog. He would have had a great time banging your boy." The pistol flashed flame, and flashed again as Tignor's body spasmed for a moment, then went still. Molly rose, moving efficiently to the old man, where she dipped the fingers of Danny's severed hand into the blood dripping freely from a variety of wounds. She walked over to the doorway leading out to the yard, tapping the fingers once or twice and dragging the hand along the wall at about the level she felt a man's hand should be if he were leaving somewhere in a hurry. She left several such markings, blurring all but one, so it looked staggered and hurried, with but a single hand imprint leaving a useful impression. She was not an expert at crime, or evidence planting or evidence gathering, and frankly didn't care to be. What she planted were the seeds of confusion, with one defining element. She was always careful to never leave traces of herself. That was enough. The competence or incompetence of those who would later study the scene concerned her not in the least.

Molly left then, carefully packaging the hand back into its bag, and choosing to walk out through the yard and around the building on the outside rather than spend any more time walking through the interior. It was now almost four. It had been less than an hour since her arrival. And still a couple of hours before the workers would arrive to make their grisly discovery. She knew Danny's father held the boy in disdain, and that would work well for her. She pictured the conversations that would take place during questioning. "Always called the boy an idiot," one would say. "It's no wonder he finally cracked," another would call out.

Opening the trunk on the Camry, Molly deposited the canvas bag inside. She placed it directly on top of what remained of Danny

Tignor, his body wrapped heavily in plastic. A few minutes later, as she guided her car back onto the highway, she popped in a CD and began singing along to the Spice Girls. "Tell me what you want, what you really, really want." She smiled amusedly, remembering Tignor's voice as he had cried out, somewhat less melodically, the same question.

CHAPTER FIVE

Michael Lair entered the room with a certain arrogance. He had fallen, he knew that, but refused to allow his demeanor to show it. Two others waited there, seated at a long table with enough chairs scattered about to accommodate a much larger gathering. But there were just the two, a suited man whose face suggested a friendly, approachable disposition, and a woman, hawkish and middle-aged, showing not the slightest hint of warmth as she nodded up at him.

"You're late," she said, her voice scolding. "We've been waiting for over an hour."

The man seated across from her waved a hand congenially. "Well," he said, looking first at the woman, then also nodding at Michael, "It's not like we have a life out here in the sticks. We're not missing out on anything."

"Sorry." Lair studied the room. The two sat at about the mid-point of the table, directly across from one another. He moved past them both, then swung to the right, slinging himself down in the end chair, the chairman's chair, where he directly faced the two, but knowing they would have to turn their heads in order to face him. Clasping his hands out in front, he slid them onto the surface of the table, then leaned forward in the chair. "It seems no one's in a hurry to get to Omaha. My plane took off late, and landed even later. I think they took the scenic route." He attempted a weak smile. "Again, my apologies."

The woman's face softened slightly. "I'm Elizabeth Warman, deputy director of field operations out of Des Moines." She nodded at the suited man. "This is Phillip Crane, an agent from my office."

"Good to meet you, Lair," said the man called Crane. He nodded at Michael. "You come with a glowing endorsement from the big chief back in Washington. We've heard lots of great things about you."

Michael Lair was well aware of the *things* other agents had heard about him. All of America had heard about Michael Lair. Of how, two months earlier, in a cabin hidden away in the backwoods of Maine, he had gunned down three members of a white suprem-acist organization who had holed up there with enough weapons and ammunition to start a minor war. Three supremacists... and one small child. Surrounded by an army of agents from the FBI, the three had waved a flag of truce, requesting to speak with someone concerning possible terms of surrender. Michael had worked his way up close to the cabin, to a point where he could view the inhabitants through a small window set into the side of the structure. It was from there he saw the boy, a tiny broken face against the glass, who for a brief instant looked out at him before he was snatched away. Then, in complete defiance of the rules of engagement, rules demanding that he stay safely behind an obstruction at all times during a negotiation, Michael had moved out into the open, climbed the steps onto a covered porch, and stood there before the door.

"Let's talk," he hollered out. "I know you have a child in there. Let's do the right thing and let me take him somewhere safe. Then we can work this out." Before he'd finished the last sentence the door swung open and a flash of flame erupted, aimed at his face. He dove to the side, drawing and firing his pistol even before he smashed into the weathered boards that made up the surface of the porch. Several of the boards gave way, cracking audibly beneath his impact and he found himself somewhat imbedded into the floor. He saw the shape of a man looming in the doorway, and he fired twice more, putting the man down. Then he rolled himself free and dove through the doorway into the cabin. Michael had been highly trained in instantaneous situational evaluation. Big words with big meaning. He was among the best at it. His eyes swept the room. One man lay close by, and appeared, if not dead, seriously debilitated. In the corner to his right stood another man, a rifle in his hands pointing straight at Michael's head. A few feet to his left was the third man. He appeared unarmed and stood there trembling with a small boy clutching at his legs. Michael took out the man with the rifle, knocking him down with three quick blasts. The first to the belly, then allowing the natural rise caused by the recoil of his weapon to dictate the next two rounds. The second caught the man in the chest, with the third searing a path right through the center of his forehead. The third man screamed out, dropping to his knees where he wrapped both arms around the boy. "It's okay," Michael called out. He addressed the man. "You just stay right there. Everything's going to be okay." Composing himself he rose, gun still in hand, and moved over to the two, reaching down his free hand to lift the child aloft. The boy cried out, but Michael pressed him in close to his chest, the whole while keeping the barrel of his pistol trained on the third man's face.

A loud sound pounded away at them then, as four heavily armored agents crashed their way into the room. Michael turned, raising his weapon in a signal that everything was under control. As he turned back, the man on his knees drew a pistol from his boot and fired one round, point blank at Michael. The blast knocked him backwards, but as he fell, still holding onto the boy, he fired a single round. The bullet caught the third man in the upper jaw, ripping its way from there all the way through his head, where it exited and smacked into a wall board just beyond. Michael dropped the pistol, his now freed hand rushing up to examine his face. He was unharmed, sprawled out on the floor with the boy on top of him. He couldn't believe his good fortune. A miss from point blank. It rarely happened, and he had not a scratch on him. He looked down at the boy who now lay limply on his chest. A slow gusher of blood seeped from a hole just behind the boy's ear. Michael thought he remembered screaming then, but during the investigation that followed no one else made note of it. But some of the armor-vested men in the room hinted that as he turned back to face the shooter, he had raised the boy up slightly in a reflex, perhaps to use the child as a human shield. So Michael had fallen, at least in the minds of those who knew him, worked with him, respected him, and those were the only minds that mattered.

A fog lifted now, as he stared blankly at the two agents sitting at the table. "I know what you've heard about me," he said. "It's not all that great. So let's cut the crap and not pretend I don't know what you're thinking."

"Hey," Phillip Crane spoke again. "I didn't mean anything by it. The report said it was a clean shoot. Who knows what any of us would have done in a similar circumstance."

Elizabeth Warman spoke next, her eyes piercing deeply into Michael's. "Agent Lair. Your sensitivities would indicate the problems unresolved from any action you took are yours, and yours alone." She shuffled some papers and flipped open her laptop. "I'd prefer to stick with the case at hand. You were sent here for a reason, I think. To help us resolve this." She drummed her fingers on the tabletop. "So why don't we concentrate on that and let whatever demons dance around in your head pleasure you in private."

Both men stared at her. "What?" they said at exactly the same time.

The case Warman spoke about had been developing over a series of months. Five families, or members of families, in the Midwestern meat industry had died under suspicious circumstances. The number of deaths totaled nine, or possibly as many as eleven, as two were still missing and considered either suspects or victims. The latest case had come out of Kansas, just a week prior, when a pork producer was found shot to death on the ground in one of his own barns. Lair looked at Warman, the woman relentless in her ability to appear cross. "You're a profiler right? I'm guessing that from all the damn psycho-babble you just threw at me."

"I used to be. Back in the day." Her look was a surprised one. "But that was a long time ago."

"Well," he continued, "is there enough viable information here to give us something to go on, or are we just bobbing for apples?"

"Fruit references." A hint of a smile might have flitted across Warman's lips. Michael wasn't sure. "At this point the scenarios are way too broad to profile." She shuffled through her papers again, selecting one which she perused. "We have no real motive yet, nor does there appear to be one on the horizon. Hog farmers, it seems, are simply dying extraordinary deaths and we have yet to figure out why."

Phillip Crane spoke. "This latest killing, out of Gallant. A little town in the middle of nowhere. Seems as though a disgruntled son had a beat down on his daddy. Right there in front of the hogs. So this one we might have to separate out. It could be just a family affair."

"What about the others?" Michael asked.

"Most of those are weirder than hell. A couple of men found dead in a pig trough. Not a lot of evidence on that one. They weren't found until after feeding time, and the hogs kind of worked them over." Crane bit down on his lip. "Another one out of North Platte, a threesome. Husband, wife and ranch foreman. Husband and wife shot in the head, and a few feet away the foreman is hanging upside down between a couple of hog carcasses. It appears he'd been working the stun gun that day, butchering up a line of pigs when someone sauntered in and added him to the line."

"Any more?"

"Yes." Elizabeth Warman took over. "We had one right here in Omaha. Just this last month. There was a farmer named Jimson, Maxwell Jimson. Found slain in a truck behind one of his barns." Warman's eyes closed, either from mentally establishing an image or avoiding one. "His pants were pulled down, and there was a girlie magazine on the seat beside him. A rasp, a rat-tailed one, had been driven through one ear and out the other, like a lance right through the middle of his brain. He must have been earnestly engaged when someone with incredible coordination slipped up and popped him."

"Was he in the driver's seat?" asked Lair. The other two looked over at him curiously.

"As a matter of fact. Where would you expect him to be? Why?"

"That's useful." Michael looked first at Agent Crane, then at Elizabeth Warman. A flush feeling of smugness washed over him. "Isn't it obvious? Our killer is almost certainly left handed. As I said. That's useful."

A touch of incredulity crept into Crane's voice. "What? Just how in the world would you surmise that?"

"Yes," said Warman, her voice as smug as Michael's. "Do grace us with your intellect, agent."

Michael smiled condescendingly at them both. "He's sitting in the driver's seat, right? I don't care how busy he is in his pants, no one is going to approach him from the front. It would be fool-hardy to even try, and if we do have a serial killer at work here, he is anything but foolish. Approaching from the front would mean you'd have to thrust with your right hand, and be easily seen. The left hand simply wouldn't work." He challenged them both. "Go ahead, try it." Both the agents turned somewhat sideways, conjuring up a vision of a pickup with a man seated behind the wheel. Picturing themselves approaching from the front of the vehicle they both immediately real-ized any thrust with the left hand would point the weapon on a path into the side of the victim's face. There was simply no way to chart the rasp on any credible course that would take it from ear to ear. Lair smiled at their frustrated attempts. "Now," he said, "picture yourself slipping up from the rear, from the direction we know the perpetrator must have come, if for no other reason than stealth. The right hand is now useless. Hell," he raised the hand, "with your right hand you'd have to ram it through the door jamb just to get it to his face, and even then it would only offer a glancing blow. But the left, agents. It swings sweetly through the air, slicing its way in deeply, ear to ear."

Michael Lair rose then, moving around the table. As he passed by Agent Crane he tapped the man on the shoulder, his eyes reaching across the table to play with those of Elizabeth Warman. Hers refused to play back. "You'll learn," he said, his voice deep and scholarly. "I'm here to teach. Let's meet back here tomorrow."

The only meaningful lead in the case thus far was a handy one. It came from a company headquartered right there in Omaha. A pharmaceutical manufacturing company named McMillan. Michael Lair headed there now. It seemed a woman who worked for McMillan, a territorial sales representative, had come up on the radar in at least three of the murders. After reading the information on her it became apparent that she was probably not a viable suspect, but the woman either served the victims as her clients or had approached them in the recent past with regard to doing business. The dossier on the woman was limited, but she was certainly a person of interest. Her name, Molly Bishop, her age, twenty-eight, and she had degrees in animal husbandry from both Nebraska and Iowa State. So she was young, educated, undoubtedly ambitious, and in no way fit into any sort of criminal profile Michael could imagine. Still, it was a lead, and she might, at the very least, offer up some information on the various farmers who had been stalked and slain.

As he pulled into the drive at McMillan Pharmaceuticals, a grin broke out on Michael's face. There on the lawn, proudly representing the company, were life size replicas of a horse, a cow and a pig, each painted realistically, and each bearing the expression of an animal well-tended. Gone was his big city world, one of bulls and bears, and statues of presidents and statesmen, replaced in this most rural of places by the animals that drove the heartland's economy. He exited the car, walked across a lot and entered the building. A well-fed country girl, seemingly only about sixteen, in a bright yellow summer dress, greeted him with a smile.

"Hi." He waved his credentials at the girl. "I'm Agent Lair with the FBI. I wonder if I might speak with a Molly Bishop."

"It's about the killings, right?" A voice spun him around. It was Carl Monroe, Molly's employer. The man was dressed as brightly as the girl, in yellow and black, with polished leather boots and a belt buckle the size of a plate plastered across his stomach. The look, Michael was certain, was intended to be cowboy, but came off as garishly city-slicker.

"Maybe." Stepping toward the man, Michael extended his hand. "Agent Lair," he said.

Monroe stepped to meet him, also extending a hand. "I'm Carl, Molly's boss. We've been expecting you. A Miss Warman called and asked that I have Molly made available to you this afternoon. She should be here in a few minutes." The two men shook hands, and Carl escorted the agent down a hallway and into his office. Horns adorned the walls. That's the first and most obvious thing a person noticed. Not heads, but horns, lots of them. Mostly from Longhorns, sweeping in long arcs across the upper walls, and a cluster of several others, shorter, stouter, more wicked looking, probably from bison.

"You like horns." It was a statement.

"Not particularly." Carl waved Michael to a seat at a small, square table set up a few feet from his desk. Two chairs waited there, one where the sitter could face the desk, looking across the table to do so, and the other where he would have his back to it. Lair chose the one facing, sitting down with his arms outstretched and laid out on the tabletop, while Carl took a position at the desk itself, but in front of it, where he could lean back against it in an informal, if not relaxing position. "I keep them around for the clients. As you can tell…" He tapped both hands against his chest, "I'm supposed to be a cowboy. If you're in Omaha, and you're trying to sell something to farmers and ranchers, you really need to look the part."

"Well it's working." Michael smiled at the yellow man, liking him immediately. "So, what's the difference?"

"Difference?"

"Yeah, between farmers and ranchers. I always thought they were about the same thing."

Carl laughed. "Don't let a farmer hear you say that. I think the main difference is in the way they treat the land. A farmer works it, toils at it, realizes that's where his lifeblood is. His whole life devoted to nurturing the soil, and getting the most from it. A rancher's more flippant, more frivolous about it. He just likes owning the land, and whether or not he does something with it is usually irrelevant. Ranchers are the ones you see running around town packing the Second Amendment on their hips. With big trucks and big noise, and always an air of importance about them." Carl's face grew sad. "But they don't care about the land, not really. They just care about owning it."

"Sounds like you have a vendetta against ranchers." Michael grinned mischievously. "Should I be writing this stuff down?"

Carl laughed. "No, it doesn't run that deep. In fact, I should keep my mouth shut. I do a lot of business with both sides. It's just that I respect the farmers, and as a matter of necessity, tolerate the others."

Michael looked around. Aside from the horns elevated above there wasn't much else to distinguish the room. A wall of books and journals on one side, then an empty bookcase topped by a bowling trophy on the other. It seemed extremely spartan for a man running a business. "You bowl?" he asked.

"No." Carl renewed his laughter. "Molly brought that in one day. Miss Bishop. The one we're waiting for. Some guy she was dating gave it to her as… well, a trophy. He was trying hard to hold onto her at the time and thought maybe that would do it."

"Did it work?"

"No. He was a pistol packer. Has a small spread east of here. Molly talked him into buying a few thousand dollars worth of pharmaceuticals and sent him down the road." Carl paused then, eying Lair carefully. "What do you want her for anyway? We've talked about it many times. She met a couple of those folks during her rounds, but beyond that she knows very little."

"Just routine stuff. We need to talk with everyone who had any contact whatsoever. Even the smallest of details might help us along the way." Michael paused, considering the question he was about to ask. "Does Molly own any firearms?"

"Bam!" A shrill voice sounded from the doorway. Both men turned. Molly stood there, locking eyes with Lair, her fingers formed to simulate a pistol, which she pointed at his chest. "Molly does," she said sweetly. She entered the office, pouting at Carl before crossing over to the table where she plopped herself down across from Michael. "Molly owns a vast array of firearms," she said, waving her arms expansively. "I've got rifles for hunting, handguns for shooting, and an old world crossbow sitting in my closet in case I ever have to work someone over in silence. I'm very versatile."

Michael studied the woman, who really reminded him more of a girl. A gorgeous, precocious, very out-of-the-ordinary girl. "Miss Bishop, I presume."

Molly smiled warmly at the agent, then turned her head around. "Carl, I've got this," she said.

Carl Monroe, being dismissed, straightened himself from his position at the desk and headed for the door. "Well, for god's sake Molly," he said as he left, "don't shoot the man."

Lair appraised the young woman sitting across from him, while Molly appraised back. Finally, he spoke. "Your boss is quite proud of you, I'm thinking." He nodded in the direction of the bookcase. "He tells me you're quite a bowler."

Molly grinned. "I bowl men, detective. I'm very good at it." Her always flirting hand moved out across the table, brushing lightly against his. "I'd bowl you anytime."

Though he tried hard not to, and completely contrary to his nature, Lair blushed. The skin on the back of his neck responded, prickling into bumps, as his lips twisted their way into a boyish grin. "Wow," he grabbed ahold of himself. "I've known you for twelve seconds, and already you're having my baby."

Molly withdrew her hand then, leaned back in the chair, and folded her arms across her chest in a more professional manner.

This would be her first adversarial reckoning, and she was surprised to find she was not particularly concerned about it. The agent sat there awkwardly, almost dumbly, as she reveled in his discomfort. She had learned long ago how easy it was to disarm a man, leaving him dazed and babbling and giving Molly time to formulate a plan that would lead to his ultimate demise. She supposed it was because life had damaged her enough to closet her own feelings, tuck them away, allowing her to focus on wit and irresistible external features which could subdue nearly every man she encountered. Women she had met over the years were not as taken, not as captivated and not as kind, often apt to assess her as cold, even calculating, with more than one elevating that assessment to exalt, "What a bitch," whenever Molly walked away. Often times she would turn cat-like on these women, and at a sufficient distance that there was no chance she had overheard the hurtful comment, smile sweetly at them and say simply, "I know." But with men it was different. With men it was easy.

An important component of Molly's personality was that she understood it, and even more important, had learned to deal with it. Most humans fail miserably at self-diagnosis, with many never even understanding a diagnosis is warranted. But Molly had spent long, agonizing years locked away in a death camp, watching friends and loved ones dragged away, or sometimes, to heighten the agony, slaughtered before her eyes. And it became even worse, exponentially so, for she was then required to feast upon them, and gratefully smile with each mouthful. So she supposed a certain amount of warping was understandable.

She looked curiously at Michael Lair. "So," she said, her voice dripping its way into formality, "what do you want with me?"

Lair studied the young woman for a long moment before he spoke. He suspected she could go from loving a man to roasting him over an open spit in about the same amount of time it takes to blink. To his mind that made her complex, and Lair loved the challenges of complexity. But he began in on her as he would have with anyone else. With the basics. "I understand you've been informed why I'm here. So I guess what I'd like to know first is whatever you can tell me about your relationship with the Tignors, the Mayfields, and Maxwell Jimson, the farmer who lived here in Omaha." He tapped on the table with a finger. "You knew, or did business with each of those parties, yes?"

"Yeah, I knew them." Molly pursed her lips. "Well, I knew of them. I had accounts with the Mayfields and Mister Jimson, saw them on occasion on my usual runs, and met Tignor only once, a day or two before he was killed, I believe."

"So, you what? Sold supplies to these people? Drugs and such?"

"Yes." Molly crossed her legs, and the skirt she was wearing, already shortened by sitting down, slid an inch or two further up her thigh, exposing a view just above the lip of the table of what Michael could see was a very impressive leg. He glanced at the skirt and the leg, then caught himself and looked quickly up again. Molly was grinning at him. "Well, I hadn't sold anything yet to Tignor. I'd just met him. But he was very interested in one of our latest products, a pacifier that immobilizes sows, makes it a bit more enjoyable for them when they're being bred."

"What?" said Lair. "Sows don't like being bred on their own? I would have thought that was the most fun part."

"Heavens no. They hate it. They usually rail against it with everything in them. I mean they've got six hundred pounds of boar coming at them with criminal intent. It's not the most fun time for a lady."

Michael nodded. "And this drug, what? Sedates them? Like date rape?"

Molly frowned. "Well, we don't quite advertise it that way, but that's about what it does. Makes them a bit more amenable to piggy-sex." Her eyes burned into his. "And who doesn't like that?"

Lair caught himself blushing again. "From what you've just said, I'm guessing the pigs." He leaned back then, also crossing his legs. "So, you meet Tignor, and what? He doesn't buy?"

"No, he did want to. I demonstrated the product to him and he loved it. I was in the process of drawing up the contracts when we heard about his murder." Molly uncrossed her legs and leaned forward. "I don't want to sound disrespectful, but his death cost me a lot of money. Around ten grand a year in commissions, just from that one sale."

"Wow," said Lair, impressed. "You must do alright for yourself. All those lonely old farmers out there just waiting for you to call on them." He nodded at her. "Especially given your... friendly disposition."

Molly laughed openly. "What are you suggesting?"

"Nothing. Just thinking you probably make a lot of sales. You strike me as someone who is very effective at her job, that's all."

Placing both hands on top of the table, Molly clasped them together. "I've been in and around the farming business my whole life. It's what I know. Selling to these people is something I'm very good at. And proud of. They like me, and I like them back."

"That's all I'm saying." Lair leaned forward, hands out on the table, perfectly matching Molly's demeanor. "You don't mind being in the business of slaughtering animals then?"

"What do you mean? And I don't do any of the slaughtering. I just keep the animals healthy and happy until it's time."

Lair was working over an idea. "I don't know. It just seems to me if it's one person doing this, and it doesn't turn out to be random coincidental killings, then the perpetrator may well have a certain sympathy towards animals. An activist maybe, an extreme one, or something like that. In three of the instances hundreds of pigs were set free at around the time of the killings. To me, that says something."

"That sounds plausible." Molly caught Michael's eyes and held onto them. "In my own case, I started raising animals when I was very young. My father gave me my first pig when I was only seven. A baby boar. He made it clear it was not intended to be my pet or my friend, just a commodity like anything else. I raised that pig, took complete care of it, and when the time came handed my father the knife which he used to gut it. I remember that night he rewarded me with a Barbie doll. Malibu Barbie. She was always my favorite, and I figured if slaughtering pigs was going to get me a collection of dolls, well then, hell, I'd slaughter the crap out of them."

Lair could not move his eyes. Molly held them transfixed. This beautiful young woman sitting before him, mesmerizing him, stunning in appearance and cunning of mind. He tried to profile her right there on the spot, but nothing registered. She was unlike anyone he had ever met. At the surface one would expect to see this girl tripping gaily down the sidewalk, flitting from passerby to passerby as she spread the joys of her presence. But deeper down he suspected another personality lurked. A darker, maybe even sinister one. He understood the logic that drove a farmer to raise meat. It was a matter of profit. An endeavor like any other, only with blood as its bi-product instead of wood or steel or paper. But Molly Bishop's eyes caught fire as she spoke of slaughtering pigs. There was a joy attached to it that went beyond all normal bounds. Lair could not have known at the time that as Molly created this story, the passion flowing from her was real, for as she spoke of gutting hogs, in her mind she was gutting men.

After a bit more conversation in which he learned Molly had very little of substance to offer on any of the murders, Lair rose to take his leave. "I'd like to talk again," he said. "You might not know it, but you've been very helpful."

Molly rose with him, taking his arm and escorting him to the door. She could feel him tremble slightly at the physical contact, and inwardly it pleased her. "It would be my pleasure. Anything you want, just ask."

As he broke away, he turned for one last question, just a curiosity. "One last thing, Miss Bishop. Are you right or left handed?" Molly raised both hands in front of her, as if waiting to be cuffed.

"I use them both equally," she said, her voice reverting back to its original sweetness. "Always have." She pouted at him. "Does that mean I'm in trouble?"

"No." Lair turned to leave. "But it doesn't mean you're out."

CHAPTER SIX

Molly woke with the sun streaming in through a large, open-curtained window. She rolled to view the clock on the nightstand. It was almost noon. Her head throbbed. Running her fingers across her temples, she tried to remember the details of the night before. She looked around. She recognized the room. It wasn't hers, but she recognized it. Rolling over onto her other side, she found a man, nestled in quite close to her. In his sleep, the man sensed her movement, reaching out an arm that attempted to caress her, but smacked into her face instead.

"Goddammit, Carl," she hollered out as she retaliated, reaching out and whacking the man on the head.

Carl screamed. "What the hell." He bolted upright, the sheet slipping down to expose a lipstick covered chest. He looked at her. "Goddammit, Molly."

Molly sat up then, and the two faced each other. The strap on the shoulder of her nightgown slipped partway down her arm, the gown shifting enough to expose a breast. She reached a hand up to brush the hair from her face. "It's almost noon," she said.

"I can see your tit."

"What?"

"Your tit." Carl pointed, then reached across and adjusted the strap for her. "It's gross. What time did we get in anyway?"

Molly rolled away, swinging her legs out over the edge of the bed as she sat up. "God," she said, still half asleep. "I'm not remembering much. What the hell was in that tequila?" She grabbed a pillow and reached back to beat him with it. "Did you molest me, you bastard?"

"Hey," Carl admonished her. "You know very well your room is right down the hall. You wandered in here of your own free will. I think it's a much more likely scenario that if anyone got molested it was me." He took his own pillow and smacked her back.

Molly laughed, shaking her head so a long mass of blonde hair swept in to cover her face. "Is that even possible?"

Carl laughed back at her. He looked down at the lipstick smeared across his chest. There were no lip prints, just a mass of hot pink lines and arrows, and a stick figure centered on his navel that appeared to show a man with a penis growing out of him that was longer than his legs. "Damn," said Carl as he pinched at his belly-button. "This guy's got some serious business going on." He looked at Molly. "You're very good at body art. You should do this stuff for a living." He pinched his stomach out further. "Who's this supposed to be anyway?"

Molly swung sideways and studied the drawing. "I'm not sure. That's just about when I passed out. I think it's supposed to be the guy over at Denny's. The one you have such a crush on. I thought maybe if you woke up lonely in the middle of the night you and he could have some quality time together."

Carl grinned then, and reached out to poke at Molly. "Well, you certainly gave him the right amount of equipment. But I was kind of hoping it was that agent friend of yours."

"Who? Michael Lair?"

"Yeah, he's freaking gorgeous."

"He's alright, I guess. In a kind of twisted sort of way. I think he's been beat up too many times."

"Don't you even tell me you don't think he's pretty. And that pistol he's packing is impressive."

Molly fired a pillow at Carl's face, pushed herself up off the bed and headed for the bathroom door a short distance away. "You are so gay," she called out as she swung shut the door.

"Shut up and pee," he hollered back at her. "I've got a fantasy going on here with my stick man. I'm about to be strip searched by an official agent of the FBI."

It was the first Saturday in September. A big day for those in the hog business. Farmers poured into Omaha from all over the Midwest for the association's annual festival and livestock auction. Ordinarily the event was held at the state fairgrounds in Grand Island, a couple hundred miles to the west, but the previous year a tornado had ripped through that facility and the barns where the main auction usually took place wound up somewhere in Kansas. So Omaha had stepped up and happily accepted the millions of dollars in extra revenue that would roll into the city coffers for hosting the event.

Quite naturally, it was also a big day for McMillan Pharmaceuticals, and Carl and Molly had not missed the event in years. They arrived at the fairgrounds around three, an hour before the auction was scheduled to begin. Molly wore her usual business attire of boots, slacks and a white blouse, as there was business to be conducted, but she also had the presence of mind to leave the top few buttons on the blouse unfastened to make her presentation a bit more palatable to the hog-men who always managed to find her and gather around. Carl had attempted to wear one of his oversized belt buckles, a flashy mass of silver the size of a cannonball protruding from his stomach. "No, no, no," Molly had said as she marched him back to the closet. "These are pig people, Carl. They have no interest in seeing how shiny you are." So when they finally arrived at the festival Carl was dressed as sedately as she, but without the cleavage.

For a while they mingled, seeking out a client or two or approaching new prospects. As usual Molly attracted a crowd and soon had a cluster of farmers gathered around her as she espoused the wonders of the company. Carl stood close by, as a wingman, one hand filled with business cards, the other a notepad to jot down possible new contacts. It was a fun time for them both. Molly's hands were kept busy as well, reaching out to touch an arm here, a shoulder there, and occasionally, if a farmer appeared to have a thicker veneer than most, wandering fingers would brush against his cheek. That was usually enough to break any man, and the contact information flowed at them in a continuous stream. One man in particular seemed to dodge Molly, walking up to Carl instead, asking him about any new products or developments in the pharmaceutical industry. They spoke for a few moments, then the man broke away, saying how hot it was and that he thought he might go have a drink. Molly, always multi-tasking, continued to flirt with her prospects while also watching Carl watch the man as he walked slowly away.

"Hey," she leaned over and hissed at him. "Are you nuts? That guy was totally hitting on you."

Carl's eyes were still on the retreating man. "No way. Besides, he's not my type." Carl looked away then and found Molly staring at him. "What?"

Molly waved off some disappointed faces, dragging Carl to the side. She pulled him behind a stack of particle board used to create the myriad display booths scattered around the exhibition hall. "Not your type?" she said, scolding him. "I've been watching you. Your eyes never left his ass."

"No way, man, you're crazy." Carl's mouth curled into a frown. "Even if I was into him, he's way too young for me. And way too hot. He'd never go for me." Molly's eyes bored into him, and even though she didn't utter a word, he retaliated against what she was thinking. "What? God, you're so irritating. How do we even know he's gay?"

"Please, do I look naive to you? That guy took one look at my open blouse and shot me a look of disgust. But for you, my friend, his whole face lit up. If your gaydar isn't tuned in, mine sure as heck is."

"You mean it? You think he's into me? No way. Not even

possible." Carl straightened himself then, trying to appear taller and more manly. "Do you think he knows I'm gay?"

Molly laughed. "Really?"

"Well I just can't go up and talk to him. You know I'm not good at that stuff."

Molly smiled with sweet understanding, then swung her arm down, slamming her fist into Carl's groin. Not harshly, but just hard enough to demand his attention. He groaned, and tried to double over, but she grabbed him, forcing him upright. "Get some balls, dammit." She left him there, with both hands clutching his crotch as she waded off through the crowd until she found the young man. She spun him around, "Hi, I'm Molly," she said, her voice stern enough that it scared him a little. They looked at each other for a long, uncomfortable moment before Molly shook her head and said, "God, you people should have to go to school for this." She began to drag the bewildered man through the crowd then, finding a certain resistance at first until she reached full velocity, at which time he conceded he was her prisoner and allowed himself to be pulled dutifully along. Soon she had him back behind the wall of wood where Carl still stood, adjusting his pants. Again she stared hard at the young man. "Your name?"

"Andrew, ma'am. Andrew Laskey." The man glanced quickly at Carl, then looked submissively downward.

"Well," said Molly, quite pleased with herself, "Andrew, this is Carl." She reached out and smacked Carl on the head. "Carl, this is Andrew. I'm going to go now, while you two bond over discussing what a bitch I am." She stepped away from them both, but turned her head back to address them before leaving. "I'll be watching, and if either of you comes out of here in the next ten minutes, you will regret it." She shook her fist in the air. "Understood?" Both men nodded obediently as Molly shrugged her shoulders and walked away.

She headed for the auction yard located just outside the hall and connected by a great indoor corridor. The actual arena where the auction was to be held had a covered roof, but the sides and ends were open to the outside. The two sides, the one now closest Molly and the one farthest away, had bleachers, partly under cover and partly not, so if the rains came everyone would have to scrunch down near the front to stay under cover. This day, however, was cloudless and wonderfully warm. As she walked along she nodded pleasantly to those around her, noticing most were now also headed in the same direction, towards the arena where the auction would soon begin. Memories began flooding back. Countless times she had taken similar walks, with her father holding onto her hand. They would sit in bleachers just like these, the excitement in her father obvious as he waited to see what the market would bring them that day. For Molly, although she would not have admitted it back then, those were torturous days, with many of the hogs on display coming from their own farm, some having been raised by her own hand. She gave them all names, individualized them, each of dozens and dozens of pigs that passed through the farm and through her life, even though she had been clearly instructed not to. In her own way she believed this would help her to remember them, memorialize them as they were each sacrificed for the betterment of the family. There was even a time in her youth when she tried hard to modify her thoughts, breaking down in her mind the actual business of raising and selling hogs for profit. The fact is, she told herself, it was true what her father said, that when looked at sensibly, hogs were just meat. A commodity exactly as she had been told. They were bought, butchered up and then became unrecognizable as anything other than slabs of flesh to be consumed by a ravenous society. The trouble was, no matter how hard she tried to accept this concept she could never quite shake the fact that this commodity came with a body, a life-force, a personality, a face. That's where Molly broke away, and insisted on naming names. She could remember them that way. Like souls passing through a holocaust, somehow they needed to be remembered.

A voice called out to her. "Miss Bishop." An authoritative man's voice. She turned and there stood Michael Lair and an unpleasant looking woman.

"Detective," she called back, the bad thoughts fleeting away as a look of happiness spread across her face.

The woman spoke, her voice stern, like a teacher's. "It's agent, actually."

Molly turned to the woman, challenging her. "I'm thinking I wasn't addressing you," she said just as sternly, but with a flippant shake of her head.

Michael laughed. "You can call me whatever you'd like, Miss Bishop. It's good to see you again."

Molly stepped up close, reaching out to pluck an imaginary bit of fluff from Lair's shirt. She stared at the woman as she continued to pat away at his arm affectionately. "This your wife?"

"No." Michael continued his laughter as his companion stepped a little to the side. "This is Agent Warman, also with the FBI. We've come to visit your world here. See if we can get a better understanding of what makes it tick." He looked at Warman. "This is Molly Bishop. From McMillan. The young woman you made me the appointment to see."

"You're out fishing? Looking for suspects?" Molly intentionally directed the question to Agent Warman, who just as intentionally ignored her.

Michael reached up, took ahold of Molly's hand and physically, but gently, pushed it away. "Actually, we're not looking for much. Just thought maybe we could get a better handle on things if we became a bit more familiar with how this business works." He looked around as people flocked past. "I never would have thought there was such an interest in pigs."

"They're not here for the pigs, they're here for the profit. And yes, it's big business out here in the sticks." Molly turned her body slightly, as if to exclude Warman from the conversation. "Would you like to sit with me? The auction is actually quite fascinating. I'll show you how it works."

Lair looked at Warman, who looked back at him. She also turned slightly away, dismissing Molly. "I'm not sure that would be within procedural guidelines. She is, after all, a person of interest in the case."

"Oooh," Molly cooed out. "Does that mean I'm a suspect?"

"No, not at all." Warman turned back, her face taking on more of a hawk-like persona than usual. "But unlike the social sector we have strict rules about our associations. It's never permissible to socialize with those involved in a case. In any way. It could be considered compromising."

"What a load of crap." Michael spoke up. "Get a grip, Warman. As you said, Miss Bishop is a person of interest. She knows it and we know it. Hell, everybody knows it. I'm interested in whatever she has to say. So let's just say I'm continuing our interview." He waved a dismissive hand at the agent, then tapped Molly's arm and said, "Lead on, Miss Bishop." As they moved away, leaving Elizabeth Warman to stare after them, Molly again made contact with Michael, this time grabbing his arm and entwining it with hers. She turned her head to make sure Warman was watching, and smiled smugly at her.

There was a good crowd filling the bleachers and they sat themselves right about in the middle of everyone. Molly, who loved to chatter, began to explain what they were about to observe. "For the first hour or so, the prize hogs will be shown. You'll be amazed at what they sell for. An average hog, say three, four hundred pounder will go for a buck-sixty, buck-seventy a pound. These first babies coming at us will fetch maybe ten times as much."

"What?" Lair whistled. "Sixteen dollars a pound for pork. On what planet is that possibly reasonable?"

Molly laughed. "It's not. That's what I'm saying. Most of them have been hand-raised by the sons and daughters of the farmers here. It's like a year-long project for them. And now they get to reap the benefits of all the hard work they put into it. As each pig is brought out, the other farmers who are friends or associates of the exhibiting farmer will begin a sort of bidding frenzy, and the price will escalate dramatically."

"How can they afford to do that? Are they nuts?"

"No. And it's not done recklessly. It's a sort of you-scratch-my-back-I'll-scratch-yours mentality. Everyone knows when it's their turn the favor will be reciprocated. It's a feel-good for everybody.

And it seems the bigger the hog farmer, the more his kids get for their pigs. There's a kind of hierarchy to it."

Michael chuckled softly. "Pig farmer high society. But I think I get it. When I was young my mother belonged to this local art club. She'd paint away furiously and produce the biggest piece of crap you'd ever want to throw on a burn pile. But come auction day the other ladies would always tell her how wonderful it was, and they'd actually bid on the damn thing, and some poor lady would wind up buying it. Then when it was their turn to sell, there would be my mama, always dragging home a bigger pile of crap than she left with." Lair scratched his chin as Molly smiled and nodded at him. "One thing though, I've been wanting to ask."

"What is it?"

"Well, I don't want to offend you, but you raise this pig, right? I can't even imagine there isn't some sort of emotional attachment to it. You raise it, you bottle feed it. At some point you must find your-self petting and maybe even talking to it. Yet you seem so glib about the whole thing. Like the animal itself means nothing to you. I'm guessing it's not just you, but everyone connected to this business." Michael searched her eyes with his, seeking something he hoped would be there. "Isn't there ever any pain involved? Doesn't it ever feel like you're selling away a friend and maybe surrendering a little piece of yourself?"

Molly's eyes searched back. They held nothing he could find of substance. She placed her hand on his leg. Inside she was trembling. She wanted to grab his face between her hands, shake it and scream, yes, yes, goddammit. I feel all of that. All of it. Instead, she said, "I think you'd need to live the life to understand it. We're not raising a dog here, or a cat, or any kind of pet. It's just meat." Her voice grew cunning. "Do you eat meat, Agent Lair?"

"Yes, of course, and I know what you're going to say. But I don't know the damn thing. Not personally. I've never met it, lived with it, socialized with it. It comes at me on a plate. I'm not sure I could eat it otherwise."

"But isn't that the same? You're what my father likes to call a cellophane hunter. You'll eat the meat if it's all wrapped up neatly, but someone else has to do the dirty work for you. You're not willing to look an animal in the eye and bludgeon it to death. But when it's all chopped up nice and pretty, you're sure sitting there at the table with a big grin on your face." Molly removed her hand, but not her eyes. "Maybe you shouldn't judge while you have all that blood running down your chin. As an agent you should know that can be used as evidence against you. I believe they call it *accessory to murder.*" Molly flashed air quotes at Lair. "Am I right? You'd be found guilty as hell."

"Wow," was all Lair could say. Their eyes were inches apart, unblinking, daring the other to move. It was Michael who surrendered first, tilting his head downward. "I don't know what to say to that." He tried to smile. "I suspect your daddy would have taken me out behind the woodshed and beat me till I killed something. And I guess I probably would have."

"You would have. If you wanted meat. There's really no alternative."

They watched the auction for a while, as hog after hog marched out as if on parade, proudly accompanied by a girl or boy. Each youngster would march their pig to the center of the arena, some using a rope to encourage the animal along, but many required nothing more than a soft whistle or call which the pig would instantly obey as it followed along. There was definitely a kinship between many of the children and their pigs. It was undeniable. Molly glanced at Michael from time to time, and was certain there were moments when pain twitched away at him. She liked this man, felt drawn to him just as surely as he must be repulsed by her. It hurt her somewhat, but also amused her, and she decided to take a look inside at her first convenience to figure out why.

Off to one side she heard a familiar sound. A man's loud laughter. Studying a group of young men who sat just below them and an aisle to the right, her face lit up. She tapped Michael on the leg, pointing. "You see that man, the one in the blue-checked shirt."

"Yeah." Michael leaned over. "One of your beaus?"

Molly punched at him playfully. "No. I knew him in college. Haven't seen him in years. Funny how you never forget a laugh. His name is David Mertle. We took animal husbandry together. They called him the pig-baller. He was very popular."

"Pig-baller? Dare I ask?"

Both of them continued to stare at the man. "He used to regale us with stories of how he and his brothers would play basketball with the baby pigs. The runts." Molly turned back to Michael. "You know about runts and pigs, right?"

"Well, I'm guessing they're smaller. Is that what you mean?"

"Yes, but what a lot of people don't know is pretty much every litter has one or two. They're not deformed or anything, just born small. No one has ever figured out why. It's sort of a hog phenomenon."

"Oh, I did not know that." Lair crinkled his face, confused. "And he played basketball with them?"

"Yeah, they invented a game. David used to boast about it. You see the runts, if left alone, would develop right along with their larger siblings, but it takes them longer and requires more feed and effort than most farmers are willing to put in. So usually the runts are culled out at birth, gathered up in buckets or sacks and discarded. At least that's the way we did it on our farm."

"You mean they're still alive?"

"Temporarily. Some farmers throw them on the garbage pit where the coons and foxes will come and fetch them. My dad considered himself more merciful than that. He'd throw them all in a sack and toss them into the pond behind our barn. That way he said they wouldn't suffer."

"Wow, I'm thinking that has suffer written all over it."

"It's life, Michael. At least for pigs it is." Molly paused, motioning at David Mertle. "Anyway, he used to brag about how he could toss a runt pig over thirty feet and bank it off a wall into a barrel. They would do that until the runt was dead, normally on the second or third toss. So the game was to see who could get the most tosses out of a pig before it was pronounced dead. Mertle there said he held the record at five. He was quite proud of it." Molly looked away so Lair couldn't see the quick flash of fire that came into her eyes. "That's why they called him the pig-baller."

The next morning the three agents met again, and again Michael was late. "Did you oversleep with your little hottie?" Warman scolded, while Agent Crane looked at them both curiously.

"No, Agent, but as a matter of fact I did garner quite a bit of information that may come in handy at some point. This business of hog raising is really quite fascinating. You should have stayed."

As he sat, she slid a newspaper across the table at him. "Were you so fascinated you failed to catch another stockman's murder going on right underneath your nose?"

Michael grabbed at the paper. "What the hell are you talking about?" He studied the paper for a moment, catching a headline that covered the right-hand part of page one. *Hog Farmer Slain at Annual Event*, it read. Next to it was the photo of a young man, and the name, *David Mertle*.

CHAPTER SEVEN

Michael Lair and Elizabeth Warman headed back towards the fairgrounds. Michael drove while she busily tap-tapped away on her laptop. There was no sun out and shining as there had been the day before, the sky closed up and grey, with a light drizzle causing the wipers to come on every minute or so. Warman spoke. "So this man was twenty-nine, and seemingly fit, but it appears he died without a lot of resistance."

"What does that mean?" Michael shook his head.

"He was found in one of the stalls under a pile of hay. There was no sign of a struggle. It looks like he went there of his own free will."

"Or he was carried."

Warman nodded, conceding this new possibility. "In that case our perpetrator is rather fit himself. This Mertle was no small man. It says he weighed in at around two-hundred pounds."

"Method of death determined yet?"

"Still trying to figure that one out. Initially it's been ruled a homicide because of the manner in which he was found, all bundled up in the corner beneath a pile of hay." Warman paused, studying. "There is a new report. It doesn't appear they have released it yet, stating a suspected needle mark was found on his neck, high up, almost under his jaw bone."

"It says that?"

"Well, it's from the coroner. Actually it says sternocleidomas-
toid and mandible. I'm breaking it down for you."

"Thanks." Lair grinned slightly. "I would have thought that was
his ass-bone or something. It's good to have you along."

Warman studied Lair for a moment, trying to judge whether or
not he was genuinely thanking her or making fun of her. Her entire
life she'd had trouble telling the difference. "You don't like me much,
do you?"

Michael looked over and examined her, determining the intent
of the question and the possible responses he could come up with
to answer it. "I don't really know you." He looked back at the windshield, tapping at the wheel thoughtfully. "You've got a pretty tough
exterior, I'll tell you that."

"I like to go by the book."

"You're very good at it."

"You're not. You don't really seem to give a damn what anyone
thinks." She flipped the laptop closed as they turned into a lot at the
rear of the fairgrounds, one that would allow them to pull up close
to the quartering stalls where livestock was held during exhibitions.

As he pulled in and parked, Lair turned to face her, both hands
still gripping the wheel. "We might as well put our cards on the table
here. Are you referring to now, to our current situation, or my past?"

Warman looked back at him, at first seriously, but then just the
hint of a smile crinkled the edges of her lips. It was the first sign of
softness he'd ever seen in her. And it was fleeting. "Well it seems to
follow you around. Your record would indicate you're an excellent
agent, one of the best. But occasionally you have a way of going off
track, of going rogue, off on your own. That could be a weakness."
For a moment it almost looked like she might reach out to touch
his arm, then the coldness returned. "It's always best to lend your
talents to a team. That way the credit is spread around evenly, as is
the blame. It makes us whole. We're an organization, not a group
of individuals running around in disarray. You don't seem to understand that."

The scene at the stalls was one of delicate efficiency. An area had been cordoned off, not with tape, but rather a line of orange cones, like highway markers that blocked off the section of corridor where the body had been found. An officer greeted them, offering to move a couple of the cones aside, but the agents chose to squeeze between them and proceed to the crime scene. Another officer met them there. "Well, this is it," he said to them. The stall was a small, partly open enclosure. It had two solid walls and two low, stable-fence barriers, one in front, facing them, and the other to the left side. The officer pointed to a corner on the right, the one bordered by the walls. "We found him over there. He was all scrunched up, almost fetally, and didn't appear to have gone through a great deal of discomfort. The coroner indicated to us this morning he was likely injected with a substance that killed him. They're still checking that out." The officer tapped at his neck. "There was a single mark, a probable injection site about here. Other than that there isn't a lot to tell. Or see." He handed Warman a folder that held a few dozen photos, first of the discovery itself, with very little of the hay disturbed, and then a varying array of photos showing the body as it lay when found, and more as it was laid out on a gurney for transport to the morgue. Michael glanced at the photos as Warman rifled through them. He selected several that showed the victim lying on the gurney.

"Those are post scene," she said. "They won't teach you much." Still, Lair studied them, his instincts crying out that something of worth was imbedded in the images. He'd done this many times before. And many times there was something so simple it was almost always overlooked. He studied the face of the deceased man first, then his shirt. The checkered-blue shirt Molly had first pointed out to him. There was something about it. Something substantive right there in front of him. His finger traced its way up the man's shirt to his neck, and there it was. Three buttons unfastened. The collar thrown loosely open. It had been warm yesterday, but not hot. Most men wore their shirt with a single button undone, with some, mostly younger ones, unfastening two. But three, never. Even in the heat of summer, two was about as far as a man would go. With three undone, it likely meant there was another party in close proximity whose interest was physical, affectionate maybe. It indicated Mertle had been quite relaxed at the time, and in a good enough mood to allow someone access to his clothing. He gave the photos back to Warman and raised his hands to explore his own shirt, testing how hard it was to unfasten a button. Could it happen nonchalantly, accidentally become undone by the careless movements of the attendants lifting and shifting the body? His shirt and the buttons on it resisted effort to fling one haphazardly open. It required a certain dexterity. He'd need to take a look at that shirt.

"What are you doing?" Warman asked him.

"Nothing. Unbuttoning my shirt is all. Is that a crime?" He smiled dumbly at her and moved away into the corner where the body had been found. The hay, once piled on the corpse, now lay strewn about, as the forensics who investigated the scene had obviously dug through it in an effort to extract evidence. There wasn't really much to see. But Michael had his own technique for the ground game. He was a great groveler. Even more, he knew exactly what he was looking for, another piece for his puzzle. He dropped to his knees. Cupping his hands and dipping them downward, he scooped through the straw in a low arc, shoveling a great pile of hay into the air. He shook his arms then, allowing the hay to flake away in small bunches until his hands were emptied.

One of the officers standing with Warman watched him for a moment, then turned to her and shook his head. She nodded back. "He's not normal," she said, then uncharacteristically added, "but he's damn good at what he does."

Lair continued his hay extraction technique for another few minutes, shifting his position once or twice to cover more of the floor. He considered it sort of like panning for gold, only sifting through straw instead of sand, and gold is exactly what he found. On one of his last sweeps, as the last of the straw drifted away, a single strand of long, golden-blonde hair was left dangling between his fingers. He glanced over in the direction of Warman and the officer. They were engrossed in conversation. Covertly slipping the strand into his shirt pocket he rose, and signaled her that his investigation had been completed.

CHAPTER EIGHT

Molly drove a backroad somewhere in the middle of Iowa. There were several smaller farms here, truck farms with patches of corn growing next to patches of wheat growing next to fenced-in ponds with ducks and geese paddling along, and with a few pigs scattered about the edges of the ponds, shoveling their way merrily through the muck. It was like a Rockwell painting of early Americana, each farm settling comfortably into the earth as though it had nestled there throughout time. It was a rare site, this section of Iowa. Most of the flatlands of the Midwest had long since been taken over by the large combines, and were not even run by farmers, but rather laborers hired by big city conglomerates who bought up the land by the square mile instead of by the acre. These giant enterprises had little respect for the fields they owned, having learned to sow immense crops by stripping the land of the very nutrients the crops needed desperately to grow, but making up for it by dumping tons upon tons of chemicals, layering the land with a thick chemical paste, and sentencing the earth to a slow, agonizing death.

Molly could feel the earth as a living thing. She talked to it, and had since she was very young. She thought it spoke back to her, cried out to her. She dreamed of a time, long past, when the earth was able to care for itself, with the rains and the soil and the seasons blending themselves in perfect harmony. But the earth was running out of energy. It just couldn't fight any more. And it was dying.

She turned into a drive at the end of an unpaved road. The fields there were sparsely tilled, the native plants and grains growing in abundance. This land made her smile. Pulling up next to an old weathered farmhouse, she parked beneath an oak and stepped from the car. A young girl came out from behind the house just then, and walking along beside her was a huge boar hog. The girl spied Molly, and calling out joyously, ran to her. Molly dropped to her knees, enveloping the girl in her arms as they collided in a ball of laughter. The hog arrived a moment later, nearly crushing them both as it tumbled headfirst into the two. Molly hugged the girl and Molly hugged the hog. "Agnus is getting fat," she chided the child as she pushed hard to get the boar off of her.

The girl giggled. "You know he hates it when you call him that. His name is Angus, not Agnus."

Molly sat up as the boar rolled over to lay next to her. She scratched at its belly and it grunted back contentedly. "How's everybody?" Molly asked.

The girl sat up then, clutching Molly's arm. "Well," she held up her hand to count on her fingers. "We've got new baby chicks, new baby ducks, a baby goat mama bought at the flea market, and yesterday I found a little cottontail out on the road. He's kinda hurt, but I think he's gonna be okay."

"Wow," said Molly. "You've been very industrious." She looked at the house. "Is your mama home?"

"No, she had to drive into Sioux City. She'll be home later this afternoon." The girl looked at her excitedly. "Can you stay over?"

Molly reached out to brush her hand across the girl's cheek. "No, sweetie, I'm afraid I can't stay this time. I'll only be here a little while. But I'll be back next week and I'll stay for sure."

The girl's eyes dimmed, then quickly brightened. "Okay," she said. "Let's go to the barn. I wanna show you the new chicks."

Molly loved this farm. She had stumbled across it four years earlier during her first week of work for Carl and McMillan. He had sent her out to the most remote of places, to test her, to see if she had the fortitude to make it in the world of cold sales. So she had driven there with good will and good intentions, not knowing that day and this place would mark her, blemish her, and set the course for all that she would become. There was no little girl rushing out to meet her back then. But a child of about four, small and frightened, who sat on the steps, her face reddened, a touch of blood running down from her nose. She was crying, and holding on as tightly as she could to a raggedy doll. Molly had quickly climbed the steps when she saw the girl, and sat beside her. "Sweetie, are you okay?" she had asked, her heart breaking a little without even knowing why.

The girl had looked at her with dead eyes, then turned to point alongside the porch. At the end of the porch, and pushed out into the yard, stood a buck-pole, a steel post with a steel cross member at its top, used mostly by hunters to hang the carcasses of their kills. There, dangling by a chain from the pole, was a young pig. Its neck had been slashed, with fresh blood still dripping to the ground.

"My Polly," the girl had cried out, her hand falling back in despair as she clutched again at the doll. A screen door had sounded then, behind her, and as Molly turned her head a man stepped out onto the porch.

"What the hell do you want?" he had snarled at her. He was ten feet away, but even from that distance Molly could tell he reeked of alcohol. A woman, small and frightened, appeared in the doorway.

"Please, Angus," she said, her voice trembling. "Please."

The man had turned on the woman, and though Molly couldn't be certain because her view was blocked, she thought he struck her. She heard a cry, a shortened scream, and then the sound of a body striking something hard as it fell. The man's voice had yelled out, "If I wanna kill a goddam pig, I'll kill a goddam pig."

It all came tumbling back now as she walked towards the barn with the girl. Molly had frozen there on the steps that day, her face ashen. She had tried to find anger, tried to call on rage to come to her aid, but all she could summon was fear. Then tiny arms had grabbed at her. Instinctively her arms reached back and Molly and the girl clung to one another, the doll now crushed between them. A moment later the man turned back. "I said what the hell do you want here?" He had stepped towards them, his face cruel and menacing, his fists waving madly about. Without thinking, Molly broke away. She tore her arms from the child and she ran. A few minutes later, when she was safely back on the road, her body began to convulse uncontrollably. She pulled off the roadway, hands moving up to cover her eyes. She knew all too well the horror the girl had faced, watching her beloved pet slashed and hung up as a slab of meat. She and this child were kindred.

After what must have been a long time, she lowered her hands and lifted her head. The fear washed away. Reaching back into the rear seat, she had fumbled through a number of cases which laid there, selecting one and placing it on her lap. She remembered opening it. Inside were three small vials, safely secured in tight little indentations carved out especially to accommodate them. In another indentation, just beneath the bottles, was a large syringe, and tucked away next to that, a two inch needle. Large letters adorned the flap on the case. *Malazine*, it read. *An equine product to be used only on animals greater than six-hundred pounds.* Molly had removed the syringe and fastened it to the needle. She took out one of the vials, inserting the needle tip and drawing back on the handle until it filled the chamber of the syringe about one-third full. The vial was then empty. She took out another and repeated the process, this time drawing out enough liquid to fill the chamber to the exact level of a bright red line painted on the outside of the syringe. The fine print below the line read, *Fatal, Euthanize Only*. Molly remembered trembling, remembered catching herself, scolding herself, and then her mind had entered a tranquil, controlled place she had not even been aware existed. Her whole life had been a crawl through pity, a crawl through the slime of acquiescence, accepting the carnage around her as something to be despised, but tolerated. That day, right there in the road, Molly would change. Her metamorphosis would be a stunning one, and it would be markedly unpleasant for a select few she deemed especially unworthy. She remembered pushing down slightly on the handle of the syringe until a tiny drop of golden liquid bubbled out, and then turning the car around and heading back in the direction of the farm. The memory flooded back at her. That was the day of her first hunt.

CHAPTER NINE

The woman awoke to darkness. She tried to grab hold of her senses, tried to reason with herself about her whereabouts and her circumstance. The one thing she knew, it was pitch-black dark. Her head throbbed. She tried to reach a hand up to feel her forehead, but the hand was restricted. It seemed to be tied down. She tested her other hand, but found it was even more restricted, having been not just tied but also wedged beneath her body and something hard and cold. A sound pounded away at her. A steady obnoxious drone. She tried to think, tried to remember. She had been shopping— no, had finished shopping— had an armload of bags and packages she'd been trying to stuff into the back of her car. Then the donuts had fallen. The damn donuts. It was her first clear memory, and she clung hard to it. The small, pink box with a clear plastic window on top. She closed her eyes tightly in an attempt to remember more, but found an irony in that, as nothing could be as void of light as the space she now found herself crammed into. So she opened them back up and laid there staring into the darkness as her mind fought its way back.

At this same time, Johnny Grimm drove south with his new girlfriend. She was obstinate, he told himself over and over. An obstinate bitch. Maybe it was time for a change. This was his fourth girlfriend in just over a year, but each one had brought with her the kind of baggage that made maintaining a healthy relationship a near impossibility. He considered for the briefest moment whether or not he could be at fault, but no, he had done nothing wrong. He'd been supportive and caring in each instance, and deserving of a kind of love and emotional commitment none of them could provide. They were all bitches. Take this new one in the trunk, for instance. He'd met her in the produce department at the market just an hour earlier. She'd smiled at him first, and not tentatively, but widely and openly, in an obvious attempt to attract him. In fact, they had spoken for only a moment or two before she professed her love for him. So he had followed behind her as she shopped, always staying an aisle or two away, but keeping close enough to have an intimate conversation about her intentions to make him happy. It wasn't until they left the store, with her pushing a cart and Johnny following along at some distance behind, that he found out the truth about her. She was leaving him. Just like the others. They all had. They would flirt and flaunt and proclaim dark passions and deep love, but always, just when he had fallen hard, they would leave, or try to.

Johnny headed now for Omaha. He'd read an ad in one of the weeklies that called for workers on a new hog farm opening up near there. The ad said only experienced hog men need apply, and he figured that would give him a nice leg up. He'd worked hogs pretty much his entire life. As a skinner, a slopper, a herder, a hook-man, even as a sticker. That was the job he really coveted. He had a special talent as a pig sticker, often arranging the stinging jabs so that it would take several to put a hog down. Most of the men who worked the stick would take their hogs down in a single jab, one thrust, low down, where the neck connected with the body. They would fire down on the trigger, and a massive voltage of electricity would smash into the creature's chest, immediately stopping the heart so the pig could be hoisted aloft. Johnny would scoff at them, pointing out several more entertaining ways to prolong the experience for man and hog. If done correctly, he would boast, an animal could remain standing for three or even four jabs before succumbing. The problem was the other workers would always become envious of his ability, and the boss man would be called in, usually assigning him a lesser duty and sometimes even sending him away. He supposed it was his cross to bear for being the best, and he was never particularly ill-willed about being let go.

About an hour outside of Omaha, Johnny turned off the highway onto a side road, drove it for a ways, then turned once again, this time into an old dirt drive that went only a hundred yards or so before it ended abruptly in a grove of trees. It was time for them to have it out. He would make one last attempt to reason with... Beth... yes, he told himself, her name would be Beth. They could stop here, talk like adults, and either work things out or go their separate ways. If she decided to stay with him, he was quite willing to make a good life for them both. But that would be for her to decide.

He climbed from the car, working his way to the rear of the vehicle where he reached down and popped open the trunk. Beth lay there, her eyes at first squinting as the light streamed in on them, then widening as she saw Johnny staring back at her. Several layers of duct tape were laced across her mouth, with one piece applied so sloppily that in crept its way onto her nose, effectively blocking one of her nostrils. "I've found a nice place for us to stop," he said. "Nice and secluded where we can talk and figure stuff out." He reached down and drew her into his arms, lifting her gently, and carried her to a nearby log which jutted out from the trees, partly blocking the roadway. He deposited her there, in an upright sitting position facing the car and the road. For a time he paced back and forth in front of her, trying to find the right words to cement their relationship or at least give them a fighting chance. Finally, he spoke. "Look, baby, I'm willing to forgive you for trying to run out on me like that." He moved over and knelt beside her. She twisted her head to face him directly, her eyes pleading as she tried to speak through the layers of tape. "I understand all that," he replied to her. "I just wanna be sure you're in this for the right reasons." The woman looked at him dumfounded, and shook her head. "Okay," he said, his tone soft and understanding. "I appreciate your honesty. But it would have been easier on both of us if you'd shared this with me a long time ago." He reached for her blouse then, tearing it open and exposing her breasts. His hand reached out and found one, massaging it savagely. She tried to scream, but her cries were muffled by the tape. "I know," he said to her, still speaking softly. "I'm just as sad about this as you are." He pushed her off the log then, and onto the ground. As he climbed on top of her, his face contorted, and his voice grew raspy. "I need you to know I don't hate you for this. I'm disappointed in you, but I don't hate you."

A short time later, Johnny drove back along the dirt road and entered the highway, turning once again for Omaha. He clicked on the radio, listened for a few minutes to the news and then turned on a music station. The music irritated him somehow, so he clicked it off and drove along in silence. Women were so confusing, and frustrating. But somewhere out there was a woman who felt the same way as he, who shared all the same wants and needs. She could be looking for him this very moment. That would make them fated, and on bisecting paths toward a shared destiny. He would search for her, and bond with her.

John Grimm would find his female.

CHAPTER TEN

Carl Monroe leaned over to grab a cookie. He munched away on it for a time, his head bowed thoughtfully. "I'm gonna kill the bastard," he mumbled to himself. "First I'll take *her*, lock her away somewhere, and then I'll take the old man down. Trap the bastard and watch him beg for his life." Molly poked her head through the doorway.

"Sounds serious," she said. "Are we having fun?" Carl looked up.

"Hell yes. I've got his queen trapped between my knight and bishop, and I'm about to make a move." He tapped at the chess board. "Only trouble is, I'm gonna lose them both before I can get back out of there."

"But you get her, right?"

"Yeah, I sure as hell get her."

"Then all you have to ask is, is she worth it?"

"Yeah, she's worth it. And it opens up a doorway right to the old man."

"Then do it." Molly entered the room and crossed to where Carl sat at an old wooden table. She studied the board for a moment, having not the slightest idea what sort of battle was raging down there. But she knew it was important to her friend, and that made it important to her. "Spank her hard, baby. No mercy."

"But I'm gonna lose two of my best men." Molly sat down on a chair opposite Carl. She reached out to tap at one of the pieces.

"Queen, right?" she asked.

"Yeah."

"And she's in your way, right?"

"Yeah."

"Then take her down. Consider your men collateral damage if it helps you achieve what you're ultimately after." She tapped at another piece, the tallest on the board. "This is him?"

"Yup."

"Then that's the prize. Do whatever it takes to get to him." Molly smiled at the thought that her knowledge of chess was akin to her knowledge of quantum mechanics, and yet she had found herself in this position many times, sitting across from Carl, as his cheerleader and coach in a game she knew nothing about. She watched as he looked down at the board, his face twisting in anguish.

"You don't get it, Mol. I don't like to give up my men." Carl looked over at her. "I'm just trying to take my time and see if there's some way I can save them. Collateral damage is just bullshit."

"Oh, god." Molly reached out across the table. She swiped at his face, and narrowly missed his nose. "Man, you are one messed up dude. It's a war, right? And shit happens in war."

"It's not a war. It's about strategy and sacrifice. It's about who can sacrifice the least and still win."

Molly shook her head disdainfully. "The very definition of war, dear. I swear you need therapy. If someone is in your way, you take them down, and it doesn't make a damn bit of difference who gets hurt along the way. Not if your goal is victory, and sacrifice is what it takes to achieve it."

"That's cold, man."

"It's fact." She looked down at the table. "I don't know why you're so obsessed with this game. All it does is make you cry." Molly picked up a pawn laying in a pile of other pawns at the side of the board. "These guys are dead, right?"

"For now they are. Till next time."

Slamming the pawn down hard on the table, she exclaimed, "Well that's it, you dumbass. They get resurrected. Every time. As soon as you take down that king, everybody gets to wake up and party, and do the whole thing all over again. No war, no sacrifice, no damage, just a joyous moment of rejuvenation." She rose then, and walked around the table where she reached out a hand and grabbed a fistful of Carl's hair, twisting it forcefully.

"Ouch," he cried out. "Dammit, Mol."

"Stop being such a big baby," she said as she released her grip and turned to leave. "Just kill the bitch."

Carl watched as Molly moved away, leaving the room and heading down the hallway that led to the kitchen. His face took on a helpless expression that went well beyond just losing a couple of players in a game. His thoughts were of the girl. He loved Molly. As contentious as their relationship was at times, she had brought more pure joy into his life in the past few years than he had known in an entire lifetime before that. They had met one night in the parking lot at a dive bar on the outskirts of Omaha. Well, that's not entirely true. They had actually met a few hours earlier when she had danced her way into his office at McMillan and asked for work. His first impression of her had not been a positive one. She had plopped down in a chair, looked him over intently, judging him, he supposed, and then just blurted out the words, "Hire me. It'll be the best move you ever make." Carl had been unimpressed, or more accurately, intimidated. He saw her as complicated, aggressive, menacing even. The sort of person who would berate and bully him at every opportunity. He'd seen her kind before, in every human form imaginable. Always pushing, always pressing to assert themselves. So he had not ended the interview well.

Shuffling some papers, he had opened and closed a drawer with blunt authority, and said simply, "Thanks for stopping by, but the positon has been filled."

Molly had leaned forward, placing both hands on the desk. "I don't believe that for a minute," she said, her eyes so piercing that he had to look away. "If it were true I would have been told that by your receptionist, and would have never made it to your office."

Carl's eyes remained down, staring at the desktop while he stammered, "I don't have to explain myself to you. As I said, the position has been filled."

Molly tapped both hands on the desk, drumming away in a quiet rhythm. "It must be sad being you. Never able to face someone squarely. Never able to tell the truth."

Carl had looked up then, a flash of anger moving in. "I don't have to answer to you." His eyes caught hers for the briefest of moments, cowered, then quickly retreated downward again. "Please leave."

Molly rose, and moved to leave, but when she reached the door she turned. "You're a sad little man," she said. Then she was gone.

It was later that evening he would next run into her, at a bar called Lola's, a local hangout for stockmen and farmers. Carl would go there about once a month or so, to hand out business cards and make contacts with the agricultural community who were the life-blood of his business. He would always dress sedately for these outings, blue jeans, plaid shirt, brown boots, trying his best to blend in as just another country boy in a world filled with country boys. As he sat at the bar nursing a beer, a young man had pulled up on the stool beside him. The man nodded pleasantly, and seemed to brush intentionally against Carl's arm. "Excuse me," the man said. "Buy you a beer?"

"Sure, thanks." Carl felt an immediate rush. There weren't many gay men in Omaha, at least not openly so. Opportunities were few and far between. And this young cowboy was not bad looking. Carl shifted his body slightly to more openly face the young man, allowing his own arm to brush back. "Maybe later I can buy you one." The man looked at him inquisitively, and nodded.

"Sure," he said. He reached across Carl, his hand aiming at a bowl of nuts shoved back against the edge of the counter. Mistaking the move for a suggestive gesture, Carl had reached his own hand out and their fingers collided over the bowl, Carl's curling around those of the other man's in intimate fashion. His heart pounded. What he was doing was risky. What they were both doing was risky, but it had been a long time since he had felt any form of attention or affection from another man. The entire action took only a second or two, and was driven by impulse rather than intelligible thought. Carl had smiled then, and turned even more in the direction of his companion. The look that awaited him was anything but friendly, and in an instant the spell was broken, crushed actually, as the man recoiled, ripping his hand away while lashing out with his other hand. It impacted Carl's face, and even though the music was loud and raucous conversations abounded around them, the sound of the impact caused everyone close by to turn and stare. "What the hell are you doin'?" The young cowboy's face became instantly heated and violent.

"What?" stammered Carl, outwardly trying to remain calm, while inside he was screaming, "Shit, shit, shit." His hand went to his face, massaging the site of the blow. "I didn't mean anything by it."

"What's goin' on, Larry?" A big man moved up beside the cowboy. He stood there looking hard at Carl.

"This sunovabitch just tried to fag on me."

"What? No!" Carl tried to laugh, but his voice choked up on him and he began to cough instead. "I was just reaching for the nuts, that's all."

The big man laughed, and soon others nearby also began to laugh. "Oh, he wanted some nuts, alright."

The cowboy rose suddenly and stood there, fists clenched and trembling with open anger. "You fag sunovabitch. I'm gonna kick your ass." He reached out and grabbed at Carl, pulling him off the stool. His hand caught a fistful of cloth, ripping open the top few buttons on Carl's shirt. There was an audible gasp from the onlookers, and then a long moment of silence as all eyes turned to stare at Carl and his now exposed undershirt which flashed brightly orange with bold, black lettering, *Bang Me Hard Big Boy*. It had been hiding behind a wall of placid fabric, and removed all doubt as to sexual preference. Carl loved the shirt. It was the only piece of clothing he had ever bonded with, the printed words a humorous way for him to demonstrate a defiance beneath the surface that he might never be able to unveil. A fear began to rise in him as the cowboy, his large companion, and a throng of bystanders began to close in on him.

"Wait, wait," he called out. "It's a joke. It's just a joke." Backing away, the heel of his boot caught on a metal railing running the length of the bar, causing him to stumble. As he fell another boot rose up from somewhere behind, crashing into his side and sending him sprawling to the floor. What happened in the next few seconds came at him as a blur. Hands groped at him, lifted him and carried him towards the exit door and the outside. His head smashed into a table, then the side of the door itself, amid loud cheering and laughter. Finally he was hoisted high and thrown vigorously onto the hood of a pickup in what he thought must be the parking lot. A fist smashed into his stomach as he was dragged off the hood and onto the ground. Loose gravel grated roughly against his face, some of it making its way into his mouth, and he gagged as dirt and tiny pebbles worked their way down his throat. "Please," he cried out."Please. I didn't mean anything." He was just about to scream when the air was shattered by the sound of a blast, a booming explosion so loud and so close that for a moment Carl thought a bomb had gone off. Then all was silent. Completely and utterly silent. He rolled over, looking up through a haze of dirt and blood and mental incapacity. There, just a few feet away, stood a woman. She wore long, black boots and a short skirt which showcased her disgustingly perfect thighs. As his eyes roamed higher he noticed the gun, a giant pistol hanging loosely from her hand. The hand rose, the barrel of the gun swinging upward until it pointed directly at his head. "Oh, god," he moaned. "Oh, god." The woman spoke, calmly and evenly.

"Anybody here willing to die for this piece of shit?" The pistol remained trained on Carl, but a sort of calm swept in, tugging away at him, and he felt more protected by the gun than threatened by it. He had already made the assumption that he was the piece of shit, and he doubted, given his current circumstance, anyone would consider him worth dying over. But there were some rumblings from the spectators.

"Screw him, man."

"Yeah, screw him."

"Fuckin' fag."

"Fuck the bastard."

"Yeah, fuck him."

"Let's go get a beer."

"Yeah, the hell with this. Let's go get a beer."

After a moment or two, the crowd had moved away, headed back in the direction of the bar. That's when Carl rolled over a bit further to gain a better view. As he looked up he noticed that the barrel of the gun remained trained on his head. "I wouldn't mind if you pointed that thing somewhere else now," he said, trying to sound grateful and jovial at the same time. Then he saw her face, and his heart slowed dramatically. "Oh, god, it's you."

"Yup, it's me." Molly stood there, waving the barrel in a slow arc. "If you had any intelligence at all you would have figured that out by the shit reference. That should have done it for you." She walked over to him, then past him, finally leaning against the pickup. "You okay?"

"I think so." He had to turn again, rolling in the other direction so he could continue to face her. "Your name is Molly, right?"

"Good memory." She reached down to tuck the pistol into her boot. "Poor decision making though. What? Did you hit on that guy?"

Carl grimaced. "No, of course not. I'm not gay. Just a misunderstanding, that's all."

Molly looked at his shirt and pointed. "So, *bang me hard big boy* is just your way of expressing your heterosexuality?"

Carl looked down, took a hand to the shirt, and stretched it out. "Oh, yeah." He smiled dumbly. "I guess I'm not too bright."

"No argument here."

"So why did you step in like that? You took a big chance."

"Not really. I know most of those boys. They're drunk and prejudiced as hell against anything that ain't them, but when confronted by a woman or a gun they pacify pretty easily." She smiled knowingly. "Incidentally, the guy that was about to kick you in the balls. Is he the one? The young cowboy?"

"I think so. I wasn't seeing so well at the time, but I think he was about to beat the crap outta me. Why?"

Molly laughed then, rich and loud. "He's gayer than hell."

"No way. You weren't there."

"You're about a dumb ass. He's gay, you're gay, you're both fucking gay. But you don't put a move on somebody in the middle of a redneck bar." She reached out a boot and kicked at him. "God, take a lesson."

"For real?"

"Yeah for real, dumbass. There's half a dozen of them in there, maybe more. They're so intimidated by public perception that they'd rather beat on a gay man than admit they are one. It's so sad it's stupid."

"How can you know that? How can you just walk in and know?"

"I have a system. I just pop a button or two on my blouse and watch their eyes. If they don't at least glance and give me a little nod, then I know. It's foolproof. I'd take you back in and demonstrate, but you'd never make it back out alive. I'm not sure you'd even make it through the door."

"You sure think highly of yourself. I'm thinking not every man is attracted to you."

"It's not about me, dumbass. It's about tits. I could look like Attila the Hun, but if I'm flashing tits, every man in the house who isn't, you know… you, is going to start to salivate. It's human nature."

"Would you please stop calling me dumbass?"

Molly had looked down at Carl pityingly. She shook her head, then turned and began to walk away across the lot to a group of parked cars. "See ya," she said.

Carl called out to her. "What about that job?" Molly kept

walking. "Well, you want it or what?" She continued to walk. He shook his head and pushed himself up into a sitting position. "What do you want from me?" he hollered out. "You want me to say thanks? Thanks goddammit." She arrived at a car, and swung open the door. His voice rose in pitch, becoming almost frantic. "This doesn't obligate me to you for the rest of my goddam life you know." Molly leaned down, entered the car and slammed shut the door. "Ah, shit," said Carl, somewhat aloud. He climbed painfully to his feet and began to limp in the direction of the car.

Molly, meanwhile, started the engine, put the car in gear and drove to meet him. She pulled up alongside, rolled down the window and said, "You say something?"

"You know damn good and well I said something. I'm offering you the job."

"I don't want it."

The frustration was mounting in Carl. "What do you mean you don't want it? You asked for a job. You need a job. I'm offering you a job." He leaned down so their faces were at the same level.

Molly looked at him. She reached her fingers up, unfastening the top two buttons of her blouse. "Beg me," she said.

"What?"

"Beg... me."

"Are you fucking nuts, lady? I'm not gonna beg you for anything. And are you actually showing off your tits? To me?"

"Goodnight, dumbass." The window started back up and the car started to move slowly forward.

"Wait, wait." Carl's hands went to his head. He grabbed at his hair, twisting it violently. "Alright, goddammit. Please take the job. I want you to take the job."

Molly looked at him for a long moment. She tapped the steering wheel with both hands, then moved one hand to her chin, where she sat for a while longer in quiet contemplation. Finally she looked over at him. "Okay. I'll take it. I'll see you tomorrow." She then continued to roll the window up and drove out of the lot.

Carl stood there watching her drive away, his pants ripped, his shirt torn, bits of dirt and blood caked onto one side of his face. Finally, he turned and limped his way in the direction of his own car. "God, how I hate that woman," he said.

As Carl thought back to that first night, he smiled whimsically. It had been almost four years ago. Since then he had come to love Molly, and need her, like no one he had ever allowed into his life before. It wasn't so much that he allowed her there, as that she had inserted herself without regard for his opinion on the matter. That was how Molly did her best work. He remembered the night he fell in love with her, and not just the night, but the moment, the exact moment. He had been on the couch sipping wine while Molly stood a few feet away, her arms folded across her chest, the look on her face a stern one. They had been talking about Carl's feeble attempts to put worthy people into his life. As he lamented, Molly's job seemed to be filling his glass until he reached a point of limited resistance.

"I still hate it when you call me dumbass," he said, his words slurring slightly.

"Do you have a better word for yourself?" she challenged back. "Because I'm not seeing it."

"You just think you have it all worked out. It's not that easy finding someone you can trust. Finding someone who isn't slicing into your back whenever you're not looking."

"That doesn't mean you get to surrender." Molly reached down, placing her own glass on the coffee table between them. She then moved around the table and sat next to Carl on the couch, sat in close, to where their legs touched slightly. "The only way you can learn to trust someone is to trust them. You just take a deep breath and go for it. There's really no other way."

"That's bullshit. I've been there too many times. That's how you get hurt, man."

"No, it's really not. It's how you find the people who are worthy. It's also a good way to find the ones who aren't. You discard those and hang on to the others."

Carl had turned to find Molly's eyes looking right back at his. Just inches away. It disarmed him somewhat. "Well I've done a lot of discarding and not much hanging on. So I'm pretty well over it."

"No, you can't say that. You don't just stop trying."

"Look, all this stuff is easy for you. You're gorgeous. You just blink your pretty eyes and men fall all over you. Everyone wants to be with you, and you can be with anyone you want. The only real friend I ever had was back in high school. At least I thought he was, until he wound up outing me and leading the pack dedicated to my personal torment. So you wind up with a hundred kids taunting you, and not one who says, hey. Trust me. Trust sucks."

"It really doesn't. And having someone want you isn't nearly the same as having someone like you, or be a real friend to you. I'll bet we've both made bad choices. Maybe lots of them. That doesn't mean we give up. We try again, and again, till we get it right. Make one good choice and all the torment fades away."

"Just how can you possibly know when you've made a good choice?"

Molly leaned to the side, Carl's side, her head coming to rest on his shoulder where it snuggled comfortably. Her arm swept down alongside his, until their fingers met and intertwined. "You just do," she said softly.

"Oh," said Carl.

Carl found himself smiling at the memory. After a bit more contemplation he rose from the table without making the move that would have captured the queen and led him to ultimate victory. That could wait for another day. Another day of survival for his bishop and his knight, and a brief stay of execution for the king and his lady.

He walked across the room to his bed where he sat. Pulling open a nightstand, he extracted a small, green journal which he opened and began to read. It was all about Molly. The first few pages catalogued her arrival at McMillan, her moving one night, unannounced and uninvited into his home, and her incredible ability to captivate, not just Carl, but any individual or audience she chose. The first entries, comprising perhaps a third of the journal, were light-hearted, and explored the early development of their relationship. Then the writing began to take a more sinister turn. He had noted down a series of dates and times, dating back to about two years ago, times when Molly had been out on the road, supposedly selling pharmaceuticals. That's when the killings had begun, not many of them, but a few here and there, scattered across the states of Kansas, Iowa and Nebraska. Carl had begun to take an interest in the murders after about the third one, when it dawned on him that Molly's route seemed to always coincide with the jurisdiction of the slayings. Now, two years and seven deadly incidents later, he had amassed a mountain of circumstantial forensics, gasoline receipts, hotel vouchers, mileage computations, not enough to nail down anything conclusive, but certainly enough of a substantive nature to arouse serious suspicion. He had tried to bring up the subject of the killings a time or two, but Molly, who was a master at deflecting conversations in an alternate direction, would always deflect. And that, he also found suspicious. The one time he had succeeded in starting a dialogue had been a few days after the murder of Maxwell Jimson, the farmer who had been found stabbed through the ears in the front seat of his pickup.

"What do you make of this Jimson killing?" he had asked her one evening while they washed dishes together in the kitchen.

"I don't know," she answered him. "It's kind of strange though, stabbing a guy through the head without his putting up some sort of a fuss."

"He was on an activist watch list, you know. Seemed he and his hands enjoyed roughing up the livestock." Carl had casually wiped a dish, watching Molly peripherally for a reaction. There was none.

"I don't think someone would kill a man for beating up on a pig. It's just a pig."

Carl had nodded agreeably, and that was the only time they had ever spoken about one of the murders. He closed the journal then, pondering for a moment what his next step should be, or whether a step was even in order. One thing continued to gnaw away at him though. Molly never spoke critically of the methods used in the raising and processing of meat animals, and seemed to place no value, one way or the other, on the cruelties employed by many in the industry. On the contrary, she was a master at selling the very products that allowed the industry to profit and to flourish. So she was by all accounts, an accomplice. It made no sense that she could be somehow involved in a plan to eliminate the very meat producers she depended upon for her livelihood.

CHAPTER ELEVEN

The fetus shifted slightly and opened its mouth for the first time, sucking in a great gulp of fluid. It still had no real awareness of itself, but there was a definite feeling of comfort and belonging as its brain began to receive tiny signals that were the preceptors of thought. The brain had no real form yet, and limited function, but over the next several days thoughts would begin to arrive, tiny scattered fragments of information which would begin to assemble as the fetus lounged there in a warm bath of cerebral pudding. Geneticists call this period simply *Mark One,* for it marks the first moments a hominid separates from a simple life form into a complex being with the ability to perceive itself. By this time in its development most of the genetic matter had already been assigned, but dozens of brave little genes still swirled around in the membrane of the brain itself, attaching themselves to tiny snippets of DNA as they scrambled to assemble into something meaningful and useful and logical. In this particular fetus a rarity occurred. Several of the genes arrived and attempted to latch onto the same snippet at the same time, colliding and merging and clinging hard to their new base. One of them, however, smaller and weaker than the others, tried to wriggle its way into the mass, but was squished and distorted before finally being dislodged and flushed away. It floated free, badly damaged but still organically viable. As it reached out to grab onto another strand of matter, an electric impulse exploded within it, causing a shockwave to pulse throughout the entire cortex of the fetus's brain. The fetus shuddered, its tiny limbs convulsing involuntarily, its face contorting, with only its lips remaining calm. They seemed to curl upwards into a sort of smile. Its brain was now primordially activated.

Rotating its body, it began to feel its way around. There were no anomalies present, at least not at first. Just the warm consistency of the liquid pressing against it, and the gentle pulsating of its own body as it completed its assembly as a human. It was still rotating and reveling in this fresh, new life, when suddenly it bumped into something hard, something with structure, something which moved closely into it, with alien limbs reaching out in embrace. Instinctively, the fetus knew it had just encountered another life force, in fact, another *it*. A twin, a being identical in composition to itself. The ordinary response to such an occurrence would be to feel comfort, a sense of exhilaration as one realizes the world is offering up companionship and a sense of belonging. Most twins, when encountering one another in pre-birth for the first time, will lock together in embrace, and revel in their combined presence. But this fetus was not ordinary, not normal, and not welcoming. The distortion of genetic material had left it somehow estranged, and worse, hostile about an invasion of its space. It reached back at its twin, but instead of grasping it tenderly, began to pick away at it, ever so slightly. It has been suggested that one human can kill another with almost any ordinary object, if given the time and opportunity. A matchstick, for instance, rubbed against the skin over and over will eventually cause the skin to break out in rash, finally opening up a small lesion where blood will begin to flow. Adding in the element of more time and more gentle rubbing and the blood will not be allowed to abate, but will continue in a tiny stream until the body can no longer sustain itself, the heart will stop, and one human will have killed another by the simplest of means. So the fetus, having an abundance of time, began, almost non-stop, to poke, to prod, to pick at its tiny sibling, who eventually attempted to pull away. But there was nowhere to run, nowhere to hide. The attack was relentless. And when some months later the twins were born, one was stilled, the other crying out contentedly as it greeted its new world.

John Grimm would have been a psychologist's dream. In the fragmented and often distorted world of pseudo-analysis many would have tried to point out the variety of factors that combine to create a true psychopath. Genetics, environment, upbringing, bullying, abuse, an abundance of candidates pouring in equal shares of responsibility from a multitude of sources. And each diagnosis of him would have been dangerously wrong. There was only one true interpretation of Grimm. He had been born a stone cold killer.

"Johnny?" A voice called out.

Grimm sat quietly off to himself, on a stack of hay in the corner of a large barn. In his hand he held a small cricket which struggled to free itself from his grasp. Very diligently he plucked away at it, removing each of the legs from one of its sides. He then leaned over and dropped the tiny insect onto a trail of ants who were already attacking another cricket he had previously dropped there. The ants swarmed over the new cricket as it tried desperately to hop away. With half its legs missing, however, it was only able to twirl about in a ragged circle while ants tore into it from every direction. There was no great amusement on Grimm's face as he watched the spectacle of dismemberment. More a look of simple curiosity as he assessed the odds that the cricket might somehow escape its persecutors. The outcome, while probably obvious, was of no concern. There would always be another cricket and a never ending supply of ants.

"Johnny!" The voice called out again, this time with greater persistency.

Grimm looked up. "What?"

"What the hell are you doin'?" A man in loose overalls caked in mud stared down at him.

"What? I'm not doin' nuthin'."

The man's voice held a certain disgust. "Well get your ass back out here and help me. They're waitin' out on the line. We gotta bring in a hundred more pigs… like now."

Johnny looked at the man, sensing his impatience. "Alright. You don't have to get all huffy about it." He shook his head as he rose from the hay. "You know, I'm not supposed to be doin' this kind of work. I'm trained to work the line. I should be stickin' pigs, not herdin' em."

"Yeah, we've heard all about it." The man snarled sarcastically, then turned to walk away. "Well right now you're bein' trained to herd pigs and shovel shit, so get off your ass."

The two men walked across the barn, exiting through a large breezeway into a chute located just outside. Hundreds of hogs milled around there, in a pen connected to the chute, snorting and grunting as they pressed themselves against a sturdy wire-mesh fence that surrounded them. As Johnny separated himself from the other man and began to move in among the pigs, a group of well-dressed people came toward them along a narrow pathway built alongside the chute. He recognized one as his new boss, Matt Culpepper. With him were two other men, both in farm clothes, but neat and clean ones, and a blonde woman who could only be described as gorgeous. She wore white slacks, a white blouse that clung tightly against her body, and her hair flowed gently around her shoulders like that of a goddess. Johnny's mouth hung open as they approached. His hands clenched into fists and a tremor of excitement flushed over him.

Stepping forward, he pushed his way through a cluster of hogs until he intersected the group. "Mister Culpepper," he called out in friendly fashion.

One of the men turned and paused, the others pausing with him. "Yes?" he answered, a question in his voice. Then, "You're the new man down from Chicago. John Grimm, right?"

"Yes, sir." Johnny's heart raced. He looked at the girl who smiled warmly back at him. He felt an instant connection with her. He could tell she felt it too. He needed to say just the right thing. Make just the right impression. Something that would make Culpepper linger and cause the girl to linger right there along beside him. "I've been workin' hogs for a long time, sir. I know I'm new here, but I think my talent is bein' wasted out here in the pens." He paused, again looking at the girl, then back at his boss. "I'm a sticker, sir. A damn good one. Best in the business. I should be up on the line."

Culpepper nodded curtly. "Well you keep at it. Do a good job out here and you'll get your chance." He nodded at the girl, as if seeking her approval. "Everyone gets their chance here. I'm very fair about that."

As Johnny stammered out, "Thank you, sir," an amazing thing happened. The girl reached out and touched his arm.

"Hi," she said. "I'm Molly." Her smile enveloped him. "So you're a sticker?"

Johnny's heart leapt. But his mind moved into a state of caution. "Yes ma'am," he said. And that's all he said as he studied her face. The look of warmth never left her. If anything it thickened, as her eyes began to play with his.

"I like a man who's not afraid to get a little blood on his hands." Her fingers continued to stroke his arm. "Most men can't make the actual kill. They'd rather just hang around for the cleanup." Grimm continued to study the girl for a sign. Some glimmer that could mean she was testing him, or teasing him. But there was nothing there except the warmth. So he basked in it.

"I'm not afraid of nuthin'," he said finally.

"Good for you." The girl who called herself Molly turned her head slightly as she pulled her hand away and motioned to his boss. "I've known Mister Culpepper here for many years. If he says you'll get your chance, you'll get it. Count on it." Her hand then returned to linger on his arm. She seemed to be marking him as hers, and Grimm had all the signal he needed. This was the one. His decisions concerning women had always been fairly quick and decisive, but this one, for the first time in his life, was instantaneous. Her eyes spoke to him, probed away at him, and matched his every thought. They were fated. She knew it and he knew it. The men in the group began to move away then, and with a final caress Molly turned to follow them.

A fog rolled in, blanketing Johnny in a haze. He couldn't contain himself, so he called out to her, "I love you."

The girl spun around, a look of joy spread across her face. "I love you, too," she cried out. "I love you so much." She ran to him then, her arms opening up in what could only be described as a torrid embrace. Their lips met, and he swallowed her up. He tasted all of her, drank her in, merged with her until they became indistinguishable, one from the other.

"Grimm, goddammit!" A voice slammed into him. "Quit suckin' on the boss's ass and get back in here and help me herd these goddam pigs."

Johnny shook himself, turning to his fellow worker with a broad smile on his face. "Did you see that? Did you see? She's crazy about me."

"What? That blonde broad? Are you stupid? She never gave you a second glance. Get your ass back over here."

CHAPTER TWELVE

Michael Lair moved around to one side of the log and peered into the woods a short distance away. "I don't get it," he said. "What makes you think this could possibly be connected to our killer?" He looked down at a tarp spread on the ground in front of him. A human foot stuck out at one end. A manicured foot. A woman's foot. "This lady obviously got caught up in a bad situation. Some bastard raped her, beat her, and took her out. There are no similarities here."

Elizabeth Warman raised a hand. There was a small plastic bag in it. "I don't know. We're only an hour out of Omaha, right in the middle of the kill zone, and the forensic over there says this bag is full of pig hair." She squinted as she studied the bag. "I don't know about you, but I haven't covered too many murder scenes where the perpetrator is shedding pig hair."

"And he found them where, exactly?"

"On the duct tape covering her mouth. Or more precisely, the end of the tape. When he unwrapped her gag, it was pressed into the last fold. Some of it even attached to her skin." Lair reached out and accepted the bag.

"I'd hardly call this full. There's like three hairs in here." Lair also squinted. "How can he be sure exactly what they are?"

Warman smiled, that condescending kind of smile someone uses when they are about to show off. "This is Nebraska. I would think you'd get that. I'm pretty certain these boys know what they're talking about."

Lair read the condescension on Warman's face and ruined it. "I guess I don't hang out with pigs as much as you folks do."

About an hour later Michael turned his car into the lot at McMillan. He wanted to have another chat with Molly Bishop and her boss. As he entered the building he noticed an anomaly on the floor ahead. A small smattering of red droplets lay directly in his path. Beyond them were even more, until just before reaching the desk the droplets merged into a small puddle. The girl behind the desk greeted him.

"May I help you?"

Michael pointed at the floor. "You've got blood out here."

"Oh," said the girl, rising and leaning forward so she could see. "I'm so sorry. I'll clean that up." She shook her head somewhat apologetically and continued. "Miss Bishop just brought in a calf. I think it got hit out on the highway."

"Ouch," said Lair. "Where can I find her?" The girl picked up a towel from behind the desk, then pointed down the same corridor he had walked on his last visit, offering to escort him. "I'll find her," he said, pointing back down at the floor. "You better stay here and clean up the crime scene."

As Michael moved down the hallway he passed by the office of Carl Monroe, the same office he had questioned Molly Bishop in a few days earlier. He glanced in but found no one there, so he proceeded to the end of the corridor. As he pushed open a door there, a soft moaning emanated from somewhere ahead. He moved toward the sound, entering into a large warehouse that was nearly void of machinery or product, except for a few crates and boxes pushed up against a far wall. It seemed like an unusual waste of space. There was another doorway off to his left, with an open door, and the sounds seemed to come from there. When he arrived at this new doorway, he paused, just leaning in enough of his head to view the room. It was far smaller than the one he was standing in, with a single table at its middle, and a couple of folding chairs. Sitting in one of the chairs was Carl Monroe, his elbows thrust forward on top of the table, his head resting in his hands. Molly Bishop stood beside him, fussing over a mass of brown and white fur that Lair reasoned must be the calf.

Molly spoke. "How in the hell can you drive along and not see a calf walking in the middle of the road?" The calf lay there, while she stroked gently at its neck. Every few seconds, in rhythm to its breathing, a soft moan would emanate from the tiny creature. "Dammit," she snarled angrily. "It's just a baby."

Carl spoke. "Let it go Mol. There's nothing we can do. People are just too damn busy to slow down." He followed that line with something he immediately regretted saying. "It was just an accident."

Molly's eyes burned into Carl. "The hell with people." Michael could see that the girl wasn't actually crying, but wasn't actually not, either. There was a definite mist in her eyes as she glared back at her boss, defying him to defend the incident further. "And the hell with you."

Carl winced, but decided not to respond to the attack. "Look, we need to put him down. He's suffering." He lifted an arm, reaching out to touch her on the shoulder. "We need to."

Molly let her hand slip away from the calf as she stepped back from the table. "I'll do it," she said simply. "I wouldn't want you to mess up your pretty shirt." She turned then, to head for the door, and that's when she saw Michael Lair. An immediate morph flushed over her. It happened so quickly that Lair was unsure if it had even occurred. He shook his head slightly.

"Miss Bishop."

Molly responded, with not a trace of emotion in her voice. "Mister Lair." She tapped at Carl's shoulder as she passed him by and walked in the direction of the agent. "Damn," she said. "You beat up on one little calf and the cops come knocking. We're about to butcher up some steaks. You care to watch?"

Michael stepped fully into the doorway. "Just came by to chat. Sorry about the timing."

As Molly arrived at the door, she paused, reaching up to brush

Lair's collar. "Something is always dying, Michael. So timing is irrelevant." Her eyes probed his, and that rare innocence he had noted when first meeting her poured back into them. "I'll be right back."

As Molly disappeared down the hallway, Michael moved into the room. Carl rose to greet him. "Good to see you again, Agent Lair." The calf raised its head, crying out desperately, and Carl reached out a hand, gently pressing its head back down on the table. "We've had an accident."

"I see that." Lair moved over to the table, his fingers tapping at its surface just inches away from a small pool of blood. "It's a messy business you're in. I'm surprised to see this much concern over a dying calf." The calf seemed to look up at Lair, still holding onto enough of its life to question his arrival. Like a wildebeest who has been taken down by a lion, but still shows concern when another shows up to feast. Michael looked down at it, his heart crying out. "Easy little fella," he said softly. He wanted to reach out to offer comfort, but restrained himself, and just stood there uncomfortably instead.

Carl spent a moment measuring Lair. "It's not so unusual," he said finally. "Just because we're in the business of meat production doesn't mean we are without feelings. Besides, our end of it is purely medicinal. We're not the butchers here. Our job is to preserve life, enhance it even, until it becomes the commodity folks like you like to feast on." He pointed at the agent. "We're all involved in one way or another."

As Michael nodded, Molly walked back into the room carrying a syringe. She moved over to the calf. Displaying not the least angst or displeasure, she slipped the needle expertly into its neck, pushing down on the plunger until it drained. The calf again raised its head slightly, and its tongue licked out at Molly's hand. She dodged the tongue, pressing down with her free hand on the calf's neck until it shook suddenly, and then went still. She nodded at the two men. "Lights on, lights off," she said, and then, "Now is there something I can do for you, detective?"

Carl spoke. "You mean agent," and Lair responded.

"No, she knows exactly what she means." Molly ignored both

men, moving past them, out the door and back down the corridor. While Carl moved over to the table holding the calf, Michael followed the girl. A few minutes later they sat directly across from one another at the desk in the office. Lair motioned to the trophy, still perched on the shelf off to one side. "Still bowling, I see."

"As long as I have breath." Molly sat there, arms folded, looking perhaps more purposeful and less relaxed than the last time they had met. Michael pointed.

"You have blood on your blouse."

Molly looked down and unfolded her arms, letting her hands move across the stained fabric. "Hazards of the job, I suppose. One never knows what she'll find when driving the magical backroads of Nebraska."

"I'm a bit surprised." Michael leaned forward, resting his elbows on the desktop, his face cupped in his hands. "I would think a girl who once slaughtered pet pigs for Barbie dolls would be a bit less… sympathetic towards a dying calf."

Molly's head came up, and her eyes flashed. "That was kid stuff. I merely traded one thing for another. I'm thinking lots of little girls would trade a pig for a Barbie."

Lair nodded agreeably, but countered, "Maybe not so many if they actually had to slit its throat first."

Molly's lips quivered slightly. "Until you've lived this life, maybe you should reserve your judgement. I didn't pick the damn calf up out of kindness. I didn't know how badly it was hurt at first. I just figured it had escaped from a nearby veal farm. I thought it would be good for business to return it."

"So your picking it up was more of an economic decision?"

"Obviously."

"What's a veal farm?"

"You eat veal?"

"Sure."

"You know how it's raised?"

"No, that's why I'm asking."

Molly licked her upper lip, then smacked both lips together

deliciously. "Well, you're going to love this." She reached out both her hands in a gesture for his. He offered them, and they clasped fingers, their hands locked together on the top of the desk. Her face then lit up and she looked at him warmly.

"It all starts with a dairy. All that milk we drink comes at a cost. Dairy cows have to stay knocked up or they won't be able to produce. And when their babies are born, they are ripped away, sometimes before they even hit the ground. They are thrown into a truck with dozens more like them. They lay there, beneath a pile of their own kind for as long as a week, or until the truck fills with enough babies to make a trip profitable. By this time many of the first ones thrown in have grown weak or have been crushed or died, but it is of little concern." Michael's eyes began to widen. "Next, the calves are dumped at a veal farm." She squeezed down on his fingers. "Things can only get better now, right? From the truck, they are dragged into a barn and thrown into tiny individual cages, each cage so small the calves can't even turn around, but must always face forward. If they ever wish to lie down, they must collapse onto their knees and stay in this somewhat upright position, as the sides of the cages won't allow them to lie down further. Those who arrive at the farm too weak or injured from the journey are bludgeoned to death with baseball bats and tossed into another truck for transport to a factory where their bodies will be ground up into dog food or fertilizer." Michael's eyes, which had grown wide, now narrowed, squinted, and almost closed, like dams trying to hold back water. Molly continued, all the while gripping down hard on Lair's hands so there could be no escape for him. "For the other babies, the stronger ones, life is just beginning to show signs of merriment. A chain is placed around each of their necks, tying them fast to the front of the cage. The chain allows workers to forceably pull their heads forward through a metal grate several times a day for feeding. The grate swings shut on their necks, so they can't pull back, and their heads are pushed down into plastic buckets filled with milk and mash or other feed.

"This wonderful life goes on for months. They are never allowed out from their cages, never allowed body movement of any kind, for if they were allowed to roam about the whole process of veal would suffer. Veal relies on the physiological fact that muscle toughens the fibers in meat. And since the whole promotional value of veal is its tenderness, muscle development must be reckoned with harshly. No movement means no muscle." Molly eased her hands open, and with a slight tug pulled them away from Michael Lair, distancing herself from the agent.

"What happens next is rather humorous. The calves are now ready for harvesting. You know it's a funny word, harvesting. Folks out in the real world didn't take so well to the terms slaughter, or butcher, so someone in the meat industry came up with a more wholesome word to describe the act and appease the masses. So now wheat or corn or nice chunks of beef are all categorized the same fun way. Anyway, by this time the calves are so debilitated that they can't even be herded off to *harvest*. So it has to be done right there in the cages. A sticker walks by, thrusting a shock-rod into the ear of each calf, usually rendering it senseless. Usually. Sometimes the shock isn't at all effective and the next step becomes rather painful. Another sticker follows the first, this one with a knife. He thrusts it deeply into the neck of each calf, and they collapse there in the confines of their cages while they slowly bleed out. Once movement has died down a bit, they are hung by the neck— some still flopping about— right there in the cage, and hoisted aloft where they are swung onto a conveyer which sends them off to the cutters. Once there, of course, they are all chopped up nice and pretty. Kind of a one stop shop, where you never have to leave home until you die." Molly's expression continued to be a warm one as she drummed her fingers on top of the desk. "Care for some veal, Michael?"

Lair looked at Molly for a long moment before responding, and when he finally did, his tone was almost a whisper. "You're an enigma, Molly Bishop. One minute you're as cold hearted as they come, and the next you seem to have feelings like the rest of us. Like something could actually matter to you." He shook his head. "I don't know what's real and what's not."

Molly's look turned playful, but then hardened. "I didn't tell you this to expose your sympathies. And it sure as hell doesn't reflect on mine. I just thought it would be helpful for you to understand exactly what's going on behind the scenes. The meat you so desperately covet comes at a cost. You have to surrender yourself to it, surrender your soul. You can't come into this business with feelings of pity or condolence. If you're not courageous enough to stand there and plunge in the knife, then it's more than hypocritical for you to judge me from the catacombs while you feast on meat at the king's table one floor above."

Lair's mouth opened slightly, but that was the only sign to indicate her speech had impacted him. This beautiful woman was brilliant. And cunning. Yet he still had no idea of her true feelings or motives. "So it doesn't bother you then, this cruelty in raising veal for profit?"

Molly began her answer honestly. "If I could change the rules I would. I don't imagine anyone wants to see an animal suffer unnecessarily. But you yourself just identified the villain here. It's profit. If that's what it takes, then that's what we do. The animal's needs have to become secondary, or better, not even a consideration. And there's no real cruelty. Just circumstance. It's their station in life. What they are born and raised for." She pointed at Michael. "Fortunately, for both of us, we're the eaters, and they're the eaten. I'm fairly certain that's the way you'd prefer to keep it." While Lair shifted his gaze to the many mounted horns adorning the walls, Molly continued to bore in on him. "So why did you come here today? You still out fishing, or maybe seeking a little female companionship?"

Lair looked back at Molly, and spoke with not a hint of emotion. "I think you'd eat me alive. I'm not sure I could survive it."

The playful look returned to Molly's face. "Oh, I'd keep you alive. At least long enough to ripen you up for consumption. Just like veal, baby," she said, even as her tone stiffened. "So again, why are you here?"

"Your college boyfriend. The pig-baller, David Mertle. I suppose you heard he's dead?"

"Yes, I heard. A terrible thing. I called his folks a couple days ago to offer my condolences. The newspapers didn't say how he died. Just said he was found in one of the stalls. Like he'd had a heart attack or something."

"He was murdered. They found a needle mark high up on his neck. Seems he was injected with something they haven't quite figured out yet. But they will. Probably a tranquilizer of some sort."

"Oh, my god, how awful. The papers gave no hint of that." Molly bit down on her lip. "I'm not sure what you want from me though."

"I was wondering if you spent any time with him after I left. Thought maybe you spoke or something and could shed a little light on this."

"No," she bit down harder. "I think I waved at him out in the breezeway. But we had no real contact. Why?"

Michael studied the girl intently. Her bottom lip flushed white where she had chewed away at it, but then her face softened and filled up with that familiar sweet innocence. "Nothing, really. It's just that I found a hair, a long, blonde hair near the body. Thought it looked kind of like one of yours."

Molly appeared to lose herself in thought for a moment, then blurted out, "Oh, wait. We did speak, but just briefly. I remember now, because we almost bumped into each other at the entrance. I think we might have hugged, but just for a second."

"Well that must be it then." Michael tapped once or twice on the desk, then rose to leave. Molly rose with him.

"I hope I've been helpful."

"Miss Bishop." Lair reached out to shake hands. "Every time I see you it is at the very least, instructional. I never leave unfulfilled."

Molly grabbed the hand and pulled herself up close to Lair. Her lips moved up alongside his cheek as she whispered, "We ever take this to a more intimate level and I assure you it gets even better."

"Can't wait," said Lair, as he broke away and headed out the door.

CHAPTER THIRTEEN

Late that same night, Molly parked her car on a side road, some distance in from the highway. She turned the engine off and sat for a long time in the dark. There was a quarter moon just above the horizon in the western sky, and she was waiting for it to set and plunge the night into an even deeper darkness. A fire had been burning inside of her since the calf had been found brutalized in the street. Her talk with Michael Lair had only intensified it. These fires were not common, but once one started to rage there was only one way to extinguish it. Molly needed to hunt. Her target this night was a veal farm, one she had never before visited. That made the venture all the more difficult and all the more dangerous, but was exactly what she needed. And it did not require her usual investigatory skills to determine the level of cruelty or depravity a certain farmer might or might not possess. If a farmer raised veal, he was already well qualified for Molly's attention.

After a time, she exited the car, heading up and over a small rise that acted as a barrier, separating one valley floor from the next. She carried with her the usual bag of accessories, all things that could be handy and welcoming in an unknown circumstance. Her pistol, a flashlight, a syringe, a ski-mask to be used in the rare occurrence that she might decide to spare a life while taking one. Some tape, some twine, and a small box of cupcakes in the event the night was so wrought with displeasure she would require comfort food. Coming off the rise, she dropped down into a gully, then out into the open where she passed by a grouping of barns and outbuildings set right up against the rise she had just descended. The night was without sound, which surprised her. Not a cricket, not a frog called out, not even the soft mooing one would expect from barns filled with calves. She suspected that the torturous routines of the day left this place exhausted by night. And that the calves probably lapsed into the deepest of sleeps in an attempt to escape, at least for a time, the barbarity that awaited them when they awoke.

A sound came at her from somewhere ahead. A light rustling, and she stiffened. Then she heard a growl, low and deep. It was not unexpected. Without hesitation she dropped to her knees, bowed her head and began to whimper submissively. The growling stopped. For what seemed a long time she just kneeled there, senses alive for anything that might come at her. Her hand slipped down alongside her leg, extracting a hunting knife from her boot. Fearing the blade might flash or glisten, even on this darkest of nights, she slowly brought it up and tucked it into her shirt, keeping a firm grip on the handle. And she waited. Finally, she heard what she'd been waiting for, a sound, soft and padded, as feet approached cautiously. Then a moist sponge splashed down on her cheek as she raised her head, reaching out her free hand in welcome. "Good dog," she said. Slipping the knife back into her boot, she extracted a cupcake from the bag, and could sense rather than see the dog munching away on it. It was a pitbull, she suspected, or Rottweiler, massively muscled and nearly bowling her over in anticipation of more cakes. She rose then, and with the dog accompanying her moved further up the drive to the front of the house. It was dark in the house, as dark as the night, but as she moved her way up onto a porch she could see just the glimmer of faint light shining through a curtain at one end. Easing her way over to the door, she tried the latch. It opened easily. Doors of country folk were rarely locked, and if the front one was, the rear one wouldn't be. Especially in homes guarded by the kinds of dogs who could take a man down and ruin his day. As she opened the door, a smile traced its way across her lips. She reached a hand into her sack, extracting another of the sweet cakes. Sensing her intentions the big dog nudged up against her, wriggling happily in anticipation. She eased her way through the door and into the house as the dog laid down on the porch, mouth filled with sweetness, to wait for her return.

Molly stood there in the dark for a long time, letting her eyes adjust. Finally, after a good bit of time, she began to make out shapes, a long curved sectional, coffee table, television, and off to the left a longer, higher table and a cluster of chairs. The living room and the dining room, right where one would expect them to be in an old country home. She moved cautiously through the dining area and found herself in a narrow hallway. Here she saw the light, just a glimmer emanating from beneath a closed door at the end of the hall. She glided down the darkened channel which led to the light, keeping one hand draped off to the side, her fingers caressing the wall as she slid along. When she came to the door she paused, pressing her face against its wooden surface. No sound came from the room. Her fingers found the latch, and it turned easily with only a tiny clicking sound. A moment later and she was in the room. A nightlight cast a warm glow, and a slight breeze washed over her. Directly ahead stood a window, partly open to allow in the fresh air of the night. It was a friendly accessory for the room, as it would allow another avenue of escape should she need one. To the right was a closet, also partly open, with clothes and toys spilling from it, out onto the floor. To the left stood a bunk bed, the top half filled with stuffed animals, and the bottom bunk holding snugly onto a small child, deep in slumber. That answered the question of the closet, with toys and clothes mingling about in equal portions. It also answered a more important question. One of discipline and obedience. This was a spoiled child, used to getting its way. Had Molly left her own room in such disarray when she was a child, her father would have reproached her with strong words and a whip. Moving silently to the bed, she eased herself down upon it, sitting only inches away from what she could now see was a small boy of around five. He lay there, looking like an every-child in sleep, his lips curling upwards playfully, while inside his head danced all the dreams a boy can dream. She watched him for a long time, and though there was no awareness of it, her lips slowly curled until they perfectly mimicked his. She poked at the boy. He rolled slightly, but remained asleep. "Hey," she said softly, poking at him again. "Wake up, sleepy head. Wake up." The boy woke then, looking at first confused and maybe even frightened, but then his face found hers, and a look of simple curiosity came over him. "Hey," Molly said again. "It's time to get up."

The boy yawned, stretched himself, and without the faintest hint of fear said, "Who are you?"

"Who do you think I am, silly? I'm your fairy godmother. Surely you've heard of me." Reaching down and into her sack, Molly extracted another cupcake. "Only fairies carry cakes when they come to visit." The boy raised his head to study her more closely, his face now displaying a most whimsical look.

"I know you," he said.

"Of course you do." Molly's hair had been tied back and fastened to the top of her head, but she now loosened it as a swirl of long, blonde hair cascaded down the sides of her face. The boy became as entranced as every male who first laid eyes on her. "It's me." She lifted the cake to her mouth, and took a small bite, then gaily waved the cake in front of the boy's face, before finally moving it up against his own mouth. Without even shifting position, the boy also took a bite. He chewed away contentedly, his look, once whimsical, now glowing from pure joy.

"Are you here about Tommy?" he asked excitedly.

"Yes, of course," said Molly, who could play boys just as easily as she could play men. "I'm here about Tommy. In fact, that's why they sent me. Tell me about him."

The boy's enthusiasm waned. "He has to go away."

"Oh, my," said Molly sympathetically, doing some math and figuring that Tommy might be a big brother or a friend. "So tell me where he's going."

"I've been praying every night for him not to go away. To stay here with me."

"So where is he going?" Molly repeated.

"Away from the farm. All the calves are leaving. Day after tomorrow the trucks are gonna come for them."

"Oh," said Molly, her voice dismantled. She rose from the bed, moving over to the window. The air from outside swirled in, cooling her face as she looked out into the blackness of the night. "So they're taking Tommy away. I know what that's like, and I know what you feel. I feel what you feel."

The boy sat upright, kicking out from under a blanket and swinging his feet to the floor. "You can talk to Daddy." There was real excitement in his voice. "Tell him to let Tommy stay. He'll do it if you ask. I know he will. You have magic."

Molly turned away from the window, moving back over to the boy. She knelt down beside him. "What's your name, sweetie?"

"Bobby."

"I like that name. And of course I already knew that. I just wanted to hear you say it." Molly reached out a hand, brushing wisps of hair back from the boy's forehead. "I had a pig named Bobby once. In fact, there were two that year. Bobby and Robby. They were terribly bad little pigs, always in some sort of trouble. Always getting me in trouble. But I loved them."

"Fairies have pigs?"

"Of course, silly." She stroked at the boy's face. "We have all kinds of pets."

"Do they get sent away?"

Molly put the remains of the cake down on the bed, reached out both her hands, and cupped the boy's face with her fingers. "Life is going to get very complicated for you now. In a short time you'll be given another Tommy to replace the one who's gone. Soon the first Tommy will become a distant memory. And each year as you grow, a Tommy will leave and a new Tommy will arrive, until at last you reach an age where it stops bothering you much, and eventually stops bothering you altogether. Finally, there will be no more Tommys at all. Just faceless, nameless animals that will come at you by the thousands. And because they are now nameless they will have no opportunity to impress you. They will move in and out of your life as meaningless blobs of flesh, and any feelings you might have felt for them will die. You'll never think to make friends with one of them again."

"But I want my Tommy." The boy began to cry, and Molly's thumbs moved across his cheeks, wiping away the tears.

"I know you do, sweetheart."

"Then help me."

Molly had an idea. "Listen, get up and get dressed. Let's go out to the barns and visit him. Right now."

"And we can keep him?"

"We'll see. Come on." Molly waited while the boy slipped into some jeans and a warm, woolen shirt. "Be very quiet," she said as they made their way back down the hall to the front door of the house. "We don't want to wake your father. He'll make us give Tommy away for sure."

Outside, the dog waited, happily pressing himself up against both Molly and the boy. Molly pointed broadly into the night. "Which barn is he in?" She brought out her flashlight, and with Bobby and the dog leading the way, they made their way to the first in a line of barns and outbuildings. The door creaked as they opened it, but then they were inside, facing a long row of cages lining not just the middle of the barn but also both sides, dozens and dozens of them. In each cage lay or half-lay a large sleeping calf, already fattened by several months of rich feed. Off to one side, and very close to the entrance, was a single cage, but a bit larger than the rest, like a small pen. It also held a single calf, but this one had more room to lay itself down, and it slept now upon a pile of fresh hay.

The boy pointed, "My Tommy." They moved over to the cage, Molly slipping open the latch. The boy ran in and knelt down with the calf, stroking its head. The calf woke then, its face lifting to greet the boy, and a great rubbery tongue pushed out to lick away at the boy's face. Soft, amber lights glowed throughout the barn, and Molly thought the scene was eerily similar to one from her own childhood, when she would slip off to the barn to be with her pigs.

"He's beautiful," she said, her voice a kind of sad whisper. Stepping over to join the boy, she also kneeled beside the calf. "I'll bet he's been a wonderful friend to you. I can see why you love him."

"Please don't let them take him away."

Molly leaned back thoughtfully, her thighs resting on the backs of her boots. She reached a hand out to stroke the calf. "I know you won't understand me." For the briefest of moments Molly's eyes closed, and when they reopened her voice sounded dismal and worn. "You are locked up in a place where the soul is to be sucked right out of you. The saddest part is, there is no redemption, and no way out. Most of us like to think we have free will about the things we do and the journeys we take. In reality, there is nothing like that. By the time we are old enough to choose, the choices have already been carved out of us, leaving a huge, empty hole that is then filled to the brim with the worst sort of garbage others have amassed in their own lifetimes. So you become exactly what those others have poured into you. There is no escaping it. You're left with no real choice at all."

The boy looked at Molly, and she could tell he was trying hard to please her, and to understand her. "My daddy?" he said finally.

Molly looked back at him, somewhat amazed. "Yes," she said. "You will become just like your daddy." She ruffled a hand through the boy's hair. "I think I love you."

The boy tried to smile, then turned back to the calf, wrapping an arm around its neck and hugging it mightily. "I wanna stay with Tommy."

"I know." Molly's voice grew as gentle in that moment as it had ever been in her life. She reached into her bag, bringing out a syringe already filled to the brim with a golden liquid. Bending forward, she slipped the needle deftly into the calf's hindquarters, at a place where she knew it would feel no pain. The boy looked at her inquisitively. "I'm giving him a little injection to help him sleep. It's a special one so he can dream about all the wonderful adventures he's going to have with you. Forever."

"And I'll be with him?"

"You will Bobby, I promise." Molly tugged the boy's arm free from the calf. Without a moment's hesitation she pinched at the arm with one hand while pricking the needle deeply into his flesh, just above the elbow. The boy cried out, but from surprise, not pain. "Shhh," whispered Molly. "It won't hurt. You're going to have the most relaxing sleep and the most wonderful dream, right here with your friend. As her thumb pressed down on the plunger, Molly trembled, her eyes closing until darkness shut out the soft golden light fighting so desperately to get in. Then her thumb stopped its compression. She withdrew the needle, having injected only a tiny quantity of liquid. "Rest now, my love," she said, as the boy laid down closely beside the calf. "In the morning when you wake, you will be fully refreshed. You can tell your father you were visited by me in your sleep. It will be like a grand adventure you can share with him. He won't believe you, but you and I will both know it's true." Molly rose as the boy's head tumbled gently onto the neck of the calf. They both lay there, one drifting off to sleep, the other drifting off to a deeper place. To a place with no more suffering.

As Molly moved back to the door of the barn, she turned briefly. "I'll see you again, Bobby," she said, her voice low and sad. "When you're older I'll come back for you."

CHAPTER FOURTEEN

Springtime had come to the mountains. Even though the weather had warmed over the past few weeks, a light dusting of snow, the last snow of the season, had fallen the night before, blanketing the trees and the open spaces with a coat of glistening white. A woodpecker flew down from a tall pine, finding the wood there unnecessarily hard and still winter frozen. It chose instead to land on some nearby railroad tracks where it hopped onto one of the wooden ties. It began to probe with its long beak, seeking out tiny caverns in the wood where termites had come to make their nests. Suddenly the woodpecker looked up in alarm. Its head darted frantically back and forth, sensing an unseen intruder. There was a rumbling sound approaching from the east. Clack-clack-clack, clack-clack-clack, the sound started out as more of a vibration than anything clearly audible, but soon the vibration turned into a solid pounding noise as a train drew near. The train rounded a turn at a point where the tracks broke free from the mountain, pushing their way out into the open, with only one more slight elevation drop keeping them from the valley floor. As the train came rumbling into view, the woodpecker surrendered its post, flying back into the very tree that had so frustrated it moments earlier.

Aboard the train, and in one of its first cars sat a young woman, an old woman, and an old man, who was mute. They did not sit in the luxury of a Pullman or other car usually associated with the accommodation of passengers, but rather a boxcar, more suitable for the storage of cargo or cattle. Huddled together in the farthest corner of the car, they sat on a thin matting of straw. The old woman spoke. "I don't see why they couldn't have given us more time. At least allow us to gather up a few of our things." She tightened the shawl around her shoulders. "I don't even have a proper coat."

The young woman smiled, and attempted to convey a bit of warmth into their frozen surroundings. "Here, come cuddle with me. There's room in my coat." Unbuttoning her coat she flapped it open and the old woman leaned into her, grasping at her until they both found a small degree of comfort. The old man, also thinly dressed and sensing a shift in the two bodies, leaned in from the other side, but there was no coat waiting for him. Crossing his arms tightly to his chest he sat there, face stony-set, but because he was mute, he said nothing.

After a time the train slowed, its whistle sounding three short blasts, its brakes squealing against the cold steel of the track. It stopped then, the only sound the constant puffing of steam calling out in a steady rhythm. A short time later they heard a latch being thrown, and two doors cut into the side of the car began to slide open. The old woman, irritable from the ride, pushed herself away from the other two. She rose and walked over to the doors. A man stuck his head in just as she stuck hers out. He did not have a friendly face. "I need to use the facilities," she growled out at him.

Another man moved in from the side, joining the first. He laughed harshly. "Go piss on the floor old woman." As he spoke, he reached in with a long pole, a prod, which he used to smash against the woman's legs. She stumbled backwards and fell. The young woman rose then, rushing to the old woman's side.

"What are you doing? She's old." The look on her face was imploring. The man with the prod leered at her.

"You'd do well to keep your mouth shut, lest we be dragging

you out here for a bit of fun." Both men laughed at that, but then stepped away, leaving the young woman to help the old back to their seats in the corner of the car.

Soon a ramp was raised from the deck outside, and with cries and sticks and prodding more people were herded aboard the car. It filled rapidly, until spaces widely empty now began to press and compress with human bodies. The three in the corner, so isolated moments earlier, now found bodies moving against them, falling against them in a massive wave of flesh. Someone in the middle of the mass hollered out, "That's enough. You're suffocating us." The voice seemed to have an impact, as soon the doors grated closed, leaving the occupants crammed together in a dim-lit world of intense humanity.

The train moved on for what seemed endless hours. And a most unusual thing happened. A hundred bodies, as tightly compacted as could be imagined, and yet no one spoke. Maybe an occasional whisper could be heard, or a cough or a sneeze, but all normal communication ceased. Finally, after much time had passed, a boy's voice spoke out. "Mother," it said. The voice was sad and tentative, like it was trying to hold back the words. "I have to pee."

A man's voice called out, "Then just do it. You won't find any facilities here, child." Another man tried to laugh at that, but the sound quickly broke off and the silence closed back in.

The boy's request did seem to have a commiserate effect on the crowd. There was a great milling around, and soon the scent of urine began to mix with the already pungent scent of human sweat and damp cloth. The smell was soft at first, sort of sickly sweet as the variety of aromas melded themselves together. But after a time the car began to reek, as the release of ammonia gas filled the air. The crowd, en masse, was pissing their pants.

After a long time the train slowed, squealing and screeching its way to another stop. Those in the car could hear the busy sounds of men working outside. Soon the doors were flung open, a ramp raised and much yelling began for the passengers to step outside to greet their new surroundings. The young woman, the old woman, and the old man, having been scrunched up in the corner and farthest away from the doors, were the last to step down. Being the last, they were the most easily beaten by steel-faced men who poked at them in an effort to move the line along. The scene outside the train was grim. Soldiers waited, each bundled up against the cold in warm, wollen military jackets, caps with flaps that muffed their ears, and each carried a baton which they waved in menacing fashion as the passengers were herded into a long, thin line. The line was single file, and anyone who defied this rule to step up alongside a friend or loved one would immediately be dragged away, beaten with clubs, and thrust back in at whatever point was convenient for the tormentors. Those who reentered the procession were noticeably more docile.

The old man, at the very back of the line, stumbled, falling to one knee. A soldier stepped up, striking him hard across the shoulders with a club. The blow caused the old man to stumble further, rolling down and onto his side. The young woman turned and fell to her own knees in an effort to offer aide. "He's old," she cried out. "And he doesn't speak."

"I don't give a damn if he speaks. He can sure as hell walk," called out the man who had struck him. He raised the club threateningly. "Now you get your ass back in line, lady. And leave him be." The young woman looked up for just a moment, saw the raw anger staring down at her, and quickly moved away from the old man and back into her place.

The line moved along until they came to a wall. A bleak wall of cement and mortared stone. That stopped them. A door opened, and more hard-faced men arrived, coming in from the side through a barrier of barbed wire and steel netting. The men shouted out, demanding that the line move through the doorway and into whatever circumstance waited on the other side. The old woman had had enough. She turned to face one of the men. "I don't understand what's going on," she said. "Where are they taking us?"

This man was different from the others. He looked almost frightened. Not frightened in the same way as those being herded, but in a way that suggested a fear of some future retribution. Like a boy waiting to be punished and knowing that, inevitably, he would be. "Just move along," he said, his voice shaking but not unfriendly. "They're taking you to the showers. To wash away any lice you might have carried with you."

"Lice," spat the old woman. "I don't have any damn lice."

Sensing weakness in the herder, another man stepped up, lashing out with a club at the old woman. The blow caught her across an ear, opening a wound and causing her to stagger. The young woman stepped up to catch her. "Get into the goddam showers before I beat you," the new man spoke with a venom, failing to consider that the threatened beating had already commenced. The young woman, using both her hands, pushed hard against the old, forcing her forward and into the doorway. But the old woman was not yet done with her scolding. Holding a hand to her head, she turned for a last word.

"They don't treat pigs this badly," she snarled out. Then she and the young woman disappeared behind the wall.

For many days the young hog had heard the screams. So when it came time to herd a new batch into the chute that led into the barns, he had always hung back, fighting his way to the farthest reaches of the holding pen. The trouble was, all of the pigs heard the screams, and many of them attempted the same strategy, a frightened mob of flesh that mashed away at the young pig as he struggled for position. The holding pen was quite plain, a rectangle of planks and wire, sufficiently large enough to hold a hundred animals at any one time. A single trough, low-slung and kept full by a dripping faucet, lay against one side, pushed right up against the wire. It was the one stanchion of normalcy in a world gone mad, where the pigs could gather and socialize and drink while they awaited the inevitable. The young hog wasn't brilliant, at least not in the way humans measure intellect, but in the world of pigs he was a scholar, having assessed the situation as a terminal one from which hogs entered the chute and were never seen again. One day, on his third day there, he noticed a narrow opening behind the trough, made even more open by a plank that had broken free of the wire and leaned inward against the tank, causing a sort of triangular tunnel just big enough for an enterprising pig to squeeze its way into. So he grunted and crammed and squeezed his way into the opening until he had secreted himself safely into the cavity created there behind the trough. He wouldn't lay there the entire day, just the few hours when he knew the chutes would open and men with sticks and clubs would enter the pen, herding the animals towards the barn. This system worked well for several more days, until the young pig was overcome with hunger. There was simply nothing to eat. Each day around noon several of the workers would enter the pen, sitting on the edge of the trough while they ate their lunches. Occasionally a bit of fruit or a crust of bread would fall from their hands as they ate, but whatever meager scraps would fall were quickly scooped up by the myriad hogs which gathered hungrily around the diners. The young pig, tucked safely away just inches behind the men, could plainly hear the sounds of eating, could hear the sounds of the other pigs as they fought over the scraps, and his hunger grew. And hunger is like an addiction. Eventually it overpowers the mind's ability to resist risk, and so the pig considered that soon he would have to emerge.

On the morning of the sixth day, the young pig was out in the yard with the others, lounging in a great hog-pile of his brethren as they pressed against the one side of the enclosure that allowed a small patch of sunlight to reach the ground. It was the only time of day the pigs could somewhat relax, warmed by both the comradery— which brought with it a small amount of security— and the sun. Suddenly the gates to the chute swung open. The hogs looked up in surprise and alarm. It was not yet time for the first calling. They knew the schedule well. The young pig hobbled to his feet, the massive ache in his stomach causing him to falter as his body began to break down from within. Still, he felt the fear, and the fear overcame the hunger as he stumbled his way over to the trough, burrowing deeply behind it. He could hear the sounds of several men who had entered the enclosure and were roaming about beating the hogs. One of them hollered, what was to the pig, unintelligible gibberish.

"What the hell," the voice said. "It's just a pig. One damn pig. What the hell."

"Eleven-sixty-five," hollered out another voice. "Just find it. It should'a gone through the chute days ago. Boss don't like it when we lose a pig."

"Lose a pig?" The first voice responded with a laugh. "You gotta be kiddin'. There's a thousand of the bastards out here. What the hell is one pig?"

"Eleven-sixty-five. Just find it." As the men searched through the hogs, pounding away on them, then grabbing at their ears to inspect the small, white tags imbedded there, the young pig burrowed deeper into the cavity, mashing himself as far into the wire as he could.

Then a third voice, very close, called out. "What's this hole behind the trough?" The pig could sense movement before he actually felt anything, but then his hind legs were seized, and he was dragged screaming from the hole.

"Well I'll be damned," someone said. "Little sunovabitch found himself a hidin' place."

"Eleven-sixty-five?" a voice asked. The pig's ear was mauled at, and then a hand came crashing down on his head.

"Yep. Smart-ass little bastard." The pig struggled desperately and futilely as more hands grasped at him, and two of the men hoisted him up between them. The pig twisted his head then, and with frightened, pleading eyes, stared directly into the face of Johnny Grimm.

Grimm stared back. "You caused us a lot of trouble, you little bastard." He reached out a hand, smacking the pig on its nose. The pain made the pig cry out, which only incensed Johnny more, and he began to beat away on the pig, this time with a closed fist as he punched its face.

"Enough, Grimm. That's enough. Just leave him be."

Johnny's eyes closed slightly, and grew cold. "Yeah," he said. "I'll leave him be. But when we get him inside the barn I'm gonna slit his fuckin' throat." The two men holding the pig slung it between them, one grabbing its front legs, the other the hind legs, with the pig hanging upside down, its head facing rearward and its back nearly scraping the ground. They then marched up the chute and into the barn like hunters returning with their quarry. Johnny followed along behind, tapping a fist against an open hand, keeping a constant vigil on the hog.

Inside the barn, Molly Bishop stood with an older man, near to where the chute poured out into another large pen, but this one indoors, and directly adjoining the slaughtering unit. She was dressed in her usual work attire, crisp white slacks, polished boots, and a white blouse opened at the top just enough to show what she liked to call *professional cleavage*. Which was just enough to allow a man to treat her somewhat professionally, while also giving him some leniency on where his eyes could roam each time she turned away. She addressed the man. "Look, Mister Culpepper, we both know you are under tremendous pressure from both the government and consumer advocates to produce bellies that are free of hormones, steroids and antibiotics. It's your cross to bear." Molly rubbed the man's arm, her mouth twisting into a mischievous grin. In her free hand she held up a small spray canister. "That's why we at McMillan have come up with this." She sprayed a bit of mist from the can into the air. The scent drifted back at them as mildly antiseptic. "Government mandates clearly state a restriction of what you can feed or inject into your animals. It's very clear cut. So instead of convention, we offer you circumvention. This is merely a spray. And there are absolutely no restrictions of any kind as to what you're allowed to apply to the skin of your hogs. A pleasant dusting of this stuff once a week, and your little piggies get their steroids and their hormones as a gift from the winds. It's perfect and it's foolproof. Tests show it is almost as easily absorbed by the skin as it is orally. But without all the red tape."

Culpepper reached out a hand for the canister and Molly handed it to him. "What's this gonna cost me?"

Molly's hand moved up to adjust the collar of Culpepper's shirt. "Is that really the issue here? That breeding treatment I gave your ladies last year made you a cool hundred-thousand bucks in extra revenue. This stuff is every bit as good. Your stock will grow fatter quicker, and be healthier than anything you've ever seen. From the results we're getting you should be able to shave a solid month off slaughter time. A month. And goodbye to all the ailments. We've stuffed enough antibiotics into that can to prevent almost any disease you can think of."

"I'd still like to know how much. Nuthin' you sell is cheap, lady."

Molly positioned herself directly in front of Culpepper. Both her hands went to work pressing against his shirt and his chest. Her lips pouted seductively as his eyes moved downward, stopping at her breasts. "You get what you pay for," she said.

Just then, the men carrying the young pig came to the end of the chute and stepped down into the barn a few yards away. One of the men turned to Grimm with a sly grin. He whispered, "Hey, Johnny, your wife's here."

Johnny looked up, past the pig and past the men, and there was Molly Bishop, blonde and lovely, standing there as if waiting for him. "What's that mean?" said the other man carrying the hog. "His wife?"

The first man spoke, his voice chiming out pleasantly. "Yeah, Grimm has this fantasy goin'. He thinks they're in love." Both men laughed, but Johnny heard not a word. His attention was focused solely on the woman.

Culpepper turned then, motioning the men closer. "You found him."

"Yes, sir." It was Johnny who stepped quickly forward, past

the other two. "Eleven-sixty-five. We found him hidin' out behind the water trough. He's been hidin' there for a whole week. He dug a hole."

"A hole? Well I'll be damned. How the hell do you think to dig a hole with a hundred other pigs millin' around? Smart little bugger."

Johnny stepped even closer to his boss and to Molly. "I got him. Ain't no pig gonna outsmart John Grimm." His eyes blazed into Molly's.

She spoke, her own eyes showing a quick spark as they glanced at the pig, then turned back to Johnny. "I remember you from the other day. You're the sticker."

Grimm blushed, warmed that she hadn't forgotten him. "Not yet, ma'am. But I'm workin' on it."

Culpepper pointed at the hog. "Take him in and put him on the line. He's dodged us long enough."

Molly grimaced, pursed her lips and stepped boldly forward, past Culpepper, past Grimm, and right up to the young pig. "Wait," she said. Reaching out, she bent down and scratched at the animal's ear, cooing out to it. "Easy little fella." Then she turned to Culpepper. "Let me have him."

"What? What in the world are you gonna do with a slaughter hog?"

Molly thought furiously. "Well, if he's been out there for a week as you say, then he's had nothing to eat. Nothing at all. That's very curious." She nodded her head. "I'd like to run some tests, check fat content, meat tenderness, stuff like that. It could be useful to study the effects of a week without nourishment. I don't think we'd actually like to starve a pig for ourselves, but here we've got one already pretty well emaciated. I'd like to explore that."

Culpepper nodded meekly. "So not only are you here to dip into my checkbook, now you want to steal my stock."

Molly returned the nod, but without the meekness. "You can keep that canister. It's worth over a thousand bucks. We'll call it a sampler."

"I knew this shit was expensive. I knew it."

Grimm turned to stare at the hog. His face crinkled up in

confusion. This was supposed to be his moment. A moment of bonding and reaffirmation, yet the woman appeared to have completely forgotten him in favor of the pig.

Molly motioned to the two men, and they lowered the pig to the ground. It lay there on its side for a moment before lifting its head slightly to study the five humans that stood over it. Sensing it was now free of restraints, it rolled over onto its other side and quickly rose to its feet. Then it backed away a few steps, and stood there trembling.

"Somebody put a rope around the damn thing," said Culpepper.

"Not necessary." Molly stepped forward again, moving close to the pig, where she dropped to her knees as she continued to coo away to it. "Easy little man," she said. Then she whispered. "Be smart. Let's get the hell out of here." The pig continued to tremble as Molly stroked gently at its neck. After a few minutes she rose, turned, and walked deliberately past the men without looking back. It was only a moment later she heard the soft sound of tiny hooves scrambling to catch up.

When she was gone, Culpepper spoke. "That's like some kind of voodoo shit."

Another voice called out. "Hey, Johnny. There goes your woman and she seems to be runnin' off with your pig. This is a bad day for you." Laughter followed.

Grimm stood there in the barn for a long time. Culpepper walked by, pausing just long enough to place a friendly hand on his shoulder. "Don't reach so high, son," he said. "Stay at your own level or you'll pay a hefty price." Then he walked out of the barn along with the other two men. Still Grimm stood there, focusing on the wall leading to the corridor where he had just seen the girl disappear. Had he missed the signs again? At the very least she should have acknowledged him with a wink or a nod or a whisper. Something to confirm that her feelings for him were intact. But there was none of that. She had taken the pig without so much as a glance, and walked away. His fists clenched and unclenched involuntarily. His face twisted in upon itself in open agony.

CHAPTER FIFTEEN

When Carl Monroe got home from work that night, he found Molly and her new pet seated in the dining room, a large box of cereal and two bowls on the table between them. Molly held up a carton. "More milk, Ramsey?" she said, nodding at the pig. The pig grunted contentedly, and seemed to nod back. It sat there like a little man, its two front hooves pawing hungrily on the tabletop. Glancing briefly at Carl, it shoved its snout deeply into one of the bowls to continue eating.

Carl paused, open mouthed, and pointed. "What the hell is that?"

Molly laughed up at him. "You've been in animal husbandry for twenty years, and you still don't recognize an ungulate when you see one? That's sad, man."

Carl moved to the table, pulled out a third chair, and sat down on it. "You know what I mean. Usually when a guy comes home from work he doesn't expect to see a pig sitting at the table. What's that thing doing here?"

"Having dinner." Molly paused, shaking some cereal from her spoon, which she then waved in Carl's face. "God, you're mean," she said. She pointed the spoon at the pig. "That *thing* happens to be a friend of mine, of ours, dumbass. You should be a little more respectful."

Carl surrendered, his body slumping forward pitifully, his

elbows coming to rest on the table's surface. "Where'd he come from? Another one of your road kill buddies?"

Molly reached out and affectionately scratched at one of the pig's ears. "Found him out at Culpepper's. They were just about to gut him."

"That's what they do, Mol. They gut pigs. That's the process. We're supposed to be aiding and abetting, not appropriating the livestock. Did you miss the memo on how our business works exactly?"

"Don't be a shit. Ramsey here is different. He deserves better."

"They all do." Carl looked at her intently. "You're personalizing again. Like in your mouse and snake story, and every other animal you pause long enough to get up close and personal with." He studied her face. "What's going on, Mol? You can tell me."

"What's going on is I brought home a pig. It's not unusual for a girl in my line of work to have a pet, you know. It's one pig, not a barn-full. That doesn't make me the patron saint to hogs everywhere. Just this one."

"No, that's not it. There's more to it than that. You're changing, Molly. You're becoming bitter somehow to the whole process. There's something going on."

Molly rose from the table. She moved over to the counter in the kitchen, drawing from its block a large carving knife. Then she moved back to the table, sliding her body right up against Carl's. The blade moved expertly in her hand, caressing its way down Carl's cheek and pausing finally at his neck. "Don't stress, silly," she said, her voice a tantalizing whisper. She pointed the knife at the pig. "Someday you and I can butcher the little guy up, maybe right there in the kitchen. We'll gut him and skin him and sit there on the floor, and drape ourselves in great slabs of flesh while we feast. We don't even need to cook him up. We'll go all Neanderthal and just cover ourselves in blood and meat while we eat." She laughed then. "Good times are coming, baby."

CHAPTER SIXTEEN

Michael Lair drove back down to Gallant, Kansas. Elizabeth Warman sat in the passenger seat beside him. She was not exactly the sort of person he would ordinarily have chosen as a companion on a three hour drive, but she was a dedicated agent with a good mind and might prove useful. He'd already spent long hours reviewing crime scene photos, several of which continued to gnaw away at him. Something just didn't add up. Something about the blood evidence, and the theory that the victim's son had committed the crime and then absconded to parts unknown. Lair felt certain there was more to it than that, and the feeling kept picking away at him that this killing, like the others, was connected, each one imbedded deeply into the next.

Warman spoke. "You know, the sheriff down there seemed pretty competent when we met him. And the crime scene is like twenty feet across. It's been looked at over and over again. I'm not sure what you hope to gain from this trip."

Michael glanced away from the road for a moment, studying Warman. "There's always something you miss, no matter how many folks look at a thing. There's always something."

"You learn that at the academy? Or back up at the cabin in Maine, when you busted through that door?"

"Ouch. The lady bites."

"I'm sorry, I didn't mean anything by that. It's just that you always seem so self-righteous. Like you're better than the rest of us. All of us make bad choices, Michael." It was the first time she had ever called him by his first name, and he accepted it as a peace offering.

"Of course I've made them, but not that day. You don't think I relive every moment of that encounter, over and over again? I can't ever shake it. But those men had already predetermined their fate. They knew it and I knew it. I had to try to get that boy out alive. It was his only chance."

"Yet you failed."

"Yes." Lair's grip on the wheel tightened, his face now pointing straight at the road ahead. "But I tried."

Warman nodded. She turned away and spent several moments looking out the side window. Then she pointed. "Pronghorn."

"What?"

"Pronghorn antelope, there on the hill. A bunch of them. They take me back to my childhood, when I would drive this same highway with my father. Whenever we saw pronghorn we would scream it out. City kids play games counting license plates. My dad and I counted antelope."

Lair smiled. "I never would have guessed you were a kid."

She turned back to face him. "It was a clean shoot. There weren't really any alternatives."

"Just how would you know that?"

"I studied it. We all did. Even though you were reprimanded and sent out here to serve your sentence in Hell, you're right. There was no other way. In another five minutes they would have blown that cabin to bits. Boy included. There was clear evidence."

"Nice of you to say so. I guess we'll never be certain."

"I'm pretty certain."

"Thanks."

Late in the afternoon they turned in at the sign, *Boomer's Pork and Pigs*. Driving along the same dusty road they had taken just a few days prior, they pulled up in front of the trailer, and just across from the barns. One of the hands stepped out from the trailer to greet them. He led them through the first barn, and down the long

corridor connecting each of the other buildings until they came to
the last one. It had been more than a week since the murder, but
under instructions from law enforcement, this barn, at the end of
the long row, was still cordoned off, brightly swathed in yellow tape
attached to a line of cones. Warman entered the space tentatively,
but Lair was more aggressive and was already probing the floors
and the walls for evidence long before he reached the taped area.
Once at the actual site of the murder, he moved over to the spot
where several large pools of blood had accumulated, drying out in
macabre Rorschach patterns on the hardened concrete. He studied
them intently for several minutes. Accompanying the blood were
several lines drawn in white chalk, marking the exact spot the victim
had been found. The lines were not as precise as he would have
liked, as every so often one would stop abruptly at one of the dried
splotches, disappearing for a time before reemerging on the other
side. Warman disengaged, walking over to the corridor leading to the
pens outside. She studied the long, jagged trail along the wall where
it appeared a bloody hand had been scraped along as the killer made
his escape. Soon Lair joined her.

"This guy must have really hated his father," she spoke in
monotone.

"Or loved the hell out of him and got nothing in return. That
could make a man snap." Lair reached out a hand, letting his fingertips brush along with those of the killer's. "I just don't get it."

"Get what? One dead. One running away and bloody as hell.
What's not to get?"

"He shoots the old man, and then what? He saunters over and
takes a damn bath in the blood? The very nature of a shooting is that
it's clean. At least for the shooter. Squeeze the trigger. Target goes
down. You walk off into the night." Lair pointed again at the wall.
"Where's all this blood come from? There's no need for it."

Warman also reached out, but her own fingertips stayed slightly
off the wall. "That's the love-hate stuff we're talking about. I can
picture this sick bastard running over to hug his father, poking all the
holes until the old man just fades away."

"I like it. It's sick as hell, but a beautiful thing." Lair nodded appreciatively at Warman, and stepped back a few steps to gain a larger perspective. He then walked along the entire length of the wall, noting how the pattern of streaks would lessen every few feet, then break contact altogether, only to be rejuvenated a step or so later until, near the entrance to the pen outside, one very distinct set of prints stood out in stark contrast to the bloody smear left by the rest of the trail. "Funny he'd stop right here and lay down one perfect set of prints. Just before leaving." Warman nodded, but said nothing, and Michael continued to stare at the wall. Finally he grunted, reaching out a hand to poke at her arm.

"What?" she said.

"You're gonna hate me for this, but that's the wrong hand."

"What? Oh, god, not again. What are you thinking, Michael?"

Lair continued to tap her arm. "You're gonna love this one. Heading out from inside, this is the right hand wall, right?"

"Yes, and duh."

"The thumb's down."

Warman sighed miserably. "Okay, I can see that. The thumb is beneath the fingers. Is that what you mean?"

"Yes." He pointed back along the entire wall. "Look. Whenever there is a clear representation of the hand, and not just streaks, you can clearly see the thumb is always hanging down. Especially here at the end. It's conclusive."

"I get that, Michael. Now why don't you tell me what it means?"

"Nope. You tell me." Lair stepped further back, leaving Warman to study the wall alone. He crossed his arms, the look on his face a smug one, and waited.

Warman closed her mouth tightly, but allowed her eyes to wander the length of the wall. Moving back inside to where the streaking blood had begun its journey, she set out to follow it again to the waiting doorway. Lifting her own hand, she moved along, mimicking the hand prints already laid out in front of her. She took only three steps before she stopped, turned, and stared wide-eyed at Michael. "Oh, god, there it is. It's so obvious."

"We've all done it countless times. Anyone dragging their hand along a right hand wall has to use their right hand. They have to. And if you're dragging your right hand the thumb points up. Always." He pointed to the final print. "This thumb is clearly down. It's a left hand on a right wall."

"Wait, what if he pushed it instead of dragged it?"

"Can't. First of all, pushing your hand is uncomfortable and unnatural, and it turns the fingers into tiny bulldozers, leaving clean streaks instead of bloody ones. Only a dragging hand allows streaks to form along behind it. No, it's a left hand."

They both stood there, side by side, contemplating the wall and the prints and the blood. Finally Warman spoke. "It doesn't make any sense."

"I know." Lair shook his head. "Let's look at possibilities. I suppose he could have been going backwards, you know, in a daze and staring back at his dying father. That would bring the left hand into play."

"No." In an instant Warman became Lair. "Then he would be moving slowly and methodically. And in agony. The blood would be dripping and not streaking. This guy was in full out escape mode. Nauseated and psychologically damaged perhaps, which is why he needed the wall in the first place, but he was definitely moving forward at a good pace."

Michael grinned. "You see, you're not just all fluff and beauty. You can be quite useful when you put your mind to it." Warman ignored the comment, remaining stoic, but inwardly she was quite pleased with herself.

"So what does it mean? How the hell does a left hand wind up on a right wall?"

"Genetics." Lair poked at Warman. "This guy is obviously genetically challenged. He's one of those guys that's just screwed on backwards. Or..." One hand reached out and again brushed against the wall. "Someone's screwing with us."

Sometime later the county sheriff arrived and filled them in on the few new details that had worked their way into the case. The

Tignor boy, Daniel, strongly believed to be responsible for the killing, had been seen in town on the evening before the murder in the company of a young woman. As Lair immediately suspected, that woman had turned out to be Molly Bishop, and she was conveniently registered at the Stockman's Inn directly adjacent to the restaurant. They had been seen briefly together at the diner, and when young Tignor had departed, Molly had gone with him. One interesting aspect of the incident was that when the diner closed and the workers went home some hours later, Tignor's truck was observed still in the parking lot.

Agent Warman spoke. "Damn peculiar that he leaves without his pickup, and your girlfriend, who seems to be keeping him company at the time, conveniently has a room booked right next door."

Lair nodded. "So what? You think maybe she meets this kid for the first time early in the afternoon, seduces him, plots with him, and they run off to kill the old man? Then what? Honeymoon in Tijuana, maybe?"

"I'm not saying it makes sense. I'm just saying it's peculiar. And apparently she's very good at the art of seduction." Warman studied Lair for a reaction. There was none.

CHAPTER SEVENTEEN

The Stockman's Inn stood as it had for the past seventy-five years, long, lean, dusty, and laying out closer to the road than it probably should, as several highway widenings over time had pushed the asphalt like lava ever closer to the buildings. Since it was already late in the day, Lair and Warman checked in for the night, planning to nose around a bit more before heading back to Omaha in the morning. Lair booked himself into room twenty-eight, the same one used by Molly Bishop on the night of the murder. Warman took a room down the row, and closer to the office. After questioning the clerk there they learned that Miss Bishop had specifically requested that the room adjacent to hers remain vacant, citing her need for rest. That caused the two agents to glance at each other knowingly, but they then frowned as they realized it was just another piece of puzzling information from which they could draw no substantive conclusion.

In his room, Michael looked around intently. He moved over to the bed and sank down heavily upon it. He leaned back, his hands pressing down on the mattress, feeling its texture and its firmness. He laid all the way back then, sprawling out, his head not quite reaching the pillows as he closed his eyes, allowing his mind to explore possibilities. He pictured Molly, laying out on this very same bed, wrapped up in the ecstasy of lovemaking with a young man she had just encountered. He shuddered suddenly as a wave of excitement passed through him, but that quickly subsided, leaving him feeling empty and alone. This girl was perhaps his greatest enigma, his greatest challenge. At the very moment he suspected her of wrongdoing, with just the tiniest bits of evidence to suggest her involvement, there was this other side of her that cried out like a child, in a voice of innocence. Nothing about her fit. But it would. Lair always found a way to make the pieces fit, even if he had to slam some of them around a bit first to make them more malleable. So it was only a matter of time until a solution materialized.

As he lay there, a sudden drowsiness washed over him, not unlike a mild sedation. Agent Warman would be waiting for him, he knew, as they had made plans to dine there at the inn. But that could wait. Right now the drowsiness closed in, called out to him, and in a brief moment he surrendered, falling into a deep sleep.

Sometime later he woke. There was a loud knocking coming from somewhere just outside his field of vision. He rose cautiously, and moved toward the sound. As he turned a corner a huge moving mass plowed into him, staggering him a few steps into another moving mass. He almost fell, but caught himself. Then the screaming of cattle could be heard, and the raucous laughter of men who stood off to one side, beating at them. The cattle were moving in a great herd, a mass of hides and horns and hooves, and Michael Lair found himself right in the middle of them. Terror struck. A massive force blasted into him from behind and he was swept into a maelstrom of dust and clamor. He cried out, but no one heard him, and he was again knocked savagely about. He reached frantically for the nearest cow, a brown and white monster with flaring nostrils, its sides heaving from the agony of the moment. Grabbing onto its neck he held on while dozens more of the frightened animals continued to press forward. Suddenly a man on a horse loomed in front of him, and he felt a burst of hope. "Help me," he cried out. "Help me." A rope lashed out, encircling his body and he was lifted aloft, where he found himself flying above the stampeding herd, floating there, only to crash a moment later into the side of a narrow chute which jutted out from one end of an old wooden barn. He lay there, barely conscious, but aware enough that his position was now to the side of the mass, and not in the middle of it. Looking up he saw the man who had rescued him just a few feet away. "Thank you," he called out. Another rope snaked out, this one catching him around the neck, the noose tightening until he could find no more breath. He coughed, gagged, and stumbled, trying hard to stand, to show himself as a human. "I'm a man," he tried to call out, but the rope constricting his throat turned the plea into a harsh moan.

"Take this one first," someone hollered. "It's a scrawny little bastard." The rope tugged at him and he was dragged away from the chute into an opening surrounded by milling cows and laughing men. Hands groped him then, pawed at him, ripping off his shirt to expose his bare chest. A man approached. A large man with eyes that burned like hot coals. In his hand, the man held a metal rod, and as Michael stared at it, he realized what it was. A branding iron, its tip white-hot, with just the faintest touches of red working their way across the edges of the brand.

"What? No, this is crazy." Michael tried to yell out, but again the ropes cut away at him, choking off any hope of an intelligible outcry. The man stepped closer, the iron plunging downward until it ripped into his chest, burning deeply into his flesh. The pain was unlike anything he had ever experienced, like molten lightning slicing through the most sensitive of nerve tissue. As the nerve ends exploded in agony, Michael screamed, but this time the restraints of the ropes loosened, as his voice blasted away at him. He bolted upright, sitting there in the bed, his head throbbing, and his chest still on fire. "It was a dream. A goddam dream," he said to himself, over and over. He began to laugh then, almost hysterically, and as he did so a giant foot crashed into the side of his face, pressing his head down into a pit of dirt and mud. Men rushed at him, four of them, with each one grabbing at a limb. In an instant he was spread-eagled on the ground, face up, watching his tormentors as they stared back at him. "I'm a man, dammit," he hollered out to them. "I'm a goddam federal agent." A fifth man walked up, kneeling beside him. He reached out a hand and stuffed a great gob of mud into Michael's mouth as he opened it to further his protest. As he gagged on the mud another set of hands from an unseen assailant ripped away his pants, and he felt his genitals jostled about, then grabbed savagely. Michael tried to raise his head. A new pain tore into him as his testicles were stretched out to their breaking point. The hand that had mashed his mouth full of mud now produced a knife, a long, razor sharp knife with a blade that curved almost halfway around upon itself. It was a wicked looking thing, as much like a razored hook as a knife, and as Lair's eyes widened in terror, the blade slashed downward in the direction of his crotch, until he felt just the faintest of impulses brush against his skin. Lair's eyes opened wider, until there was no further space for them to grow. A new and unidentified hand waved into the air directly over his face. Dangling from the fingers of the hand was a set of bloodied testicles. As the blood dripped onto Michael's face, he screamed a final time, and then an explosion of sound rocked his senses.

"Michael! Michael! Wake the hell up." Lair bolted upright. Staring at him from the open doorway was Agent Warman, a look of concern spread across her face.

"What?" he called back to her.

"You're having a nightmare. You woke up the whole place."

He shook his head, clearing it. "I'm alright. I just fell asleep for a minute."

"Asleep?" Warman stepped further into the room. "It sounded like a war going on in here."

"No, nothing like that." He grinned, but just for an instant, and then his face tightened. "But all this animal crap is wearing me down. I think I just found out what it feels like to be branded and castrated."

"Anything left in there?" Warman nodded at him.

"What?"

She smiled playfully, and pointed. "Well, your hand seems to be having a search party in your pants. I was just wondering if anything's missing."

Michael looked down curiously, moving his hand slightly and

causing his pants to bulge outward. "No, I think I'm good. But god, it was close."

Warman turned to head back out the door. "You're one messed up dude," she said. "Now put some ice on your balls and let's go get some dinner."

CHAPTER EIGHTEEN

The fair had come to town in Grand Island, Nebraska, west of Omaha. A new stockyard had been installed in the months leading up to the fair. Adjoining the yard were several pens surrounding a new arena replete with barns and stables and, under an awning off to one side, a bleacher sat, filling fast with fair folk, farmers, and meat processors who had driven in for the exhibition and auction. It was sheep day, with the pens stuffed full of bleating rams and ewes, each crying out mournfully as it waited for a final distribution. Some, in separate cages adorned with ribbons, would come out of this day unscathed, as they were the more prized specimens, breeding stock, or woolers, who could survive for several seasons if they dropped a sufficient quantity of healthy lambs, or grew thick enough coats of wool. They were the lucky ones, and the few. Mostly, at least on this particular day, the sheep trucked in here were meaters, or worse, culls that a particular farmer deemed unworthy to fold into his flock. They would be sold by the ton rather than by the animal, then stuffed onto train cars for a swift ride to the processor, who would grind them— before this day was out— into feed for dogs and cats. Consumers all across the country considered pet food with the word *Lamb* emblazoned on the label superior and coveted. So for most of these sheep the day would consist of more milling around, followed by a solid beating as they were herded onto the nearby tracks, and then a final ride off to a death camp.

Before the auction could begin, several long, grey busses pulled into a lot near the arena. A string of passengers began to flow from each, the strings merging at the rear of the lot, forming what at first appeared to be ranks, but then so many new strings arrived that the ranks became overwhelmed and began to mill about, losing all form and function. New busses arrived, with even more people piling out, this new batch trying hard to assemble into something meaningful, but soon losing themselves in what quickly turned into a mob. Signs were produced from the bed of a pickup parked in close beside the busses. Two men standing on the truck began to throw the signs into the crowd, and a great cheering erupted. At first there were no discernable words, just a blathering of loud voices, but after a few seconds a rhythm began, a sort of chant, and as it caught on there was a roar of synchronized sound screaming, *"AAPT... AAPT."* Soon the lot and nearby arena were overcome with the sheer ferocity of the chant. A police car pulled up, braking hard and nearly slamming into the gatherers. A uniformed man popped open the driver's door and began to step out. Instantly he was overcome by the mob, which swarmed around the car. Frantically he dove back inside the vehicle, slamming shut the door behind him. Encased in a dome of glass he sat there as the car began to rock violently back and forth. His eyes grew wide as he gripped the wheel, turning it to oppose the rocking motion, as if he was navigating some hellish ride. Soon the mob tired of this game and turned its attention on the exhibition area. There was a swirling shift in momentum as it turned suddenly and began marching deliberately forward down a long, open corridor which led directly into the arena.

Carl and Molly sat down low in one of the bleachers where they could more easily communicate with the ranchers and showmen who also clustered together in the lowest rows. They had brought with them a small case that contained samples of a new vitamin supplement, intended to increase wool production and cut down on ruminant disease. As the raucous sound pounded out, Carl leaned forward, tilting his head towards the corridor. "What the hell is that?" He coughed uncomfortably. "Sounds like bloody Jesus himself is coming."

Molly knew exactly what the chanting meant. "I don't know," she said innocently. "It's louder than hell." Even as she spoke the mob swarmed through the gates and swung itself out into the open. It moved like a great nest of ants, a ball of life, as tightly bunched as could be, until it arrived directly in the center of the arena. There it stopped, not stilled, but stopped, its defiance now a living, undulating mass. Signs were thrust about, waving madly up and down or side to side. Some read, *Meat is for Predators*, and others spelled out *Blood is on Your Hands*. But most of the signs, drawn in bold, red letters, said simply, *A A P T*.

"What the hell is that?" Carl shouted again, pointing at one of the signs.

"They're protestors," Molly hollered back, scarcely hearing herself above the din.

"I know that. God, Molly. I'm not stupid. What do the letters mean?"

Molly reached out and grabbed Carl's chin, turning him slightly as she leaned into him. She shouted out her words. "I think it's *Animals Are People Too*. Or something like that. I've read about them. They're extremists. They think animals should have rights, just like people. Crazy bastards."

"What the hell do they want us to do? We eat meat for chrissake. It's how we survive. They want us to make pets out of these damn things and start eating bamboo shoots?"

While Molly punched at Carl's arm, the sound of sirens could be heard in the distance. At first the sound fought against the chanting of the mob, but as the sirens grew near they became the more dominant force. Finally, a few moments later, a dozen heavily armed state troopers burst through the gate and entered the arena. Instantly, the chanting stopped. The mob spread then, fanning itself out until it spanned from one side wall of the enclosure to the other. There were hundreds of protestors, and because the arena was perhaps only thirty yards at its widest, they began to pile up, one behind the next until there was a thick slab of combatants directly facing the officers. One trooper stepped forward, a bullhorn raised to his mouth.

"Cease and disperse," his voice coughed out at the crowd. "Lay down your signs and leave for the exits immediately."

"Damn," Carl whispered, as this time his voice could be easily heard. "This is gonna be interesting." The protestors, now less of a mob and lined up in more of a disciplined assembly, began to slowly advance. Their movement was precise, tactical, and most certainly rehearsed. No one from the group spoke, or chanted, or made sound of any kind, and it became eerily quiet in the arena. The spectators, several hundred of them— fair-goers, livestock judges, sheepmen and others like Molly and Carl— sat as silently transfixed as the marchers. The lead trooper took a half step backwards, an instinctive move, drawing him nearer to the safety of his comrades. Again he bellowed out on the horn.

"I said cease and desist at once. I need you all to back away and disperse." The protestors continued their advance, ignoring the order, slowly and deliberately moving in on the officers. The trooper lowered the horn and, turning to his companions, hollered out, "Gas the bastards." Instantly several of the officers pulled canisters from their belts, popping pins on the tops of the cans and tossing them in the direction of the oncoming human wave. The canisters hissed out great bellows of white smoke, and in seconds the protestors were engulfed in a gaseous mist. They broke ranks then, their discipline crushed as fumes of tear-gas tore into them. There was coughing and gagging and wild screaming as the wave became a mob once again. Several of the officers raised rifles, opening fire without instruction, but elevated their weapons sufficiently so that bullets whizzed out a few feet over the mob and not directly into it. It was a warning, and it went unheeded. Burning canisters of hot gas were gathered up by protestors then, and thrown back into the line of troopers, until, in a very short time, the entire arena was engulfed in a white fog. The mist began to blow into the spectators, and the whole mass of them began to panic, rising up and crashing down through the rows of bleachers until they, too, reached the floor of the arena. There was no other avenue of escape. Molly grabbed Carl by the arm, pulling him quickly to one side just as a huge man crashed past them, his leg smashing into another man as he tumbled and fell over a railing and into the crowd.

Carl started to sob, so Molly smacked him on the ear. "Let's get out of here," she shouted. More gunfire rang out as the mob and the troopers and the crowd mashed together, all trying to reach the corridor which led to fresh air on the other side. The gas, as it reached out, thinned somewhat, and the thick fog that had blanketed everything moments earlier now became thin and wispy, but still sufficiently potent that it sought out and burned into the eyes of everyone it touched. Molly held on fast to Carl's arm, dragging him against the flow until finally they had cleared the crowd and ran to the far side of the arena. There were no gates here, but Molly reached up, pulling hard on a lever as a fence partition opened, exposing one of the chutes the livestock used to enter the exhibition area. They entered the chute, walked along its narrow channel, and exited into a holding pen. There Carl collapsed, crumbling to his knees, his back falling against a wooden slat bracing the corner post of the pen. He was still crying softly.

"Sunovabitch," he said. "I thought we were gonna die. I swear to god, I thought we were gonna die."

"I know, crazy right?" Molly spoke, her voice showing not the least distress.

Cark looked up at her. "What the hell is wrong with you?"

"What?"

"We could have died out there. I think people fucking died out there." He shook his head savagely, pointing a finger up at her face. "Why aren't your eyes burning? We just got gassed for chrissake."

"They're burning. Just not making a big deal out of it, that's all."

"A big deal? What the hell are you talking about? Did you just miss that whole freaking mob scene? We almost got sucked into it. We could be laying out there right now, choking our guts out."

"But we're not, are we? We're here, and we're safe. So calm your ass down and let's get out of here." Molly slapped Carl's finger away and climbed to the top railing of the fence. "Come on, dumbass." Carl rose then, choosing to walk alongside the barrier instead of climb over it, and he and Molly moved in the direction of the parking lot on opposite sides of the fence. Finally a gate presented itself, so Carl opened it and walked through, finding himself in an open field. Molly stood a few feet away, a tiny lamb pressed snugly against her chest.

"Oh, god. Where'd that come from?"

Molly pointed. "Over there. There's a whole truckload of them waiting to be ground into mash."

Carl looked at her, trying to mount some sort of reasonable defense against keeping the animal. "You're not bringing it home, Molly."

"I am."

"You can't just walk over and steal a sheep."

"I did."

"Look, you can't keep doing this. You can't save the whole world."

"Not trying to. Just this one little piece of it."

CHAPTER NINETEEN

As Michael Lair turned off the main highway, he entered a country drive with only a few homes scattered along on either side of the roadway. He noticed an old green pickup parked ahead, beneath a cluster of oaks situated just off the drive. As he pulled alongside, he also noticed a man sat in the driver's seat. The man was peering through binoculars and appeared to be studying one of the houses. There was no license plate visible from the front of the truck as Michael drove past, and he found the situation curious enough that for a moment he considered investigating. But while it was unusual to spy on a residence, there was nothing illegal about it, so he continued on. Pulling into a driveway near the end of the road, he stepped out and looked back. The pickup was gone. Making a mental note of it, he walked along a brick pathway until he reached the house.

Carl Monroe answered the door. "Mister Lair, what a surprise."

Michael took a half step backwards, gaining perspective. "Sorry to bother you," he said. "I was just out and about and thought I'd come by to see if Miss Bishop is available."

"You know it's Sunday, right?" Carl scratched his head, eying the agent suspiciously. "This a social call?"

"No, not really. Just informal." Michael half turned. "I can see her another time."

"No, no. It's okay. Please come in." The house was typical of many Midwest suburban areas, only perhaps a bit more upscale. A low, sprawling ranch with a large living area open to both the front and rear entrances, with a den and fireplace off to one side and a dining area off to the other. As they walked through towards the back of the house Lair could see a mass of trophies, plaques and ribbons along one wall and stuffed onto the mantle in the den. Atop most of the trophies was a golden casting of a bull or a ram, or some other farm animal. This surprised him.

"I thought you were strictly a drug merchant." He pointed into the room as they passed. "This is quite impressive."

Carl laughed. "Not really. Molly and I bought those at an estate sale for one of the old ranchers around here. When we have guests over she'll pick one up and tell a tale of how hard we worked to win it. By the time she finishes her story I almost feel like I raised the damn thing from a baby. The girl has a way with words."

Michael nodded. "So I've noticed. She's already put me in my place a couple of times." Carl caught the tone in his voice and paused.

"Look, agent, Molly's an incredible woman. She has a way with people, that's all. There's nothing bad about that. When Molly's with you, you can't help but feel good about yourself. She brings out the best in everyone she touches."

"Especially men." Lair looked directly at Carl Monroe.

"You don't know what you're talking about." Carl's tone lowered, offering a challenge that surprised even himself. "Yes Molly flirts, and yes, she's good with men. But there's not a damn one she talks to who doesn't feel the better for the conversation. Or who doesn't step a little prouder when she leaves." Carl's eyes elevated, meeting Lair's, and again surprised himself. "If you've come here on a witch hunt, you've got yourself the wrong lady."

They moved away from the den then, and a few steps later arrived at a pair of sliding glass doors which opened onto a tiled terrace surrounded by a low wall. Just beyond the wall stood the garden, impressively manicured, with floral displays in abundance, each one bordering the central theme of the garden which was a lawn and a fountain. Sitting at the edge of the fountain was Molly, with a pig nestled up contentedly at her feet, and a lamb, sucking from a bottle she held in both hands. Michael stood there at the doors, thinking the scene would have made a splendid painting. "Wow," he said, as he tapped at the glass. "Your backyard could be a whole city park. It's lovely here."

Carl pointed. "She's playing with her pets. She's always bringing something new home. Nothing I say seems to faze her. God, you'd think we were running a petting zoo here."

Lair scratched at an ear. "So she's an animal lover? I would have thought otherwise, you know, considering your business."

"You city folks just love to sit in judgement." Carl slid open one of the doors. "Go find whatever it is you came to find," he said sharply. Then he turned and walked back into the interior of the house.

As Lair approached the fountain, Molly looked up from her feeding, and for the faintest of moments he thought he saw confusion on her face. But whatever he thought he saw immediately vanished, as the face before him brightened and warmed.

"Mister Lair," she called out cheerfully. "What a nice surprise."

"Just in the neighborhood."

"Of course you were." They each appraised the other, and then Molly spoke, her lips pouting playfully. "So have you come to interrogate me, arrest me, or have sex with me? I'm never sure when you're around."

Lair felt himself blush, but not as badly as he usually did in her presence. He was evolving, learning better how to handle this woman and the uncomfortable challenges she always threw at him. "I wasn't aware those were all options, Miss Bishop. It's certainly something to consider."

"I like to give a man options." Molly aggressively pushed the lamb away and rose. "It makes for a more interesting encounter."

Lair pointed at the pig, now lifting its snout curiously at the intruder. "I was under the impression you weren't all that fond of nature's creatures."

"I'm not. The pig was a gift from one of my clients. He'd been starved for a week and I'm running some tests to see how that affected him. You can check it out if you want. And the lamb," Molly pointed with the bottle, "is receiving a new formula we've developed, that's all." She raised the bottle and shook it in Lair's face. "There's no love fest going on here, detective, if that's what you're implying."

Lair tried to sound affable. "Mister Monroe seems to think you are just loaded up with affection for critters. Says you drag them home all the time."

Molly stiffened, as all the warmth drained away. "Well Mister Monroe is mistaken. He's my boss and he's my landlord, and that's it. I don't hang with him. I don't fuck him. And I sure as hell don't allow him any emotional access to know what I'm thinking." Her smile returned then, like the sun breaking out after a storm. "I'm sure you think you know all about me. Well you don't. In fact, you know nothing about me. I'll bet they trained you up wonderfully at the factory where you were assembled, hot wiring your brain with all the psychological tools you'd need to enter someone's private space, to break someone down. I know you're desperate to tie me in somehow to all the crap that's been going on around here. But you can't and it's frustrating the hell out of you. All you've got is a hair that had every right to be where you found it, and a hunch. That's not much, is it? The fact is, the real fact is, you need to turn around and head in another direction. But you're too stubborn to see that. Like a man standing on the tracks, looking only one way for a train and refusing to consider that one might be closing in on him from behind. And then, bam! It's a sad way to end the day."

"You were with Daniel Tignor the night his father was murdered."

"What?"

"You were with the Tignor boy. You sort of forgot to mention that when we talked. I've certainly got evidence on that."

Molly looked away for a moment. The lamb moved in close to her, pressing its head against her leg, seeking comfort and nourishment. "Look, Michael," she said, her voice sullen, and her face still turned away. "I've already told you I was out there." Molly turned back then, her eyes meeting his firmly and directly. "I met him that day while I was making a deal with his father. I guess he became enamored with me and followed me into town. But that's it. He tried to hit on me and I turned him down. He wasn't too happy about it, but that's all there was to it."

"You didn't sleep with him?"

Molly's eyes flashed. "What the hell is the matter with you? Do you even listen?" She shook her head violently. "And it's really none of your business who I sleep with, is it?"

"Except you just told me you didn't."

"You know…" Molly reached out and touched her fingers affectionately to Lair's cheek. "There was a time when I thought you had potential. I used to look at you and think I could totally wrap my legs around that. But you're just another asshole in a long line. There's nothing special about you, not really. Your misguided persistence really does you a disservice. It takes you from likeable, even doable, to laughable." Molly turned to leave. "We're done here," she said.

As she walked away in the direction of the house, Lair called out to her. "One last thing, Miss Bishop. Do you know anyone who drives an old green pickup? I saw one parked up on the hill, and the man sitting inside seemed to be looking this way."

Molly continued to walk away, but turned her head slightly. "No, I don't. But if I meet the guy I'll fuck him for you."

Johnny Grimm sat in his pickup, waiting for Molly to appear. He had studied her and stalked her enough to know that each afternoon she strolled out into the garden to sit beside the fountain with her animals. He enjoyed watching her, envisioning a future filled with happiness for the two of them. Her disrespect earlier at the farm could be easily explained away. There had been other men present, and she had been in the middle of a business transaction. Then there was the squealing pig, and the laughter of the men, more distractions which were all understandable. She simply needed to be taught that his needs should always come first and never go untended. Given time she would learn. So he would give her another chance.

Grimm thought back to his youth, and to the only other girl who had ever impacted him as deeply as this one had. Her name was Emily Foster, and she also had long, blonde hair, and the face of an angel. There were many boys who vied for Emily's attention, but Grimm could tell early on that he was one of her favorites. She was very coy about it. Whenever he tried to speak to her directly, she would flip her hair so that it swept over her eyes, enveloping her in a shroud of mystery. Then she would laugh and rush away. It was a grand game, this laughing and running, one where she openly teased him, all the while wanting him as badly as he wanted her.

One day, at a bus stop, some bigger boys were taunting Emily. They pulled her hair and plucked at her dress, and the whole time she spun around gaily, pretending to revel in their attention. Johnny had jumped in, grabbing the largest of the boys. "Leave her alone," he spoke out in his toughest voice. That stopped the game, with everyone turning to stare. Emily ceased her spinning, the look on her face concerned and confused. "I won't let them hurt you," he had called out to her. The next thing he knew, the boys had surrounded him. The one he was holding turned suddenly, swinging a fist which connected with Johnny's nose. Intense pain rocked his head, bringing him to his knees. That's when all the other boys began to kick at him, slap him, punch him. He tried desperately to flee, but the wall of boys kept pummeling him back into their circle. Johnny couldn't remember much after that. He supposed he laid there on the sidewalk for some time. When he had finally regained enough of his senses to look up, the boys were gone, and so was Emily.

That day and that incident taught Grimm a valuable lesson. It changed him. He wasn't put on the earth as a protector, some grand guardian of virtue. If he wished to possess a female, it was not reasonable to assume that he must fight for her, or even court her in an attempt to win affection. The only absolute way to assure the kind of devotion he required was to find his woman, and take her.

As he sat there in the truck, thinking about the past and exploring possibilities for the future, a car rolled by. The car slowed somewhat, and its driver, a man, seemed to look intently in his direction. It was Michael Lair, suspicious of a vehicle parked in such an isolated location. Lair moved on, but the encounter made Johnny nervous, and after a few minutes more, he drove away.

CHAPTER TWENTY

Molly had grown up with every expectation that she would follow the same path as those around her. Her parents, her family, her neighbors, all heavily invested in the world of meat. Well into her youth she tried earnestly to fit into this mold, wishing to pacify, to purchase stock in the idea that her family was indeed producing a commodity and not sacrificing farmyard pets, exactly as her father had so many times suggested. But there were too many instances that nagged away at her, days when she would beg her father to give one more week of life to this friend or that. And there was another black-blinding incident that ripped away at her heart. She had accompanied her father to the slaughterhouse one day, with a truckload of squealing pigs sounding off from the bed of the truck. It marked the first and only time she would make such a journey. "How do they do it?" she had asked, her voice trembling. "I mean, it doesn't hurt them, does it?"

"No, Molly, of course not." Her father had squirmed a bit before answering, and refused to quite meet her eyes. "It's very humane. They just go to sleep." Molly had nodded respectfully, not yet ready to throw a wall of doubt or resistance at her father. And with this particular circumstance, she wanted desperately to believe him.

He had parked the truck up close to a huge, metal barn, telling her to wait there with the pigs while he went off to make arrangements. She had stepped down from her seat, moving to the rear of the truck where she stuck a hand through tightly meshed wooden slats to offer reassurance to the pigs. "It's gonna be okay," she said to them over and over. Most of the pigs immediately quieted and began to mill around, each trying to wriggle its way through the mass to where it could rub its head against Molly's hand. These pigs knew her, and trusted her.

Suddenly a door at the end of the barn nearest Molly burst open, and as her eyes widened in horror, a hog crashed through the doorway, screaming as it broke free and began to run across the yard. Seconds later two men emerged, each carrying stout metal clubs. The hog ran right for Molly, dodging her as it came alongside the truck, then frantically dove beneath the front wheels. The men were on the pig before she had time to blink, one of them dragging the screaming animal out from beneath the floorboards of the truck, while the other began a brutal assault with his club. The screaming intensified, and then amplified, as it was joined, first by Molly, and then the other pigs squished together in the bed. It was over in an instant, and the quiet that followed was as intense as the screaming had been. Molly stood there, mouth open, arms hanging limply at her sides. The faces of the pigs in the truck drooped low, with eyes only able to glimpse strips of the slaughter through the narrow slats of wood. The hog on the ground lay there humbly on its side, blood oozing from a massive wound on the top of its head. Its eyes were open, but inefficiently so, as there was nothing left for this hog to see. One of the men, the one who had snatched it from beneath the truck, gathered the hind legs of the pig and began dragging it back in the direction of the barn. The other man, still wielding his club, looked briefly at Molly, nodded, and began to follow a trail of blood back into the building.

When Molly's father returned a few minutes later she said nothing. She climbed back into her seat in the cab and sat there while the pigs were unloaded and taken away. But she made all of them a promise. She would never become like the others. Never become one of them, no matter what lies or deceptions were placed in her path. She was not yet certain how to respond to ripening feelings about her father, but she would never trust his word again.

That incident became a defining moment of her youth. There was more agony to follow, more indelible imagery that could never be erased from her mind, but she was evolving day by day, with one resolution which became unshakable. She would keep her promise.

One day, in her thirteenth year, and while playing *What If* with a friend, Molly evolved further, and achieved an elevated level of understanding about herself. It was pure, it was honest, and undeniably revealing.

"What if," her friend had asked, "there was a boy drowning in a lake, but you had on your very best dress. Would you jump in to save him?"

"Of course," Molly had replied. "That's a dumb question."

"Alright," said the friend. "Now let's say it was one of your pigs who was drowning?"

"Same answer, and still dumb."

"Okay, okay," said the friend, bobbing her head in thought. "What if both a boy and a pig were drowning, but you could only save one?"

Molly's face had scrunched up. She cupped her chin in her hands while she stalled for more time to consider. Finally she blurted out, "The boy, of course." The friend nodded, satisfied that Molly had successfully passed the *What If* challenge, and the game went on. The only problem being, Molly was certain she had just been less than truthful. The answer given had been the one anticipated, the obvious one, handed out in exactly the same manner as every programmed response that had been infused into her over a lifetime.

The truth is, Molly had been raised with pigs. At some point, her affinity for them began to outweigh her desire to mollify the humans around her. Just as Mowgli, the jungle boy, had his wolves, and Tarzan, the jungle man, had his apes, Molly, the farm girl, had her pigs. Once she realized this, and the horror that she was expected to participate in the mass slaughter of innocents as a life's calling, a rebellion started. It was obvious the pigs could not, by themselves, articulate their desire to live, so she would have to learn to do it for them. As a young girl she could only sit there and feel shame that she was not able to properly defend them, but as she grew, her defenses grew as well, until as an adult she was armed and ready. Her feelings were not unlike a mother who has seen her child raped or murdered and decides to seek revenge. Molly would attempt to create a better circumstance for the pigs, and a much worse one for those who showed up to abuse them.

She remembered one particularly painful conversation with her father just before she went away to college. "I think it's time you consider raising corn or wheat," she had said to him. "Or soy. I hear there's really good money in soy." She had touched her father then, letting one of her hands brush against his arm, trying to find a comradery she hadn't actually felt in a long time. "You could spend the last of your years without blood on your hands."

"I'm a hog man, Molly. You know that. At some point in your life you need to throw away all those silly little fantasies." Her father pushed the hand away. "You've never been like the rest of us. I've worked hard for this family. For you. So you can have every advantage. Yet the whole time you've always resented me for it. Always trying to bond with the pigs like they're your little puppies or something." He had looked at her, inspected her, trying to find something of value. "You should be proud of us, proud of me. But all I ever see you do is judge." He had turned away, avoiding her eyes. "Well you're not my goddam judge, and you have no right to be."

Anger rose in Molly, an anger she had never before unleashed on her father. "You're wrong. You have no right to dictate who lives and who dies. It's not only cruel, it's barbaric."

"For god's sake, girl. You talk like they're human." It was her father's turn to make contact then, as he reached out both his hands, grabbing onto her arms and shaking her violently. "They're just pigs, Molly. They have no rights."

Molly allowed herself to be shaken with no resistance. When her father's anger finally abated he released her and took a step back. Molly took a step forward, refusing to allow him the distance he sought. "You sicken me," she said with as much venom as she possessed. "The very fact that they have no rights means they need someone to stand up for them. Someone to protect them." She had laughed then, and pointed at him derisively. "And along comes my beloved father. Only instead of bringing a blanket of protection, he shows up with his goddam knife."

Her father had slapped her then, one of the few times in her life she had ever been struck by him. This slap brought with it a finality. A conclusion that suited them both. It was the last time they had spoken.

———

Molly drove now, heading east to the outskirts of Omaha. After a few more minutes she turned in at Lola's, the same dive bar where she had rescued Carl from a beating a few years earlier. She liked to come out here every now and then, immersing herself in a culture she felt little in common with but was somehow strangely drawn to. As she pulled into the lot, she noticed an older green pickup that pulled in and parked just a few spots away. Michael Lair had mentioned a green pickup, so her curiosity piqued that one would suddenly appear so closely beside her. She exited the Camry and moved in the direction of the truck, but when she arrived it was empty, the driver's door still slightly ajar.

It was Tuesday night at Lola's. Ladies night. Molly especially enjoyed Tuesdays, not because she felt more secure strolling into an environment where an abundance of women would offer her some anonymity, but because she enjoyed the sexual tension brought about by an excess of women in a bar usually filled with men. Walking up to the bar, she knew a hundred pairs of male eyes were feasting on her, pining for her attention, while at the same time a hundred pairs of female eyes shined bright with the hope that she would trip

and fall on her face. This amused her. Carl often referred to her as
an attention whore, and she supposed that was as close to a fitting
description as one could get.

The barroom was crowded, as it usually was on Tuesdays. She
squeezed her way in between two men at the bar, then turned to the
one on her left. "My seat," she said, reaching out with one hand to
remove the Stetson from the man's head, while the other brushed
its way affectionately through his hair. The man surrendered his seat
without protest, also happily surrendering his hat which Molly placed
on her own head, tilting it back to showcase the mass of blonde curls
that swept out from beneath the brim. She turned to the second man,
who swung himself around enough so their knees interlocked, with
one of Molly's legs reaching out to caress the man's thigh. "Vodka,
rocks," she said to the man, whose hand went immediately into the
air as a signal to the bartender. Swinging herself around in the stool
she scanned the room. Off to one side was a small stage, elevated
slightly above a large, open dance floor. Several members of a band
were hard at work there, adjusting mic heights, keyboards and drum
stands. A guitar player in the center of the group twisted the dial on
an amp, then hit his strings once or twice, producing an off-key riff.
The crowd roared out at the sound in anticipation, but the player
soon stopped his strumming and began to work on the guitar.

As Molly looked around at the room, she noticed a man standing
alone near the entrance. There was something different about him,
something familiar. As she studied him further, it came to her. He
worked at one of the nearby hog farms. A man she had met a week
or two earlier. Something about him made her uneasy. She had
great instincts about people, refined over a lifetime of working with
animals who had even greater instincts. Perhaps she had borrowed
from them, learned from them. A hand tapped at her shoulder and
she turned to the barkeep who handed her a drink. She nodded
in thanks just as the cowboy who owned the Stetson leaned in to
whisper something in her ear. The band started then, with the guitar
leading off loudly, followed by the crashing thunder of a drum, and
the whisper was lost. Molly laughed aloud, the laugh also swallowed

up by the music, and the man at the door was forgotten. She reached
out, grabbed both her suitors, and dragged them in the direction of
the dance floor. Molly loved to dance. Music, especially loud, raucous
music always carried her away, closing off her mind to all things
unpleasant. Bodies brushed against hers, most accidentally, entering
her space as the floor became compacted by a horde of undulating
flesh. Others came intentionally, men who reached for her, caressed
her, the boldest grinding themselves against her in their own weirdly
concocted mating ritual. That was always the most fascinating part,
and the most amusing. That males could feel themselves somehow
connected by merely being in the presence of, or casually touching
a desirable female. To further their fantasy, Molly would always find
these males with her eyes, bond with them, and feed their hunger.

Sometime after midnight Molly broke away. She walked over to
a young man who had been assigned to guard her purse, kissing him
lightly on the lips in thanks. The man blushed, his mundane night
composed of standing on the sidelines watching her dance having
just become a spectacular one.

Arriving at the parking lot she was still humming, the sounds
of the band pulsating through Lola's thin walls. She moved towards
her car, but stopped suddenly, a movement off to the side catching
her attention. Half-turning, she noticed a man approaching from the
far end of the lot. It was the hog man. The one she had seen earlier
by the door. "Miss Bishop," the man called out to her. Molly looked
around. The lot was empty except for the two of them. Something
about the way the man moved, or something in his tone caused her
concern, an inner voice crying out for caution. Molly was a hunter,
but more than that, her senses were finely tuned. It was obvious
that this wasn't a chance meeting, two familiar faces running into
one another in a darkened lot. It was much more likely this man had
stalked her here. Turning her head she glanced at her car, a few paces
away, and then looked at the space where the green pickup had been.
She was surprised to see it was gone. Swinging around to again face
the man, she noticed a similar truck at some distance behind him,
isolated at the very rear of the lot where it was darkest.

She spoke then, as the man drew near. "Yes?" she said, her tone low and steady. "What can I do for you?"

The man moved up very close, only a few steps away, and paused. "It's me. Johnny Grimm. From the farm." He glanced away, just for a moment, as he looked over at the entrance of Lola's, studied it, and then briefly scanned the lot around them. That was a sign Molly had been waiting for. Grimm was checking for observers, intruders, someone who might interfere with this meeting and his intentions. It was possible the man simply wanted privacy so he could ask her out, or make some sort of aggressive romantic gesture. She'd dealt with plenty of men like that in the past. But this seemed different somehow, and the look on Grimm's face became wild and twisted, though she could tell he fought hard to control it.

Again Molly spoke. "What do you want?" This time her tone grew demanding.

Johnny attempted a smile. It failed, his lips trembling miserably. "I saw you inside. I thought you looked pretty." He was stammering, stabbing at the words. "I wanted to say hello."

Molly's lips also trembled slightly. Her right hand nonchalantly slipped into her purse, held waist high in front of her. She turned, stepping in the direction of the Camry. "It's nice to see you again," she said benignly. "But it's late and I have to get home." She moved away, taking a few brisk steps towards the car, her senses on full alert, waiting to see if the man made any attempt to follow her.

"I have a pig." Grimm blurted it out, and Molly turned.

"What?"

"A pig." He pointed. "Over there in my truck. I caught it out on the road. I thought you might like to have it." A sneer formed on Johnny's face, the first genuine expression she had seen in him. It offered a further warning. "Otherwise I'm gonna butcher it up." Molly almost smiled, her lips curling upwards slightly into a familiar pose, but at the last second she stifled it. The situation was intimidating, and potentially dangerous, but she found a certain humor in it. She thought back to her childhood, with all the warnings issued to the children of her community about strangers bearing gifts. Most abundantly offered, she had been told, were candy or kittens or puppies. By strange men in dark clothes driving white vans. No one had ever warned her about a man bearing pigs.

"Alright," she said. "I'd like to see it." Taking the last few steps to the car, she bent down, removed her heels, and placed them on the hood. Then, barefoot, she turned, still clutching her purse, and accompanied Grimm in a walk across the lot. Once at the truck she could sense the tension mounting in the man. She knew there would be no pig. But she was still curious as to his intentions, exactly what he had in mind, and how he would put his plan into action. An excitement shot through her. There was still a chance this could turn out to be an innocent encounter, but the odds were growing long. More likely it would soon turn into a confrontation, and John Grimm had no idea of the capabilities of his potential victim, nor the fact that while he was hunting Molly, Molly was hunting him back. She moved slightly ahead, stepping up to look into the cab of the pickup as they arrived. She knew that would offer Grimm her back, and if anything was to happen it would happen now. She spoke. "So where's the pig?"

Johnny stammered out, "Right there in the seat. Don't you see it?" As he spoke he moved, quickly closing in on the girl, throwing up one hand to grasp her mouth, while the other hand drew around her waist in an attempt to contain her. Molly spun around, facing him, and was slammed back against the door of the truck. This was not an unexpected move, and was exactly as it had played out in her mind. Grimm was now pressing hard against her, his eyes filled with an evil lust. But as quickly as the lust had arrived it drained away, his eyes now confused, glazed, and broken. Something was terribly wrong. He pushed back away from Molly, both hands which had been on the attack, now lowering to his midsection where they clutched his stomach. Blood flowed out over them. "Oh, my god," he stammered out. He raised one of his hands, waving it in front his face, mesmerized by the blood that poured from it. "Oh, my god."

Molly stepped away from the truck. She allowed her purse to fall to the ground. In one hand she held a knife, its four inch blade flashing silver and crimson. Her other hand held a small caliber automatic pistol. As Grimm staggered back, she swung out her arm, the pistol impacting the side of his face. The blow rocked him, the cold barrel of the gun ripping a gash deeply into his ear. He screamed out, staggering further before crumbling to the ground. He began to cry. "Shut the hell up, pervert." Molly raised her arm again as Grimm cried out, with both his hands rushing up to protect his face.

"Please, no. God no. I didn't mean nuthin' by it. I didn't mean nuthin'." Tremors wracked his body and he lay there sobbing.

Moving up close to the fallen man, Molly bent low, the hand holding the knife reaching out, and expertly flaying a small patch of skin from Grimm's cheek. "Don't you ever fuck with me again," she hissed at him. "Next time, I'm gonna hurt you."

CHAPTER TWENTY ONE

The next morning Michael Lair received a phone call from Molly Bishop. Something had happened, she told him, something important. He arrived at McMillan a short time later, finding both Molly and Carl Monroe waiting for him in Carl's office.

Molly sat at the desk, dressed in her white work attire, while Carl sat in one of two chairs set up to face her. Michael took the other. "So," he said as he sat, turning his chair slightly so it would better face them both, "why am I here?"

Molly held a pen in her hand, and she now leaned forward, tapping it lightly on the desktop. "Someone tried to rape me last night," she said simply. "Or kidnap me."

Carl also leaned forward, his head falling miserably into his hands. "I should have been there. I've told you, there are too many crazies out there. Dammit, Molly."

"Nothing happened, Carl. I said the man tried."

Michael spoke. "Are you alright?" There was real concern in his voice.

"Yes, I'm fine." Molly rose and walked around the desk so she could lean back on the front of it. They were now both forced to look up at her. "His name is Johnny something, I think. I don't remember exactly. He works for one of my clients. You can check it out later."

The detective part of Lair came gushing out. "I don't mean to be insensitive, but you said a rape never actually occurred, yes?" He squirmed a bit, completely contrary to his nature. "How do you know that was his intention? Did he actually attack you? Or was he just aggressive towards you?"

Molly's face hardened. "A woman can tell if a man is attempting to rape her, Michael. Or is just being overly amorous. There's a difference. The man attacked me. There was no question as to his intent." Molly reached out, kicking one of her feet at Lair's leg. "He drove a pickup. An old green one. I thought you might find that interesting."

Michael looked up at her, his attention now fully activated. "Our stalker."

"Yes, our stalker."

"Did he actually grab you? Do anything physical?" Molly turned, walking back around the desk where she sat back down. She placed both hands out on the desktop, drumming her fingers.

"Yes," she said finally. "He grabbed me and slammed me up against the truck. I think his intention was to choke me out and drag me off somewhere." Molly's mind swept back to the night before. She could feel cold hands groping her, trying to contain her. And the smell of sweat and hogs, mingled in with the scent of his breath as his face had pressed in close. A normal person recalling such an experience would once again feel the fear, the danger of the encounter. They would tremble at the violence of it. Molly also trembled, but from excitement, not fear, and as Lair watched her, he seemed to sense she was reliving it.

"You okay?" he asked her.

Carl moaned, still sitting with his head lowered. "I should have been there."

Molly spoke kindly to her friend. "It's okay, Carl. It turned out fine. I'm fine. You're fine. We're all fine." She then looked directly at Agent Lair. "This guy's dangerous, Michael. I'm ashamed of myself for letting him get away. That's why I called. He's going to hurt someone. I'm certain of it."

"How did you get away exactly?"

Molly pushed her chair back and spoke almost casually. "I rebuffed him."

"What does that mean? The guy grabs you, tries to take you down, and you rebuff him." Lair looked at her curiously. "How do you rebuff a rapist?"

"I just did."

An idea came to Lair. "You said this guy works for one of your clients. Wouldn't happen to be a hog farmer, would it?"

"Yes, as a matter of fact. A big one." Molly sat upright. "Why?"

"Just thinking. We know this is undoubtedly some sick bastard. I've already had a visual on him stalking you. He sounds like a pro, like this is what he does." Lair cleared his throat. "There was a young lady found not far from here just last week. Raped and murdered. There were pig hairs all over the place."

Molly's face lit up and she cried out, "It's him. This is your guy."

"Let's not jump to conclusions. There's a big gap between grabbing a lady in a parking lot and dragging her off somewhere to kill her."

"Wrong." Molly stood, once again towering over the two men. "There's no gap at all. That's what this sicko was going to do to me. I can feel it." She pounded one of her hands down hard on the surface of the desk. "It's him."

Lair also stood, placing both his hands down on the opposite side of the desk. He looked directly across at Molly. "I don't doubt you. It's just that I live in a world of proof. Of hard evidence. Right now we've got nothing but a blotch of unknown DNA on a piece of duct tape at a crime scene. We need to find your guy and see if he matches up."

Molly's expression never wavered. She continued for a moment to lock eyes with Lair. Then she reached down, opened a drawer in the desk and extracted a small, white rag. It seemed to have something wrapped up in it. Placing the rag on the desk top, Molly very deliberately unfolded it. And there was the knife, its blade still coated with fresh blood. "If you need more," she said in a soft whisper, "I've got some on my gun."

Lair looked over at Carl, whose face had grown ashen. Carl opened his mouth to speak, but no words came out.

Finally Lair spoke. "Lady, I hope to hell I'm never in a situation where you feel the need to rebuff me."

One hundred miles west of Omaha the land changes abruptly, the flat, open plains erupting into massive bluffs that punch towers of sandstone high into the heavens. It is such a remarkable geological spectacle that visitors pour in from all over the heartland. Tucked back in one of the canyons there, just a mile or so in from the highway, is a park, and set alongside a creek near its center is a camp where tourists can come and stay in cabins or trailers while they enjoy the natural splendor of the place.

Late one night John Grimm's old green pickup made its way up the winding road that led into the park. Johnny slumped at the wheel, wincing and crying out at every pothole the truck rolled its way into. There were towels tied and stuffed around his waist, stemming but not altogether stopping the flow of blood that had seeped from his wound for many hours. The pickup slowed as it rounded a final turn, Johnny nearly passing out from loss of blood. As he entered the campgrounds, his head lifted. He flicked on the high beams, searching for a place where he could park and rest and heal. There were two trailers ahead and off to one side, so he pointed the truck in their direction, just managing to slide in between them before braking, turning off the engine and passing out. Hours later he woke, with the morning sun beating down on him through the windshield. A raging fire burned in his stomach, and his head throbbed miserably. Moaning softly, he rolled in the seat, momentarily escaping the sun.

A voice called out to him. "Hey, Mister, you alright?" Lifting his head he tried to focus on the passenger side window which was rolled down. A woman stood there, and next to her stood a young girl of perhaps twelve or thirteen. The woman spoke. "We're sorry. We don't mean to intrude. But we heard you calling out." A look of concern spread across the woman's face. She pointed in at Johnny. "My god, you're hurt."

Johnny looked down at the towels, some of which had slipped free from his stomach and lay there on the seat beside him. The towels and the seat were both heavily stained in blood. Shaking his head to clear it, he tried frantically to think. Looking up at the woman he managed a slight smile. "I'm pretty sure I got hit by a car," he said. "I had some plywood in the truck. It blew off on the highway, and I was tryin' to gather it up." He grimaced, as though fighting for a memory. "I remember I got the hell knocked out of me, and the bastard just kept on goin'." Without waiting for instruction or invitation the woman swung open the door.

"We've got to get you inside," she said. Grimm struggled into a sitting position, and with both the woman and the girl grabbing his arms, they managed to get him out from the truck and over to their trailer.

Johnny stayed there with them for five days as he regained his strength. At first the woman argued that he needed medical attention, but he argued back with a story. That as a boy still in his teens he had been a soldier in Bosnia, ordered with the rest of his platoon to plunder the very village where he had grown up. The woman's eyes had grown wide, and she pushed her daughter away into a side room as he told of how one night they had gathered all the young ladies of the village together in a field, where they were ordered to ravage them. "I remember lookin' into the eyes of one girl," he told her, his voice trembling with shame. "I knew her. I grew up with her. She looked at me, her eyes pleadin' as the men threw her to the ground." Real tears began to flow from Johnny's eyes as he told this story. He had no idea where they had come from, but he basked in their presence, and was quite proud of them. The woman's eyes also began to mist, and he knew then he owned her. He finished by saying he had stood there helplessly, for he was just a boy, and then had slunk away, where he ran, day by day and night by night, crossing one border after the next. It had taken him a year, he said, to make his way to America, to a place where he could finally hide his grief and start a new life for himself. But he had no documentation to be in this country, and a hospital would undoubtedly uncover this deception and he would be forced to return to his homeland. "I would be found a traitor there," he said. "Because of my refusal to obey. God knows what they would do to me." The lie struck a hard chord with the woman, as she patted his cheek tenderly and began to tend to his wound.

In reality Grimm's heritage was indeed Slavic, but he had never set foot on foreign soil. He had been born on the south side of Chicago, his father the true Bosnian, a legal immigrant, and his mother sprinkled with a variety of lineages that blended themselves perfectly into the American gene pool. Mostly, he had been told, she was Greek, but her skin tone reasoned that she was likely more black than anything else. As a child John Grimm had been loved. He remembered cold wintry nights when his mother would sit with him before a coal burning stove, singing hymns and hugging him close while they rocked together in an old wooden chair. Those were his earliest memories. He also remembered that by the age of five the hugging had ceased abruptly. He had reached an age where physically he could begin to offer resistance against the close contact his mother desired. So he began to kick at her, or push away whenever her hands would reach for him. Soon she stopped trying, and he found himself isolated much of the time, left unchecked and unrestricted. That's when he began an examination of the world around him. Mostly, he looked for weakness in those he came in contact with, and found it in abundance. Physically weaker boys he could knock down and bully, psychologically weaker adults who thought they could manipulate him, twist him into shapes that would better conform to their world. He learned early on an important tactic that would serve him right into adulthood. Beat down upon anyone weaker and acquiesce to anyone stronger. It was the perfect formula, and allowed him to move about through the layers of society unobstructed.

At any rate this woman accepted his explanation, even seemed to revere him for it, and she and the girl took on the task of caring for him. He lay there in the trailer and grew stronger each day. The woman even seemed to develop a fondness for him, fussing over his bandages and spoon feeding him by hand as often as he could eat. But Grimm felt no attraction to her. His eyes, when he could finally focus them properly, zeroed in on the girl. She was lovely, a fresh young thing not yet familiar with the ways of life or the ways of men. Sometimes late at night while the woman slept the young girl would wake and the two would talk. He could sense their growing bond, and the girl's longing for him. She never spoke of it directly, but every now and then her hand would reach out to adjust his pillow, or she would giggle playfully as he reached out to tickle her.

On the morning of the fifth day, Johnny had regained enough of his strength to swing himself out of bed and stand. It felt good to be up again. The wound in his side, which had closed by then, began to itch more than hurt. That was a positive sign that the healing process was well under way. The girl, excited that he was finally up and about, came rushing over to see him. The woman was nowhere in sight.

"Where's your mother?" he asked her.

"She's doing laundry down by the stream." The girl looked at him inquisitively. "Should I go get her?" Johnny laughed out lustfully, excitement rising in his voice.

"No, baby. We won't need your mama for this." He grabbed her, catching her by the wrists, then twisted her arms and threw her down on the bed. The expression on her face changed abruptly, morphing into what Grimm perceived as raw passion. He pressed down on her, one hand on her chest, while the other clawed at her dress. The girl screamed. "Shut up," he yelled at her. "We must be quiet, you little fool." Instead of quieting down, the girl began to struggle, her own hands racing up to claw at his face as she continued to cry out. Nails dug into his cheeks, and he also began to scream. "You bitch! Shut the hell up." His hands shifted, seeking her neck. The girl twisted onto her side, kicking out as hard as she could with one of her legs.

A knee came up, impacting his stomach directly on the site of the wound. An explosion of pain rocked his midsection, causing him to lose grip and stumble backwards until he collided with a wall. The girl bolted upright. Leaping from the bed she landed prostrate on the floor, rolled onto her hands and knees and crawled her way out of the trailer. It all happened so quickly that Johnny had no time to react. He stood there for a few moments, clutching his still burning stomach and stared at the empty doorway. "Sunovabitch," he said finally, repeating the words over and over. He then gathered himself enough to stumble over to the door and make his way outside to the truck.

Fifteen minutes later, he arrived back down the canyon at the base of the park where the road ran into the main highway. For a moment he sat there contemplating. To the west lay Wyoming and Colorado, to the south Kansas and New Mexico. All perfect destinations to lose himself amongst the thousands of farm workers who migrated back and forth as the seasons called out to them. That would be the sensible choice. To lose himself. Then he thought of Molly Bishop, and how she had attacked and humiliated him. She needed to be taught that Johnny Grimm wasn't just another man to be toyed with. He thought of how gratifying it would be to own such a woman. To bend her to his will. To dominate her. There were no further feelings of lust or affection or longing for the pretty blonde. Those had died in the parking lot when he had laid there begging her to be merciful. But there was still a burning need in him. To see her grovel. To see her beg him back. That's what he needed most. To see her beg. Then maybe he would return for this young one. He'd like to see her beg, too.

CHAPTER TWENTY TWO

Four men sat on a wooden bench inside a barn. The interior of the barn contained all the usual things one would expect a farm building to hold. There was a tractor parked at one end, with piles of tires and plows and spare motor parts tucked in close beside it. Several large stacks of hay lay off in a corner, contained by low walls of old boards, some of which had broken loose, allowing much of the hay to spill out where it began to spread its way across the floor. There were several stalls built along the wall opposite the hay. At one time they sheltered horses or other livestock, but now they lay dormant, emanating the musty scent of manure and straw, mixed in with animal sweat and time. The men were in good spirits, as one of them told a joke while the other three laughed in merriment. Directly in front of the men stood a cage, maybe eight feet across, its lowermost portions composed of metal bars, heavily screened. Rising above the metal was a mass of chicken wire, curving into a dome that encased the entire structure. While the men chatted away, a door built into the wall closest them opened, and a fifth man entered, this one carrying two large animal traps. Each of the traps contained a cat. One was an average sized house cat, but the other was considerably larger, causing the man carrying them to lean heavily to that side.

"Wow," one of the men on the bench said, pointing. "That's a big bugger. Is it a bobcat?"

The new man laughed. "No. He's sure as hell big enough though. Big-ass tom. Caught him out at the dump." The man nodded at the smaller cat. "I got this one off a porch. Dumb bastard came right up to me. Licked my hand. Some old lady is gonna be sad tonight." One of the men came off the bench and moved over to the cage. He loosened a latch, swung open a door and the man carrying the cats stooped to enter the enclosure. Once inside he opened both traps and dumped the cats into the cage. Then he backed away. Both cats, now freed from the constraints of the small cages, immediately began to seek freedom from the large one. They ran madly about, crashing into the metal bars, the smaller one then climbing the chicken wire in a frantic attempt to escape. The giant tom ran around for only a moment before sensing the futility of his situation. He then backed himself into a corner and lay there hissing.

"Hey, Lester," called out one of the men, "why don't you go back in there and pet him?"

"Hell no," called out another man. "We've been waitin' for over an hour. Go get the main event." The man called Lester turned and walked back out through the door. He returned a moment later, leading on a leash a large pitbull. The men gasped. "Holy crap. That's a lotta dog."

Lester moved back over to the cage, opened the latch and pushed the dog inside. Reaching in, he unsnapped the leash before stepping back and swinging shut the door. The pitbull looked around. Its body began to tense up, then began to quiver. It looked first at the smaller of the cats, still clinging to the wire a few feet over its head. Then it focused in on the big tom. The cat's back arched instinctively, doubling its size to appear more intimidating. It began to growl out a warning, the growl starting low, from deep in the animal's chest and then rising in pitch until it became a scream. This cat had survived many battles, but never faced anything like the mouth and teeth connected to the dog that now stared across at it. The pitbull took a step forward and the muscles in its shoulders began to twitch with anticipation. It growled back at the cat, low and deep and hungry. It took another step. "Steady," Lester called out, and the big dog froze, its eyes still locked onto the tom's. "That's called trainin', gentlemen. He don't move until I tell'em."

"Shit," said one of the men, as the four sat there mesmerized. "That's one helluva dog." Reaching into his jacket Lester produced a stopwatch, holding it high in the air.

"Ready?" he asked. No one answered as each man focused in on the cage. Lester leaned forward, extending his body out across the top of the enclosure and smashed his free hand against the wire very close to where the smaller of the two cats clung. Startled, the cat released its grip and leapt for the ground. "Fight," Lester yelled out as he stepped away from the cage. The reaction of the pitbull was instantaneous. Momentarily forgetting the large tom, it shifted attention to the falling cat, its teeth lashing out while the animal was still in the air. Teeth sank into fur, then flesh as the cat cried out. It rolled itself over, with claws raking at the sides of the dog's face. The pit mashed it into the ground then, using its face like a battering ram, smashing and tearing at the same time. Blood erupted from somewhere, a great smear of it swiping across the cold concrete floor as the dog shook its head savagely. In seconds it was over. The cat went limp, its body battered and broken, its life force extinguished. The dog paused for just a moment, turned its head and looked at Lester, as if awaiting further instruction. "Fight," Lester called out again, his own face covered in a sick bloodlust. The other men sat entranced on the bench, their eyes shifting back and forth between the dog and the big tom.

The pitbull lunged at the cat, but the tom had seen this move many times before. Tensing its muscles it leapt high in the air, so that when the teeth arrived there was no cat to clamp down on. The tom landed squarely on the dog's back, sinking its claws in deeply in an attempt to hold on. The dog grew instantly furious, slamming itself against the metal bars. The cat tumbled to the ground. It did not attempt to run away as most creatures would. It had already calculated its odds of escape. There was really nowhere to run. As the dog closed in the cat rolled onto its back. It screamed out, a short, high-pitched wail and then the dog was on it. Its huge head slammed into the belly of the cat. The tom's mouth came up, its teeth sinking into the dog's face, all four of its claws imbedding themselves into the pitbull's neck. The dog began shaking its massive head then. Teeth ripped into the stomach of the cat, as he shook it back and forth violently. In desperation the tom let out one more shriek, but this one ended abruptly as its bowels were torn open, its intestines erupting into the air in a spray of blood and flesh. The splatter was intense enough that it reached the four men on the bench.

"Holy hell," one of the men hollered out as he wiped droplets of blood from his face. "That bastard can fight."

"Holy hell," echoed another.

"Damn," said a third man, rising from the bench to stare at the dog.

Lester clicked off the watch, all of the men now transfixed on the pitbull. It stood there in the cage, completely subdued, its own blood gushing from several wounds on its face. The dog appeared not to notice. It glanced briefly around the cage to see if there were any more cats to play with, the whole while wagging its stub of a tail. Then it looked out at Lester, seeking his approval.

Lester held up the watch. "Twenty-two seconds, bitches." There was a smug, proud look on his face. "He'll take down another pit in thirty. You can have him today for two thousand bucks." Grinning wickedly, he extended the hand that held the watch so they could all marvel at the dial. "Or you can bring your own dog over Sunday night and we'll grind him into meat for you."

Sometime later that same afternoon, Molly turned off the main highway onto a drive that led up and over a small rise. On the flat-land near the highway lay a farm, its barn and outbuildings freshly painted, the farmhouse across from the barn well-kept, with an arbor

of roses that led up a pathway to the house. A sweet fragrance began
to fill the interior of the car. Off to one side she could see a tractor
pulling a mower through a field just off the road, its blades slashing
through thick layers of alfalfa, releasing into the breeze the scent of
fresh-mown hay. Lumbering along behind the mower, and trying its
best to keep pace, came the baler, with long metal arms sweeping
along the ground, churning the hay into great, round bales. Although
it was still early afternoon, with the outside temperature far from
cool, Molly lowered the window slightly to allow even more of the
rich fragrance into the car.

Continuing the drive, the road began to slope upwards until,
after a few minutes, she arrived at the top of the rise and onto the site
of another farm. Here the scene changed dramatically. There were
no painted barns or well-kept houses standing as the proud patrons
of this place. No arbors or flowers or rolling fields of hay. The land
had turned abruptly stark and barren. Untilled earth blanketed by
weeds and thistle spread in every direction. There was a barn, but
it sat weathered and worn, with loose boards and broken ones in
about the same abundance as those still properly affixed. The house,
at some distance from the barn, appeared to be in better shape, but
marginally so. Everywhere hung long strips of peeling paint, with
cut pieces of plywood covering several of the windows, and a porch
with an overhang that sagged uncomfortably low. Whoever owned
this place might use it, even profit from it, but certainly had no
respect or affinity for it.

Molly pulled in and parked. It wasn't until she exited the car and
walked around to its front that she noticed the dogs. A long line of
them, chained up against one wall of the barn. Huge dogs, pitbulls
mostly, and a few Rottweilers. Each animal had its own leash, a
shortened chain which started out anchored to the base of the
building, then clipped onto a leather collar tightly belted around each
of their necks. Molly's presence seemed to agitate them. Especially
the one at the end of the line, and nearest to where she stood. It was
a huge, black monster, foam forming at the sides of its mouth as
it strained against the constraints of the chain in an effort to reach

her. The dog growled, low and menacing, and she considered the likelihood that it could be won over with a smile and a cupcake, but wasn't sure she liked her chances.

A voice rang out. "You sonsabitches knock it off. Knock it off, I say."

Molly swung around to face a man approaching from the direction of the house. He was a short man, and slight, who walked slowly and cautiously, with a look on his face that showed he was not used to welcoming visitors. His appearance was slovenly, and he hunched a bit, his clothing well-worn and filth-encrusted. Molly thought she had never seen a more perfect match between a man and his land.

"Are you Lester Macon?" she asked.

"I am." The man stopped, still several yards away. "Who're you?"

Molly had heard all about Lester Macon, a dog breeder with a reputation that preceded him throughout the Midwest. The claim on all of his advertising was that he bred championship pitbulls for show, pets, or guard dogs, but the more sinister print spread out across the internet claimed he was a dog fighter. That news alone probably wouldn't have brought Molly out here, as she much preferred her own entourage of hog farmers who were plentiful enough to keep her busy. The problem she had with Lester Macon were the many reports filed against him for gathering up innocent animals as fight-bait to use in training his pits. Stray cats and dogs, even pigs that fell into his grasp were taken out to the farm, never to be seen again. Over the years he'd been hauled into court to answer these charges, but because a dead cat has a limited vocabulary, nothing had ever been proven against him.

Molly looked at Macon and flashed a disarming smile. "I'm Molly Bishop. I work for a pharmaceutical company over in Omaha. One of my colleagues said you might have a guard dog for me." She stepped toward him, and he began to move tentatively towards her as well. Pointing at the barn and the line of dogs, she said, "My uncle used to raise these." Though she was about to concoct a lie, her tone was measured and friendly. "He was thrown in jail for fighting his dogs and they were all taken away from him."

Macon stopped, still a few feet away, eying her warily. "Yeah," he said, his voice doubtful. "Where was that?"

"He had a place outside Des Moines. The happiest dogs you've ever seen. That was quite a few years ago, but I remember he loved his dogs and they loved him back." Molly moved even closer, and shook her head slightly, allowing the long tresses of golden hair to cascade down the sides of her face.

The man's look softened somewhat, but his voice was still wary. "So did he?"

"What?"

"Did he fight 'em? Or just raise 'em to sell?" The man looked down, stabbing his boot at the earth.

"Yes, he fought them." Molly's voice grew wistful. "But the dogs never complained. I even used to help him set up the matches. It was my job to patch up the losers. In fact, I can remember a lot of them, laying there bleeding, when all of a sudden they'd jump up and try to get back into the ring. Those dogs loved to fight."

"Damn straight." Macon clapped a hand down on his leg, now somewhat disarmed. "That's what I'm always sayin'. That's what folks don't understand. The animals love it. The government is always on my ass, accusin' me of fightin'." He paused, sweeping his hand in the direction of the dogs. "I'm not sayin' I do, but if I did, they'd love it. It's what they're bred for." Macon caught himself then, and coughed uncomfortably. "I mean, you know, if they wasn't bred to be pets."

Molly reached out her hand to shake. "It's good to meet you," she said.

Still inspecting her closely, he took a half-step forward, closing the distance between them. Most of the wariness left his face. "Well," he said, with a certain amount of pride. His hand swept out, pointing. "Those there are my dogs."

Macon led her in the direction of the barn, passing very close to the big black dog at the end of the line. The dog strained at its leash, still wanting a closer look at Molly. "Steady," hollered Macon. "You stand fast or I'll kick your ass."

Molly tiptoed cautiously past, her usual confidence compromised and replaced by trepidation. "Is he looking to guard me, or consume me?"

Macon laughed. "He'll do what I tell'em. It's all in the trainin'." Soon they arrived at the back of the barn where there were two large cages, one holding several frightened cats who huddled together at the rear of the cage, and the other, a large feral hog. Molly stepped up to the pen holding the hog. It immediately backed into a corner, keeping its face and its tusks pointed out at the intruders.

"What's his story?"

"Just a hog. One of my friends trapped him out in the woods."

"What are you going to do with him?"

"Eat'em," came the curt reply.

There weren't many dog breeders on Molly's usual route, although she was not unfamiliar with them. Most were good people, or at least not bad people, raising Border Collies or Shelties to sell to the bigger sheep and cattle producers who needed worthy herd dogs. Their animals were well treated, respected and even loved. She thought back to a Collie breeder she passed by every month or so. The big dogs would always be playing around in the yard, tumbling and wrestling with each other, or lounging up on the porch. An observer could tell right away their lives were pleasant. This farm was markedly different, with the movements of each dog heavily restricted.

She looked down at the hog, already feeling anguish at its prospects. For the pigs the fight was never a fair one. Before entering a cage for a match with a pitbull in training, each one would have its mouth wrapped in twine or tape, so that its tusks— which could rip open the belly of even the largest dog— were ineffective as weapons. The game was to see how long it would take a dog to rip off enough hide and flesh to incapacitate the pig, finally dropping it to the ground.

"What about the cats?" Molly asked, turning her attention away from the pig.

A wry grin broke out on Macon's face. "Just pets."

One of the cats hissed, its front paw lashing out in warning. The other two cowered just behind it. Molly spoke. "Well I can see they certainly feel the love." Spinning around, she looked directly at Macon. He managed to look back at her for a brief moment, then turned his head away. The grin remained.

"I ain't had time to tame'em much yet." He tapped at the wire running across the top of the cage. "They'll come around."

He led her over to the barn then, and even before entering she could hear the whine of puppies. There were four of them, about a month old, enclosed by a large pen that was open on top, as pitbulls are not famous for their jumping ability. Hanging from the ceiling of the barn were a couple of long ropes, each dangling down and into the pen where they stopped a foot or so from the floor. Tied to the end of each rope was the carcass of a rabbit, with just enough fur and flesh left on it for a positive identification. "I see you also raise bunnies." Molly's voice contained just enough sarcasm to remain inoffensive.

Macon laughed. "Just a little trainin' aid." One of the pups reached out and batted at a carcass. It swung back and forth for a moment, and then the pup lunged at it, tearing off a great fluff of fur. "This might be what you're after. I'm trainin' these little guys up to be guard dogs."

"That'll be very handy for me." Reaching out, Molly placed a hand on the top rail of the pen. "You know, in case I am ever attacked by rabbits."

She glanced around, scanning the interior of the barn, looking for things that might be helpful should she decide to return and seek retribution from this man. She could already feel the steady flow of hate building up inside. The innocent animals that must have passed through here over the years. Probably hundreds of them, trapped, beaten, thrown into tiny cages where they would lie in fear until Macon called for them. Then they would have to face the killer dogs who waited ravenously for the chance to tear them apart. Men would come, gleeful, shouting men, pouring in for what they deemed to be *fights*. As though that somehow authenticated the event, sanctioned it as fair, convincing themselves that the outcome was somehow uncertain. In reality there was no fighting at all. Just frightened, desperate animals clinging as hard as possible to their last bits of life.

Molly took a step back, removing her hand from the pen. A wave of dizziness passed over her, bringing with it the warm acid-taste of nausea. Revulsion always seemed to follow the hate. Inseparable companions pounding away at her. That's all she needed to begin to formulate a plan. Her eyes grew wide and wicked. She turned away for a moment so he couldn't see them. When she turned back, they had softened, leaving behind no trace of emotion. Reaching out to tap at Macon's arm, she spoke. "So you can train one of them to protect me?"

Macon studied Molly carefully, and still cautiously. This woman had driven in uninvited, with no connections and no references. They had spoken of fighting dogs, but he noted that she had not probed him too deeply about it. In fact, most of the chatter about the sport had originated with her. She had asked him very little about his own inclinations. Finally, somewhat satisfied with his evaluation, he answered her. "Lady, you give me a thousand bucks and about two month's time, and I'll give you a dog that'll tear the ass off anyone you say." Macon wasn't finished. His tone lowered, and became pointedly conspiratorial. "He'll also tear the ass off any dog you say."

Molly understood immediately. She grinned, and matched his look which had become defiant. "Mister Macon. You've got yourself a deal." She stuck out her hand, and Macon took it.

"You wanna pick one out?" he asked her.

Molly stepped back up to the pen, this time resting both hands on the railing. She pretended to study the pups. Pointing to the smallest dog, a brown and white with a head massively out of proportion to the rest of its body, she said, "That one. He looks like he could do some damage."

Macon nodded. "Good choice. I had a young cat fall in there a couple days ago. That brown and white of yours about took its head off. He's a good one."

"Just sort of fell in, did it?" Molly turned to face the man.

Macon grinned, boyish and mischievous. "Yeah, damdest thing. By the time I got over here it looked just about like those rabbits."

Molly considered for a moment how much satisfaction she would get from plunging a syringe into Macon's neck. Maybe even keeping him alive for a while so she could grace him with one of her stories. That would make for a most profitable outing. But she had come away from the car with no purse and no weapon. Looking around the barn she noticed, at the far end, the fighting cage where the pitbull had dispatched the two cats a short time earlier. Although she had no knowledge of the slaughter, she could tell by the wire covering that whatever was thrown into the cage was not likely to make its way out again.

A few minutes later they left the barn, passing once again close to the cages holding the cats and the hog. Breaking away from Macon, Molly moved back over to visit with the pig. "This guy has good meat on him. He's done pretty well for himself."

"Yeah." Macon joined her. "He's been feastin' alright. He's a big bastard. Probably king of the whole valley."

Off to one side, and leaning against a board bracing a corner of the pen, was a short length of pipe. Molly could see that one end was splattered with dried blood. She hadn't noticed it before. Looking at the boar, she also noticed one of its front shoulders had been injured, causing it to limp heavily. Reaching down to pick up the pipe, she said, "What's this? Your enforcer?"

As Molly tapped the pipe in her hand, Macon looked at her curiously. "It's just a pipe."

"It's got blood all over it."

"Oh, yeah, now I remember. I don't think this bad boy wanted to cooperate." As they talked the hog backed away again, seeking the far wall of the cage. Molly found it interesting that even though she was the one waving the pipe, the boar's eyes remained glued on Macon. She looked around, back at the barn and over in the direction of her car. Several of the dogs were up and had moved in their direction until tension from the chains restrained them. The big black pit on the end, the one who had shown such an interest in Molly, strained mightily against its leash. Its whole body wriggled excitedly as one mass of moving muscle. Turning her attention back to the cage, she pointed at the ground inside.

"What's that?"

"What?" said Macon. His eyes swung down to join hers. "What?" he said again.

"There in the corner." Molly pointed and shifted slightly, turning her body somewhat in the direction of the man. "Coiled up over there in the far corner. Is that a rope or a damn snake?"

Placing both hands on the top of the cage, Macon leaned in for a closer look. "Where? I don't see nuthin."

Molly's heart began to pound, and her palms became sweaty. It was completely out of character for her to act rashly without at least a minor consultation with her brain. But there was no time for counsel. No time for careful consideration. A voice shouted out, rocking the inside of her head. "You can do this another time," it cried. "You don't have to do it now." The voice grew louder. "We're not prepared. We need to talk about this, Molly."

Sensing something sinister was about to happen the big pitbull began to growl out, and strained even harder at its chain. It barked then, low and mean. As Macon turned to look at the agitated dog, Molly swung the pipe. She aimed it at the right side of his head, just above the ear, but the sweat on her palms and a lack of rehearsal with the weapon caused her to lose grip slightly. The pipe slipped in her hand, more flopping into Macon's head than slamming into it. He staggered into the screened side of the cage, his fingers entangled in the wire. As he tried to free himself, Molly swung the pipe again. This blow caught him across the top of the head, indenting a portion of it, and creating a shallow channel which began to run blood-red through his hair and down the front of his face. Molly was amazed by the amount of blood, and how quickly it arrived. Macon spun around, one hand still stuck in the mesh. He swung the other feebly through the air, with the blood blinding him enough that he missed Molly by a wide margin. He slumped forward onto the top of the cage, the wire there offering little support as it buckled beneath his weight. The boar wasted no time. The object of its hate and its pain had just come within reach. It lunged forward and upward, ripping away the wire and stripping away a great slab of flesh from Macon's stomach.

The black pitbull had by now gone insane. It thrashed against its constraints, the tight leather collar around its neck weakening. Macon tried to call out, but there wasn't much left of him. One arm and the hand connected to it slipped through the hole in the mesh created by the boar's lunge. It dangled there inside the cage, and the hog began to work it over. Its tusks tore the arm open just below the elbow, before swinging downward and savagely ripping away at the hand. Several fingers were neatly severed, the hog swallowing one and scattering the others across the ground almost playfully. Finally it paused and looked inquisitively at Molly. Moving around to the far end of the cage, she lifted a latch, and swung open the door there. Without hesitation the boar limped over to her, greatly favoring its right side. She could see how badly it had been hurt. "I'm sorry I didn't get here sooner, boy," she spoke out to the boar. As it looked up at her all the rage drained away from the animal, leaving behind what appeared to be a kind of simple sadness. They looked at each other for a long time. Finally the boar limped past her, crossed the yard and disappeared behind the barn.

The pitbull meanwhile had grown eerily quiet. So quiet, in fact, that Molly forgot it was there. It continued to strain away at its chain, but silently, twisting and pulling, weakening the collar further, until it began to fray. The dog's eyes focused in on Molly, and what was left of its master. Macon still lay there, partly atop the wire, and partly imbedded into it. For a while he flopped around like a salmon in a net, his one good arm trying to extricate him from the trap. But he was losing great pools of blood, and growing weaker by the moment. Molly moved back to where the attack had begun, to be closer to the man. She reached out, tapping at him with the pipe. "Damn," she said. "That's some mean hog, huh? He about ripped your guts out." Bending down she poked at Macon's stomach with the pipe. "I think I can see your insides." She grimaced. "Man, that's rough."

Macon groaned, using the last of his strength to roll his head to where he could look up at her. "Why?" is all he could manage to say.

"Hey," Molly continued to poke at him. "It's nothing personal. It's just a game I like to play. Every now and then I like to find a man and just beat the shit out of him." She shook her head and frowned. "I can't help it. It's hard to explain, really. Some men get their rocks off torturing animals. I get mine off torturing men. It's probably a simple matter of perspective." She laughed suddenly. "I'm gonna have to look into it. It's quite possible I need therapy."

Macon began to spasm violently, and there erupted from his throat a raspy cough. He gagged, but feebly, as finally his body began to shut down. A grin broke out on Molly's face. "Well I really have to go," she said amicably. "You're beginning to bum me out." Raising the pipe for a final blow, she brought it crashing down upon Macon's face. His cheek bone exploded, spraying blood and bone matter across the yard. Moving then to the other side of the cages, she swung open another door, this one leading in to the cats. They had witnessed the entire spectacle, and huddled together in the farthest reaches of the enclosure, too frightened to move. Molly dismissed them, pointing loosely at the door. "Whenever you're ready." Then, still carrying the pipe, she headed for the car.

The pitbull had been straining at its chain now for many minutes. It, too, had witnessed the slaughter, its eyes growing wicked and cold as Molly drew near. She moved off to one side, to safely circumnavigate the dog which was struggling wildly to get at her. "Calm down, junior," she said. "Your daddy's dead and you're just gonna have to deal with it." The other dogs, in their long line, were also straining to get at her. But there was no real insistency about it. For them it was more of a duty-bound thing to investigate the stranger. But for the big black, it meant much more. It had seen Lester Macon bludgeoned, and although its intellect had been somewhat stifled by a brutish upbringing, it still understood the rules of fighting, and the loyalty that accompanied them.

Molly was only a few steps from the car when the collar snapped. She was so confidently close to the vehicle that she had already turned her attention away from the dog. Then she heard a loud popping sound, similar to that of a whip crackling through the air. As she swung around to locate the source of the sound the pitbull was on her. In a few mighty leaps it crossed the yard, lunging, just as Molly turned, right at her throat. Instinctively she threw up her arm in a protective motion, and the dog's teeth slammed hard into the end of the pipe still held in her hand. It was an astounding stroke of good fortune, but only a temporary one. The dog crashed to the ground, its mouth stung by the disappointment of finding cold steel instead of flesh. Molly dove for the door of the Camry, finding it with her free hand and flinging it wide. The pit, having been knocked to the ground, now attacked from the ground, sinking its teeth into Molly's leg as she clawed her way into the car. She flung out the hand holding the pipe, and felt it impact the side of the dog's face. For the briefest moment its grip loosened and Molly was able to free her leg, holding the pipe out as a shield as she slammed shut the door. Pain shot through her calf. Intense, agonizing pain. The bite had not been a clean one, but because she had torn herself free, nerves and flesh had been equally mangled. "Shit," she screamed, dropping the pipe on the floor and beating on the steering wheel with both fists. "Shit." The pitbull, meanwhile, wasn't yet ready to surrender its prey. It leapt up, clawing at the window of the car. Its teeth found the side mirror, and in an instant the mirror was ripped from its bracket, its only lifeline with the car a piece of shredded plastic and a few wires. It hung there, defeated. Starting the engine, Molly punched the gearshift into drive, rammed her foot down hard on the gas and spun her way out the drive. The pitbull stood there in the yard, barely winded and proud of its victory. It flung open its mouth, and a piece of white fabric covered in blood fluttered its way to the ground. A low, warning growl sounded from deep in its chest. Then the big dog turned and headed to the back of the barn where its master waited.

CHAPTER TWENTY THREE

Elizabeth Warman took a step closer to the wire enclosure still holding on to the body of Lester Macon. Two men from the coroner's office worked on the body, one cutting away at the wire to free the top of the torso, while the other tugged at Macon's legs in an effort to disentangle the corpse and swing it to the ground. Michael Lair, who had been standing beside Warman, now hung back a few steps. She turned, eying him curiously. "What's the matter, Michael? Death make you nervous?"

"I've got nothing personal against death." Lair took another step backwards, further distancing himself. "But this boy is getting a little ripe. They said he's been sunbathing out here for two days. That's just about long enough to put a real damper on my lunch."

Warman continued to stalk in closer. "Looks like his head was bashed in by a hammer. By someone with a lot of animosity." She bent down. "At about the same time his stomach was ripped open by..." Warman lifted her hands and looked at one of the men working on the body.

"Probably a pig, ma'am. A big one." The man spoke without looking up. "A boar, I'm thinkin', with about the same level of animosity as your hammer-man."

"How do you know it was a pig?" Lair spoke out loudly, making up for the distance between himself and the crime scene. "Do they leave some kind of special bite marks?"

This time the man paused, one hand wrapped in the chicken wire, while the other pointed at the ground. "No, sir. But they tend to leave a lot of pig shit."

Warman laughed aloud at that, pointing at Lair. "He's famous back in Washington."

A few minutes later the two agents worked their way around the barn and back to the driveway in front of the house. There were no dogs present, as a friend of the victim had come by some time earlier in the day to gather them up. Lair looked down at the long row of chains still anchored to the barn. "So, pitbulls, huh?" Noting the shortness of each chain, he bent down to pick one up. "It seems each dog has its own little orbit where it can go round and round using the radius of the leash, and never collide with any of the other dogs. Very circular animals, but not very sociable."

Warman moved over to the very end of the line, bending down to pick up a chain laying there. "Look at this," she said. In her hand she held the end of the chain, with a clip still attached to a collar that had been torn apart. "It appears this one didn't like the whole orbiting principle."

A voice called out to them, and they turned to greet a young sheriff's deputy who approached with a small plastic bag in one hand. "Thought you'd like to see this," he said. In the bag was a piece of white fabric matted with dried blood. The deputy pointed across the drive. "We found it over there. It looks like one of the dogs might have tangled with the killer."

Warman elevated the bag, inspecting it. Lair joined her. She looked at him, her face lighting up. "This is big. Someone has a heckuva chunk ripped out of their arm, and we've got all the forensics we need, right here."

"Leg." Lair reached out, relieving Warman of the bag.

"What?"

"It's a leg." They both stared through the plastic at the fabric. "It's heavier material than you'd usually find on a summer shirt, and there's a bit of a crease. It's pretty blotched up with blood, but it's there."

Warman studied the fabric further while this new information sunk in, then lifted her eyes to meet Michael's which were staring straight back at her. "You'd have to look a long time to find a man around Omaha who's wearing white pants," she said.

"You're reading my mind, lady."

"It's her, isn't it?"

"We've certainly got enough DNA on this cloth to find out."

"I'm sorry, Michael."

"I'm kind of sorry myself."

John Grimm pulled into a rest stop some miles to the west of Omaha. He knew law enforcement would soon be looking for him, and it was time to trade in the old green pickup for a newer model. It was after two in the morning and the lot contained only a few vehicles, with one red pickup parked away from the others at the farthest edge of the stop. Sliding his truck in beside it, he carefully opened the driver's door and stepped out. The night was very still. He looked across the lot to the building that housed the lavatories and vending machines. Not a single person was in sight. A sixteen-wheeler moved in off the highway just then, carrying a huge load of cement block. Johnny paused to watch it rumble along the frontage road. It slowed as it neared the building, but then accelerated slightly and drifted on past. Finally it slowed again, just before reentering the highway, the driver pulling off to the right into a pocket of mowed grass where he brought the big truck to a halt. After a few moments the engine shut down, and all was quiet again. Johnny walked over to the red pickup. Glancing in through the passenger side window he noticed a magazine lay on the seat nearest him, while on the other side, slumped behind the wheel, was the figure of a man. He had a coat or blanket drawn up around his shoulders, and even through the glass Johnny could hear the man snoring. He leaned in closer, pressing his face right up against the window, his hands forming a cup around his eyes as he directed what little light there was into the interior of the truck. It was an older man, or at least bearded and grizzled and having the appearance of age. He also appeared to be a small man, taking up very little room on the seat. Johnny grinned at that. He was no large man himself, but kept in good physical condition with the knowledge that anyone his size or smaller would be easy to manage.

Moving around the truck, he stopped at the driver's door, just inches from the sleeping man. Reaching into a side pocket he extracted a knife, not a large one, but rather one with a four inch blade. If thrust in correctly it had ample range to reach the heart or slice deeply into the cordage protecting the neck. And it was handy. Most large knives prove to be unwieldy, especially in close combat. They can also be easily grabbed or deflected. The one in his hand could be deployed in seconds, flashing in on a victim before there was any chance of rebuttal. Easing his free hand up, he tried the door, pressing in gently on the handle. There was a tiny click, and the grin on Johnny's face thickened. Backing away a half-step, he leaned in on the door, braced himself, then pressed down on the handle and flung it wide open. The man inside quickly tumbled outside, slamming down hard onto the pavement. He awoke suddenly, startled, and tried to call out. But before he'd even made full contact with the concrete, Johnny was on him. One hand grabbed the man's hair, pinning his head in place, while the hand holding the knife slashed in, sinking the blade deeply into the tissues of the neck. It was over in seconds.

Five minutes later John Grimm reentered the highway, this time driving in a shiny new truck. His body shook from the excitement of the attack. He thought of Molly Bishop, and how grand it would feel to plunge his knife into her stomach, at the exact same location she had plunged hers into his. There seemed to be a sense of fairness about it that he found especially appealing.

CHAPTER TWENTY FOUR

It was early the next morning when Michael Lair returned to McMillan Pharmaceuticals. This time he was accompanied by Agent Warman. The two had spent the previous day at a horrific crime scene a few miles outside the city, where a dog breeder had been bludgeoned to death in his own yard. Warman spoke. "We're still not sure though, right?"

"We're pretty damn sure." Lair tapped his fingers on the steering wheel. "I mean, this thing has gone way beyond circumstantial. We've got real evidence now."

"If it matches up."

"It'll match." Lair's voice lowered. "I was hoping it wasn't her. When that rapist bastard turned up I figured he'd be our guy. Or at least a helluva good candidate, what with the pig hair and all."

"There's still a chance."

"No, it's her."

"You know," Warman shifted in her seat uncomfortably, "I don't want to sound all judgmental here, but if you hadn't gone off and banged the suspect you'd be in a lot better shape on this."

"Dammit, Warman." Michael's fingers stopped their tapping and gripped down hard on the wheel. "I've told you before. I did not *bang* the girl. I spoke with her a few times, and that's it." He growled over at her. "Frankly, who the hell I bang is none of your goddam business."

As they pulled into the lot they noticed Molly's white Camry parked by itself at one end. Lair pulled up alongside the car and they exited. Immediately he heard Warman whistle. "What?" he said. Walking around the side of his own car, he also whistled and spoke out, "Damn." They could both see the Camry had suffered through an attack of some sort. The driver's door had a series of long, raking scratch marks dug into the paint, extending up onto the glass of the window there. And the side mirror had been ripped away, leaving an area also gouged out by marks. Lair looked through the window and noticed the mirror, still attached to a strand of wire and laying in plain view on the passenger side seat. "She's not terribly good at covering up a crime scene."

They found Molly sitting behind the desk in Carl Monroe's office. "Detective," she said pleasantly as they walked in unannounced. She addressed Michael first, then turned to Agent Warman. "And other detective." She spoke calmly, her tone indicating not the least surprise. "What can I do for you?"

Michael Lair studied the young lady before him, as he did every time they came into contact. As always, he was surprised that nothing ever seemed amiss with her. She sat in a leather-back chair, confidently erect, the edges of a smile perpetually playing with her lips. It was as if she expected him, always expected him, and no matter how clandestinely he presented himself she was always in a state of readiness. This time though, would turn out differently. This time they would break her.

Molly spoke first, slicing through the tension that only Lair and Warman seemed to feel. "You can both sit, you know." Her tone turned playful. "Unless, of course, you feel the need to pounce on me or something."

"We have a warrant." Warman spoke, spitting out the words.

"Do you now?" Molly's voice showed just a hint of interest. Lair marveled at the girl, almost loving her. "Am I under arrest then?"

"No, not yet." Warman stepped up closer, until the desk stopped her. She held in her hand a single piece of white paper. Holding it a foot or so above the surface, she released it and watched intently as it fluttered down onto the desktop. "This gives us permission to search this facility, your home, and your car."

Molly's eyes locked in on Michael Lair's. Her expression never wavered. "This is a sad day for us, Michael." The grin, which had been barely perceptible, intensified. "I thought maybe we had a real connection, you know, with you fucking me and all."

Warman turned to face Lair, as his face reddened. He raised both hands, his face twisting miserably, while his index fingers pointed straight at Molly. "Never happened, dammit." He then turned to directly face Warman. His face flushed red, already knowing whose side of the accusation she would be standing on. "Never happened," he said again, this time with less demonstration but an equal amount of conviction.

Warman's face showed a certain disgust, but she turned back to Molly, her voice at once calm and professional. "Do you always wear white, Miss Bishop?" she asked.

Molly couldn't help herself. She laughed aloud. "To work, yes. Always. White blouse and white slacks. When I'm not working I like to dress up, look nice." She pointed at Agent Warman. "You know, not like that."

Warman found herself flinching as if she'd been struck. No one would ever have described her as pretty. Or fashionable. She'd spent a lifetime being singled out by the Molly Bishops of the world, the gorgeous ones who just couldn't help dispensing pain.

Though Warman attempted to conceal it, Molly noticed right away the discomfort her comment had created. It was more her intention to demonstrate a certain domination than it was to inflict injury. Still, Agent Warman had not come to her as an innocent, but as an accuser, an attacker. Even so, Molly did attempt to soften the conversation. "What I mean is, I usually dress for the occasion." She pointed a finger at her own chest. "And yes, I always wear white to work."

It was Michael Lair's turn to play. Reaching into his pocket he

produced the swatch of bloody cloth, wrapped in plastic, found at
the scene of the murder. He placed it on the edge of the desk, one
finger sliding it across to Molly. "Recognize this?"

Molly didn't even glance at the cloth, but continued to stare
straight up at Michael. "No. Should I?"

"We're thinking it was torn from your pants the day before
yesterday, at a farm not far from here."

Molly stood, and moved out from behind the desk. She walked
up very close to Elizabeth Warman. "These pants?" she said innocently, pointing down at her legs and the crisp white slacks that
covered them.

Warman ignored her. "Were you in the vicinity of Culver Road
two days ago, and did you happen to stop by a farm out there? A dog
breeder's place?"

"I don't know. I'll have to check my records on that. The roads
around Omaha are very confusing."

Lair spoke up impatiently. "Look, Miss Bishop, let's cut the crap
here. We've got another man dead, and as usual a lot of the forensics
are pointing straight at you. We've got blood evidence, we've got
fabric evidence, we've got vehicular evidence. I've wrapped up cases
with a helluva lot less than this." He nodded at Warman, then quickly
shifted his attention back to Molly. "Why don't you just come clean?
Tell us what happened."

Molly turned, moving back to the chair where she again sat
down. She looked at both agents, finally tilting her head to one
side so she could glance over at the door. Then she leaned forward,
whispering conspiratorially. "Can we speak in confidence? You know,
off the record?"

"No." Warman brought a hand down hard on the desk. "Are
you not getting the message here? This is an investigation. Anything
you say we're going to use." She lifted her hand off the desk and
stepped back. "Do you understand that?"

Molly's face showed surprise for the first time. But a kind of
innocent surprise, not a particularly concerned one. "My, my," she
said, her voice still soft. "This is so official. I simply wanted to

inquire exactly what in the world you two are talking about. You come in here, start blathering about a dead farmer, and imply that I had some sort of relationship with him. Then you shove a piece of bloody cloth in my face and insinuate that I'm in trouble." Molly stood, her face surrendering a good portion of its innocence. Her tone hardened. "Look, if you have a search warrant, why don't you search? Otherwise, get the hell out of my face."

Lair spoke. "We need a sample of your DNA."

"Is that part of your warrant?"

"No, not yet. But we'll get it if necessary. You could save us all a lot of trouble and just volunteer it, right here, right now." He cleared his throat. "If it's your blood on the cloth, you've got a problem. If it isn't, you're home free. Just help us all out here."

Molly nodded. "Just what exactly is the cloth meant to imply? What's it from?"

"You know exactly what it's from. We believe you were attacked by a dog defending its master. A master you probably just finished bludgeoning to death. Then while you were attempting to flee, this dog got ahold of you and beat the crap out of your car." Michael stared at Molly. "Ring any bells?"

Molly laughed then, a sweet laugh, the one someone uses when they open an unexpected gift. She even used the same response. "I love it," she said gleefully. "It would have been nice if you had started with that. And yes, I was attacked by a dog. A big damn Rottweiler or something. Bit the hell out of me." She flung one of her legs up on the desktop, pulled back a length of material and exposed a matting of bandages, with a slight tinge of blood seeping its way across their edges. Then she pouted, again sweetly. "So, tell me exactly how this makes me a murderer?"

Warman spoke. "You mind telling us the circumstances?"

"No, not at all. I was out a couple days ago, running my usual route, and I stopped in at a dog breeder's place. I've passed it before, but never stopped by. We've got some great new meds that just hit the market and I thought maybe the guy would be interested." Molly paused, and scratched at an ear. "I mean, you people do know that's what I do for a living, right? Anyway, when I arrived all these damn dogs are barking but no one comes out to meet me. The dogs all seem restrained though, so I climbed out of my car to see if I could find the owner. And bam! That's when one of the bastards broke free and came at me. I tried to jump back into my car but I didn't quite make it. He tore the crap out of me. Then went to work on the car when I tried to drive out of there." Molly shook her head apologetically. "That's it. I never saw anyone, never got more than two steps from my car." She raised a hand like someone being sworn in. "I sure as hell never bludgeoned anyone along the way. If you'd have seen that dog you'd know just how crazy this all sounds."

Warman and Lair exchanged a look. Things weren't looking quite as promising as they had expected. "So this is your blood then?" asked Warman.

"I don't know. If that cloth was ripped from my pants it certainly will be. But that's for you to determine." Molly's grin, dampened during her explanation, now reappeared. "Hey, I'm just here to help out."

"What about the dog? Are you saying it was chained up when you got there?"

"Again, I don't know. I think so. I remember seeing a whole line of dogs chained up. When I got out, one of them was on me. It all happened very quickly. So I don't know exactly where he came from."

Warman wasn't ready to surrender. "So why didn't you report this to anyone?"

"Of course I did. I was terrified, but I still had a responsibility. I called animal control while I was still in my car. I got a call back from them an hour or so later. They said when they arrived at the farm the dog attacked their van. They had to shoot it. It's kind of sad, because it was most likely just doing what it was trained to do. But the guy certainly never mentioned anything about a murder. I guess he didn't see it either. And like I said, I never got more than two feet from my car."

"And there's an official report on that?"

"There certainly should be. If you were doing your job, you'd already know that."

Michael Lair reached across the desk, retrieving the bloody cloth. "It seems every time we have a killing you're right there in the middle of it. It's long past coincidental."

"And yet, that's just what it is. A coincidence." Molly stood then, and reached out to play with Lair's collar. "I'm kind of mad at you right now, Michael," she said, as he pushed her hand away. "You're really disappointing me. But if you're prepared to apologize and be nice, I'll take you back."

As they drove away a few minutes later Warman spoke caustically. "Never banged her, huh? Well this investigation is going to hell. I thought we'd be dragging her out of there in cuffs. Your lady friend is very slick."

Ignoring the *banged her* comment, Lair said, "I thought we had her. Damn, we're so close. We need to get back out to that farm and find something that will prove she moved away from the car. Way the hell away."

"She makes sense, you know. If the dog was already loose when she arrived it would be hard to believe she could have been out there roaming around with a hammer."

"It wasn't loose. We both saw that busted collar. That took anger. And rage. A car pulling into the driveway might serve as an irritant to an already irritable dog, but it's not likely to fly into enough of a tantrum to break free. But seeing its owner beaten and left for dead; that would do it. That would push the big sunovabitch right over the edge. That dog got her on the way out, not the way in."

Carl Monroe met the two agents at the door. Elizabeth Warman held out a hand containing the warrant, but Carl shook his head dismissively and stepped back, away from the door. "Molly called and said you'd be coming," he said, attempting a smile that appeared more sardonic than welcoming. "Mi casa es su casa." He paused, then added, "At least since it appears I have no choice in the matter."

Michael Lair tapped at Carl's arm as they entered. "It's nothing personal. Just routine stuff. It seems your lady is always showing up in the vicinity of chaos."

"She'd be here to defend herself, but she called and said her car is swarming with cops right now."

"I know, and again, it's just a routine search. Sorry for the inconvenience."

"There's going to be blood in her car, you know. And probably here at the house."

"Yeah, she told us the story on that." Lair turned to face Monroe squarely. "I suppose she confides quite a lot in you, huh?"

"When she comes home bleeding after a dog attack she does. I had to help clean up the mess." Carl studied the agent carefully, trying to read the man. "I don't know how in the hell you could suspect her of anything with a damn Rottweiler on her back."

Lair nodded. "The report said it was a pitbull actually, and it was on her leg. Thirty yards away there's a man with his head bashed in and his guts ripped open. It seems like it was a joint effort by a killer and a pig. And your Molly seems to work very well with pigs."

"That's ridiculous."

Lair laughed a little. "I know, right? But that's what they tell me happened."

Warman, who had already begun her inspection while the two men talked, walked out from a side room, carrying in her hand a hammer. She held it carefully with two fingers pinching about half-way up the handle. "Look what I found." She raised the hammer somewhat triumphantly, like a fisherman holding up a trophy trout. "Top dresser drawer, underneath a pile of panties." With her free hand she turned slightly, pointing. "Miss Bishop's room, yes?"

Carl's eyes widened in surprise at the sight of the hammer. "I don't know," he stammered.

"You don't know if that's Miss Bishop's room? And this is your house?"

Michael spoke, reaching out a hand to steady the man. "It's alright, Mister Monroe. We're not really interested in who belongs to the panties, or the room." Pausing in his speech, Lair moved over to Warman and physically removed the hammer from her hand, his own fingers curling around the base of the handle, at the place where one would ordinarily grip it.

"Michael, what are you doing?" Warman gasped, then tried to wrestle the hammer back. "That's evidence."

Gaining complete possession of the hammer, Lair briefly inspected it, then tossed it onto the cushion of a nearby couch. It lay there innocently and completely compromised. "It's nothing," said Lair. "Anyone who hides a hammer in with their underwear either has a sick, twisted fantasy about carpentry or is trying to insert a bit of humor into a very serious investigation. This is just another one of Miss Bishop's little games."

Within minutes, with both Warman and Lair searching the contents of that same room, they uncovered two more hammers, a crow-bar and a tire iron, the last found bathing in the tank of a toilet. Piling the tools on the bed and shaking their heads in disgust, they moved to the next room in line, which was a den. Here they found guns. Lots of them. Several rifles, a shotgun, a variety of pistols and a desk full of knives and other hunting paraphernalia. Carl hawked the two agents, following along and watching their every move. He hung there in the doorway as Lair picked up one of the rifles. "Yours?" Lair asked him.

"No. They happen to belong to Molly. She hunts."

Lair raised the rifle, pointing the barrel out a window. "Is she good at it?"

"I don't know." Carl was carefully guarding each of his answers, not knowing which ones could be potentially harmful. "She doesn't go very often, and we seldom talk about it."

In reality, Molly had only picked up her first firearm a few years earlier. A rancher she was dating at the time had taken her to a range for an afternoon of shooting skeet. The rancher had bragged about his prowess with a shotgun, but before the afternoon was over a great silence hung between them. Molly couldn't miss. She was a natural, knocking down clay after clay, and after that day the man never called on her again. The event sparked in her an incredible excitement. The thought that she could hold in her hands a weapon so destructive that a single light squeeze from one of her fingers would send forth a tiny merchant of death. Her first emotion was one of revulsion, with harsh visions of plains coated with dying buffalo and waters littered with wounded fowl. Visions of men cheering wildly as they held up the head of a fallen stag. Visions of the earth, rich and deep in blood as an animal's life drained away into the soil. An anger had built in her that day, a quick anger, but a quiet one. It lay dormant just beneath the surface as she created for herself an antithesis, a bullet sent out and a bullet returned, not necessarily in vengeance, but in retribution. It seemed to her as a perfect alliance, and a very holy resolution to a most unholy endeavor.

With these thoughts picking away at her it was a natural transition to progress from target shooting to actual hunting, and that's when she began to take long trips into the wilderness. Losing herself in the woods she learned to crawl and stalk, becoming at one point so proficient at pure stealth that an animal could be grazing only steps away and never even know she was there. Then the real beauty of the game became apparent. Molly would raise her weapon, zero in on a branch or distant rock and fire a round with deadly accuracy. The branch would snap, or the rock would shatter, while the surrounding woods exploded with the intensity of the blast, and the animal she had been stalking would vanish into the wild. It served three purposes, this game of hers. First, her ability to move in close to a target unnoticed became uncanny. Second, her marksmanship, even in cramped or awkward circumstances, became highly honed, and third— far and away Molly's favorite phase of the game— the animal who was at the heart of the encounter learned a valuable

lesson about caution, making it more difficult for the meat hunters
who would follow.

It wasn't until many months later that Molly evolved yet again,
and achieved the highest level the game had to offer. She had been
stalking a mother mule deer and her two fawns on a huge tract of
land in the heart of Colorado. The deer moved cautiously through a
stand of trees before coming to a halt at the edge of a large meadow.
She could tell the mother wanted to move out into the open to
feed, but because of its protective instincts, it was extremely wary
of exposing the little ones to any danger that might lurk there. The
doe froze in place. Molly crept in closer until she was only a few
yards away. She lay there quietly. Suddenly the explosive sound of a
shot rang out, booming from across the clearing. One of the fawns
leapt into the air, straight up at first, but then twisting in midair as
it crashed back down again. A geyser of blood erupted from the
fawn's neck as it crumpled to the ground. The doe and the remaining
fawn immediately panicked, turning and crashing through the brush
in an effort to escape. In seconds they were gone. For a long time
Molly continued to lay there, immersed in the numbness of shock.
As her senses rebounded a raw anger moved in, an anger so intense
that her body began to shake. She rose then, standing behind the
last of a few clumps of cedar that stood guard over the meadow. A
hunter approached, crossing the clearing with a rifle clutched loosely
in his hands.

Molly stayed there, hidden by the trees, and waited. When at
last the man— who now appeared to be more of a man-size boy—
arrived at the site of the killing, he knelt beside the fawn, brushing
a hand along the fur on the animal's back. He did this several times.
Molly's vision was unobstructed. In fact, had the boy looked up just
then he would have easily seen her staring back at him through the
trees. She studied the boy, her anger still a seething presence, but
tried hard to find some sign of remorse in him, some signal that
the shooting had been unintentional, an accident perhaps, and that
he felt guilt as he kneeled there stroking the fawn. There was none
of that. The look on the boy's face was one of pure jubilation, even

pride over his prowess as a hunter. After a few minutes he stood, prodded the dead fawn with a boot and began to move away, back across the meadow. He was what Molly derisively called a joy killer. Someone who would simply shoot an animal because it was there and he had the means and ability to do so.

Molly stepped out into the open then. "Hey," she called out. "What the hell do you think you're doing?"

The boy spun around, the voice startling him so badly that he dropped the rifle. He stared back at Molly. "What?" he stammered.

Molly raised her own rifle, pointing it at his chest. "Was it fun?" she called out. "Did you enjoy murdering a baby while its mother stood there watching?" Flipping the safety on the gun, she lowered her eye to sight along the barrel. Her anger abated somewhat, and she made a rational decision that she was not going to shoot this boy. But he would certainly depart this land more contritely than he had arrived. He looked back at her, gauging her, trying to grasp her intentions, a warrior avenger who had sprung up out of the forest.

"I didn't do nuthin'," he said finally. "I just now come across it." He leaned down to pick up the rifle as Molly's voice boomed back at him.

"I wouldn't do that if I were you." She moved then, out from behind the trees and into the open, facing the boy squarely from a few yards away. The barrel of the rifle never wavered, still centered in on his chest. "I don't know whether to shoot your ass or just turn you in. It's not an easy choice."

The boy stiffened, and then straightened back up. Raising his hands to about shoulder height he turned both palms until they were facing outward. "Look. I don't want no trouble. I was just out for a walk in the woods," he said, his voice struggling to sound innocent. One instant later, and without warning, he spun around and began to run. Molly stood there for a moment, surprised. There had not yet been a lesson handed out, and one way or another, there needed to be one. Rage began to build up, replacing its more subordinate cousin, anger. And rage is not as easily contained. Tracking the boy as he ran, Molly centered her crosshairs between his shoulder blades, high up on his back, then lowered them somewhat just before she began that slow, steady compression on the trigger. It was the first time she had ever actually aimed at a living target, and her body began to shake uncontrollably. The crack of the rifle came as a conclusion to the entire set of circumstances as they had been presented. The boy went down, disappearing into tall grass. It had been his choice. No one forced him to run. She walked over to where he lay, crumpled up on the ground, a neat hole bored through the back of his right thigh. The boy cried out, clutching at the wound as a trickle of blood oozed out onto his fingers, staining them a bright, liquid red.

"Did you really think we were done here?" she asked him, her voice trembling. The boy looked up at her, his face whitened by shock.

"I don't wanna die," he pleaded.

Kneeling beside the boy, Molly brushed his hand aside and leaned in close to inspect the wound. "Well then, this is your lucky day," she said finally, as she pushed herself back up into a standing position. She stood there for a moment, still shaking, and feeling much like a bear cub does when it has finally trapped its first salmon in the rocks, and has it pinned there with no idea what to do next. This boy had clearly seen her, and could identify her, but Molly's evolution as a hunter was not yet complete, and she was not yet prepared to hand out the ultimate penalty in defense of her ideals. She leaned back down until her face was very close to the boy's. "I'm here in the woods a lot," she said to him, her voice now even and tempered. "I don't ever want to see you out here again." She poked at him with the rifle. "I'm thinking you had a hunting accident, and shot yourself in the leg. If I hear anything different, I'll look you up and we'll finish this."

The boy's eyes had been glazed over, but now sprang to life, flashing out at her. "Yes, yes… god yes. I won't say nuthin'. I swear to god I won't. I swear it." Molly prided herself on an innate ability to judge members of the male species. What she judged now was that this boy was broken, perhaps irreparably so. He would slink back into the folds of his community humiliated— not better for the experience, but badly damaged— and with a story that would almost certainly contain no elements of a woman having brought him down.

Turning away from the boy, she moved over to the fawn. She knelt down beside it, and began to stroke its fur, much like the boy had done a few minutes earlier. A soft noise caught her attention and she looked up. There, a few yards away where the meadow broke into the woods, stood the doe. She looked briefly at Molly, and then her head drooped down as she looked longingly at the dead fawn. "I'm so sorry," Molly had called out. "I'll get better at this."

That day had been an important one for her. It demonstrated that if others could flaunt life so recklessly, it was eminently fair for Molly to flaunt back.

Michael Lair, placing the rifle back against the wall, reached out to extract a knife from a shelf. He held it up to the light, flashing it at Carl. "We already know how good she is with a knife. I wonder if she shoots as well as she cuts."

Carl's face lit up. "I don't know. As I said we don't talk about it. But Molly's very competent at whatever she does. You can count on it."

Sifting through a mess of clothing on the floor near the closet, Warman spoke. "It would be nice if you'd stop playing with all the weaponry, Michael, and start helping with the search."

Lair laughed. "Nothing to find here, Warman. Like Mister Monroe says, Miss Bishop is very good at whatever she does." He put the knife back on the shelf. "I'm thinking that also applies to hiding evidence. We're not going to find anything here." Nodding to Carl, he headed for the door. "I don't think she brings her work home with her."

Completely contrary to his nature, Carl moved to block Lair from exiting. "Are you nuts?" he said in a tone that implied both judgement and condemnation. "How can you actually think she had anything to do with this? With any of this. Molly's a good person. A great person. My god, she'd do anything to help someone out. You've got the wrong lady. You should concentrate on the sick bastard who attacked her, and leave her the hell alone."

Reaching out both his hands, Lair physically but gently picked up Carl Monroe, depositing him to the side of the doorway. "Thanks, Mister Monroe," he said as he signaled Warman and headed out the door. "We'll keep that in mind."

CHAPTER TWENTY FIVE

John Grimm sat on the rise overlooking Carl Monroe's house. Parking beneath the trees in the same place he always parked when he came there to spy on Molly, this time he had moved out and away from the pickup. He found a spot half-way down the hill that offered a more unobstructed view of the street below. There was also a small cluster of hemlocks here, which rose to less than a man's height, but offered perfect concealment for someone who wanted to crouch there behind them and hide. His anger at Molly Bishop had moved on, swept away by time. The attack on her had been a mistake, a personal failure. Not the undertaking itself, that had a specific intent, but the miscalculation of his victim's capabilities. He wouldn't make a mistake like that again. This time he carried with him a knife, considerably larger than the puny toy he had been stabbed with. Tucked into his waistband was a .38 revolver, found in the glovebox of the stolen pickup. The playing field was now leveled, and beyond leveled. He sat now, waiting for the girl to show herself. There was no real plan in place, nor did he feel the need for one. It wasn't complicated. As soon as she appeared he would simply rise up, move down off the hill— his hands filled with weapons— and kill her. It was the same sort of non-plan he'd always employed. See someone, attack someone, take someone. Only this time it would be even easier, for there would be no taking. Just leveling.

As the two agents drove away from the house, depression settled in over them both. Elizabeth Warman spoke out. "She's always one step ahead, and doesn't make mistakes. How the hell does a twenty-something bimbo make no mistakes?"

Lair laughed. "That's the funny part about all this. Everything she does is a mistake. She just doesn't give a damn. You accuse her of being at a murder scene and she'll say, 'Of course I was there, it's my job to be there. Tra-la-la.'" His laughter intensified. "And who the hell whacks somebody and then calls animal control to report that she's right there on the site at the time of the killing? It's so stupid, it's freaking genius."

Warman thought a moment, then shook her head. "That leaving hammers and stuff all over the house really pisses me off."

"I hear that. Who puts a hammer in with her panties?"

"But you're still sure it's her?"

"Hell yes, it's her. A week from now there will be some other poor bastard laying out there in a pool of blood, and our Miss Bishop will be sitting next to the body with a bag of popcorn and a coke."

The laugh now infected Warman. "She'll have a club-stamp on her wrist. There will be music and everything, like a damn nightclub."

As they drove along, Lair slowed suddenly, and stiffened. Warman noticed. "What?"

Turning his head to look out the side window he slowed even further. "That's our guy."

"What?" Warman said again, mimicking Michael's actions as she turned to look out the same window. "What guy?" She studied a red pickup parked beneath some trees off to the side.

"The rapist. That's him." Lair felt the hair raise on the back of his neck, and his throat went dry. He pulled in off the road and parked some distance away from the truck. Both agents now had to turn further, twisting their necks as they looked out through the rear window instead of the side one.

"That's a red truck, Michael. Not green. And there's no one in it. What are you talking about?"

"It's parked in exactly the same spot. Exactly. And farther off the road than one would need to just pull over. There's no need for a truck to be up here, there's no reason for it, and it's the only place on the hill that offers a perfect view of the house." As Lair spoke, he opened the driver's door and stepped out. Reaching to his side he unholstered a pistol, lifting it to chest height and holding it with both hands. "It's him. I can feel it." Warman asked no further questions. She knew Lair was filled with quirks and eccentricities, but she also knew he was an effective agent with good instincts. Exiting the car on her side, she moved over to join him, drawing her own weapon.

"I don't see anyone," she said finally. "Maybe he's asleep on the seat, or in the bed of the truck."

Together they moved in on the pickup, approaching from the passenger side, knowing that if a driver had merely laid down to rest, his head would be up against the passenger side door, making it nearly impossible to fire a weapon in their direction. The seat was empty. The truck was empty. Warman's instincts were by now also kicking in. She fought to control her breathing, but seeing Michael alongside of her in such a state of readiness only provoked a deeper anxiety. Turning to face a grove of trees a short distance away, Lair motioned with his head and the two agents separated, arriving at the trees from two different directions. There was nothing there. "I don't know, Michael," Warman spoke in the first tone above a whisper. "Maybe the driver just walked out of here, or got a ride from someone."

"No." Lair spoke the single word, then turned in a new direction, one that would take them slightly down the hill in the direction of the house. This time Warman moved over next to him. Lair paused, looking around as Warman went on a step or two ahead.

Johnny Grimm heard something. The grating of a rock against gravel or another rock. A slight clicking sound. Spinning around he saw a woman with a gun, only a few yards away. Behind her walked a man. Frantically he grabbed at his pistol, cocking back the hammer and firing in almost the same motion. He was not a trained marksman, nor in any way proficient with firearms. His weapons of choice were knives and ropes and clubs. Close contact, subduing weapons designed for silence and efficiency. Still, this target was very close, and would not require much skill to conquer. The gun boomed in his hand, but he fired too quickly and the bullet bounced off into the hillside. The woman screamed out, and tried to raise her own weapon. Johnny fired again, this time taking the split second necessary to ensure a more accurate result. At the precise moment his pistol spit out a blast of flame, the man standing behind the woman leapt forward, knocking her to the side.

Lair felt the impact as the bullet struck. There was no pain involved, just a massive jolting as a missile slammed into his side. He landed on top of Elizabeth Warman, rolling over and across her body as he began to fire his own pistol. He felt the gun bucking away in his hand, but had no feeling or recollection of hitting anything or even seeing a potential target. There was just a blur of light, then long, loud blasts of sound. And then silence.

Finally, he heard Warman speak. Her voice sounded frightened and distant. "Michael... Michael... are you okay?" He tried to sit up, but failed miserably. Before he could try again, she was on him, pressing him back down. "Stay down," she said. "You've been hit." He could both hear and feel her voice choking with emotion. Twisting his head around, he looked frantically for the shooter. "Did we get him?"

"No." She began to laugh then, a sick, disheartened laugh, cradling his head in her lap. "I think we fired in every possible direction except his. We were all tangled up." Reaching down, she picked up a pistol and waved it dramatically in Michael's face. "I'll bet we scared the shit out of him though."

Lair also tried to laugh, but it wasn't working for him. "Sorry. I think I sort of fell into you."

Warman reached out her free hand and began to stroke Michael's hair. "You know damn good and well you didn't fall." Pausing then, she lowered her face until it was very close to his. "And we learned something valuable today."

"What the hell could we possibly have learned?"

"It's about you, Michael." The usually hardened voice of Elizabeth Warman grew soft. "Now we know."

CHAPTER TWENTY SIX

Molly stuck her head around the corner of the doorway. Thrust out in front of her was a bouquet of flowers. "Hey," she called out sweetly. "You decent?"

Michael Lair turned his head to face her. For the briefest of moments his face lit up. "Miss Bishop. What a completely unexpected and inappropriate surprise." Lair lay there in a hospital bed. Wrapped in a single sheet with his side exposed to show off a mass of bandages, he tapped at the site of the wound. "I always figured if anybody was going to shoot me, it would be you."

Molly danced into the room. "Hush, silly. There's plenty of time for that later."

"What are you doing here?"

Setting the flowers down on a bed stand, she pulled a chair closer to the bed and sat. "I figured we should talk. Maybe figure this thing out."

Michael shook his head, not unhappily, but warily. "I don't know, Miss Bishop. It seems every time I run into you the results of the meeting are not all that pleasant."

Laughing lightly, Molly reached out a hand, patting at the sheet. "That's your fault, not mine. If just once you would arrive bearing gifts instead of accusations I'm thinking we would get along famously."

Lair studied the young woman as he studied everyone who came into his life. It was never enough for him to just know someone, or interact sociably with them. He needed to know what made them tick, what prompted their actions and their thoughts. That's what made him such a worthy detective, and a less than worthy companion. If he were honest about it, the number of his true friends could be counted up very quickly. He had the usual number of associates, and a few acquaintances who would circle around him from time to time. But because of his caustic nature, and his need to psychoanalyze everyone who crossed his path, near-friends who might have become friends soon drifted away to dally with less analytical playfellows. This young and precocious woman who sat in front of him now was his own personal enigma. He supposed under less stressful circumstances they might have become close. Even been lovers. But that never particularly worked out for him either. Throughout his life, whenever a woman he felt connected to graduated from small talk to the bedroom, the relationship had an abrupt and final conclusion. The conversations could be substantive, and the sex substantial, but the combination of the two brought out in him a whole new set of analytics. He would begin to feel trapped, suffocated, by both the woman and the very nature of the encounter. But Molly Bishop was different. He had no doubt she would be able to handle him and his eccentricities. He also sensed his attraction to her was a dangerous one. She could drain any man, steal his substance, and then simply dance away.

Looking over at her, he tried to harden himself. "I'm still not certain you understand how serious this situation is. I'd also appreciate it if maybe you could stop telling people I'm banging you?"

Molly smiled playfully. "I usually say fucking, actually. Banging has such a coarse sound to it. Like someone beating madly away on a drum instead of locked up in a passionate embrace. Fucking really captures the essence of the act."

Lair looked at her in wonder, then shook his head in surrender. "Well, fucking then. Do you think you could stop saying that? Please?"

"Of course. I'd do anything for you." She paused, adjusting the sheet until it covered the bandages. "Warman thinks you're fucking me."

"I know, and it's really pissing me off." He stared at her for a moment. "So why are you here?"

Pulling the chair up even closer, Molly leaned in, her voice lowering to a whisper. "I think we should talk. You know, about our… situation. Consider the possibility that this Johnny guy might be your man. For everything."

Lair pursed his lips before responding, wishing to borrow more time. Finally he spoke. "His name is John Grimm, and we're going to get him." Michael's eyes narrowed, and his hand moved down to poke at his wound. "For this, and a lot more." Then his voice grew hoarse. "But he's just one guy, Molly. We both know there's another guy. And that guy is you. You know it and I know it. I just have to prove it, and I'm getting damn close."

Molly leaned back, but not far. "Do you know I think that's the first time you've ever called me just Molly? If you would consider calling me that on a regular basis I think we could make real progress here."

Lair's voice flew harshly at her. "What the hell is the matter with you? You're so damn flippant. Do you care about anything? Did you ever care about anything?"

His tone, the venom in it, and the content of the statement startled Molly. For a moment her face went blank. Then she stammered out, "Yes." The enormity of the word slammed into her, and all feeling drained away. It had been such a long time since she'd admitted anything, confronted anything. No one had ever asked her to before. No one had even brought it up, her caring or lack of caring. It seemed treasonous. But now this man, for whom she realized she had as much respect as anyone she'd ever known, lay there demanding that she expose herself. It was stunning and it was revelatory. For the first time since her childhood, she sat, ashen and isolated and somewhat broken. Michael sat up in the bed, as startled as Molly. He reached out to touch her hand.

"What?" he said to her after a long pause. "Talk to me, dammit."

Molly's head came up. She straightened her shoulders then, elevating herself slightly until she and Michael were at exactly the same level. "I never traded a pig for a goddam doll," she said. And that was all she said.

They sat there together for several long minutes in complete silence. Lair asked nothing further of her. He continued to hold on to her hand, not grasping at it, or clamping down, but rather laying his fingers gently against hers, so their two hands could keep each other company while their two minds decided on the next path.

"I grew up on a hog farm. You already know that." Finally, Molly began to speak, and once started the words flowed from her like a spring bursting forth through a wall of rock that has been holding it back for a long time. "When I was young, around ten, I was given this pig to raise. I named him Edmund. He was my third pig, in my third year of raising them. On a hog farm you learn very early on who is destined to be meat and who is destined to be master. There's a whole indoctrination process involved. It's quite numbing. Edmund was a runt, just a tiny newborn thing when I rescued him from a bucket, and my father— like he always did— warned me not to become attached. There was something different about Edmund, something special. It was like he knew me, could see inside of me and read my thoughts. My father noticed the inordinate amount of time I was spending in the barns, and warned me again. But I was just ten. And Edmund was pure love. He refused to allow me not to love him. We'd run together through the woods, splash about in the creeks and ponds, and sometimes I would even sneak him into my room late at night so he could feel as safe and warm and protected as I did. Edmund even learned all of my moods. He could predict them by studying my face or my movements as I walked up to the pens. If I was especially happy that day, he would dance, spinning joyously, reveling that his girl was in such fine spirits. My being happy made him happy. If I had been punished or disappointed, Edmund would seek me out, demand that I sit there beside him while he laid his big head on my lap and cried right along with me. He was my best friend."

Molly pulled her hand away, but gently. Placing both elbows on the bed very close to Michael's face, she leaned in, cupping her hands and allowing her chin to fall into them. "Have you ever had a best friend, Michael?"

Lair shook his head, not willing to consider prior acquaintances, and not wishing to disrupt the moment. So Molly continued. "Edmund stayed with me for the better part of a year. Each day and every day I cared for him, took care of him. I don't believe there was ever a moment when he doubted my devotion. He had complete faith in me, complete trust. Then came the day my father called for him. I was always told it would happen, and hey, I'd already faced it a couple of times in previous years, so there was no deception there. I should have expected it. But time is so irrelevant when you're a little girl; there seems to be so much of it. So, with me standing there in the driveway just outside the barn, I watched as Edmund was loaded onto the back of a truck for a ride to the slaughterhouse. Pork prices are sky high, my father said. There would never be a better time to capitalize on Edmund. And he was, after all, a family commodity. This is what we do, Molly, my father said. This is how we live." Molly's face slid downward, and while her hands had been comfortably supporting her chin before, they now reached up to cover her eyes. "I can still see it, Michael. Like it was yesterday. I can still feel the emotions that poured out of me. I remember grabbing my father, remember him pushing me away, and then falling down and crawling after him, trying to latch onto one of his legs, begging him for more time. I remember Edmund, his face staring out at me from the bed of the truck. I can still hear him crying out. Where are you, Molly? Where are they taking me, Molly? Do something, Molly. Do something."

As Michael reached for her, Molly began to cry, her first real cry for as far back as she could remember. Maybe as far back as Edmund, and all the other friends she'd had to surrender along the way. She clung to Michael then. "Let it out, baby," he said softly. "Let it out." He'd never shared a moment like this before. One of raw, naked emotion, exposed and badly wounded. Of all the women he'd ever known, this one had come at him with the toughest exterior. Unbendable, unbreakable Molly Bishop. A little girl of ten, who now lay there crying in his arms.

When the gunfire erupted John Grimm had stumbled to his feet. His mind numbed over as shock set in. It came as a surprise when, sometime later, he discovered two rounds had been fired from his own pistol. His perception, distorted by panic, was that all the shooting, all the blasts of flame and hot air had been coming at him, with none having been sent out under his direction. He had no recollection of the shooting of Michael Lair. Of seeing the bullet smack hard into the body of the agent. He did remember the running. The turning to crash through the layers of brush and trees that separated him from freedom. His first thought was to reach the truck, but he immediately realized that would be a hopeless task. And there would probably be others waiting for him there. So he headed down the hill instead of up, racing down into the street, then crossing it to lose himself in the thick brush that waited on the other side. For more than an hour he clawed his way through thicket after thicket of a thorny wasteland, never slowing, even when the brush became so thick that at every step it tore at him, ripping tiny pieces from his clothing and his flesh. His wound, not yet fully healed, throbbed terribly, and when he moved his fingers down to check on it, they came away dampened and red. Finally he reached a small clearing with a creek running through. The weather had been warm and the rains few, so very little water lay in the creek. What remained was tepid and filled the surrounding air with the stink of rotting vegetation. He stumbled down the bank, losing his footing on the way, then collapsed into a muddy pool where he lay until the sun sank low and darkness moved in to protect him.

Molly looked up through her tears. Michael was so close she could feel his breath on her face. His eyes were also filled with tears. Pushing herself away, she attempted a soft laugh. "You're crying," she said to him, her voice choking with emotion. "What a baby."

"Shut up," he answered. "You started it."

The hand that had been at work brushing away her own tears now swung over to Michael. Molly's fingers moved gently across his face. "I don't know where that came from," she said. "I've never shared anything like that before."

"You've got a lot of strength in you, Molly Bishop. Maybe more than anyone I've ever known. Crying isn't a weakness, you know. I've seen a lot of people break down over the years. Usually it just means they are cleaning something bad out of their system." As soon as Michael had spoken this last line, he knew he'd made a mistake. It was the way an interrogator would talk, not a friend. Molly's hand immediately withdrew from his face, her eyes, once caring and tender, now reverted, and she instantly morphed into the old Molly, the one who could slice a man open with a glance.

"What the hell does that mean? You think maybe you've broken me now? That you're about to get a confession out of me? That would be just dandy, wouldn't it? The great Michael Lair breaks down another suspect. Hail the great Lair." Kicking her feet out to catch the railing on the bed, Molly pushed her chair back until they were well separated. "It's not housekeeping day, Michael. There's no cleaning going on here. I just allowed myself to have a stupid moment where I thought somebody cared."

"No, Molly." Michael tried to win her back. "That's not what I meant. It's just the way I was trained to speak. You once accused me of being robotic, even assembled from parts as I remember. That was a pretty damn close assessment. But that's not at all what I meant, and I'm sorry. I simply meant it's not a bad thing to cry." Stabbing at his own eyes, which were still puffy, he attempted a laugh. "Hell, girl, you had me crying. That's not something that happens every day. Don't think this is some sort of game I'm playing to break you down. It isn't. I do care, Molly."

Molly looked back at Lair, evaluating him. Finally her face softened. "Well you suck at it."

"I know, right?" They both laughed, a short, sweet burst that reconnected them.

"So what's next?" Molly leaned back in, not fully committing herself as she had previously, but close enough to show that there had been some mending.

"I don't know." Michael tried to sit up fully, bending his upper torso into a more upright position. Pain grabbed at him, pulling him back down. "I need to get out of here, though. This guy is hunting you, and he's very dangerous."

Molly reached out both her arms, guiding her hands as they pressed Lair back down into the mattress. "You're in no shape for this. I can deal with it."

"Molly, you have no idea what he's capable of. I saw his last victim. It wasn't pretty. I don't want that to be you."

A grin broke out on Molly's face. "I appreciate your concern, and I don't want to go all Rambo on you, but the last time I saw him, he was laying out in a parking lot with his stomach sliced open." She patted her hands against Michael's chest, drumming softly. "How'd *your* meeting with him turn out?"

"Ouch." Lair shook his head, taking the time he needed to connect his thoughts. "There's a big difference this time. He knows you now. He knows what you're capable of. The very fact that he came back for another run shows just how deep his obsession is. He won't stop till you're dead."

"Or he is." Molly leaned over, almost kissing Lair on the cheek. Stopping just short as a sort of punishment, she spoke out hopefully. "You know, with him out of the way this can all finally end."

Michael looked back at her, amazed. He shook his head, displaying profound confusion. "God, Molly. Do you actually think that's going to end anything? There's a helluva lot more on the table that needs to be resolved."

Pulling her face away, she clapped both hands together, suddenly excited. "Let him be your guy, Michael. It's not me. It really isn't."

"All the evidence would indicate otherwise. We both know that. This guy is just peripheral garbage. He needs to be disposed of, but that won't end it."

"You don't know that. Not for sure." Molly's look became imploring. "You're not going to get me Michael. No matter how hard you try. Because it's not me. He's your guy." Her eyes flashed at him. "For god's sake. The bastard shot you. And we know he murdered at least one woman and likely more. He's perfect for this." Molly leaned her face in so they were once again very close. She whispered, "I can help you."

Michael's face hardened, his lips twisting as he turned away. He looked across the room and out the window. Molly could sense his rejection of her, or of anything she might offer. But when he spoke the words surprised them both. "Well, first things first, we need to put this man down. Before he hurts you."

She gasped aloud, relief flooding over her. Michael cared. She almost cried out the words. "Then let's get him. Let's get the bastard."

Michael pointed at her, then turned the hand toward himself. "Just remember I have a job to do. Personal feelings are not going to get in the way of that."

"You're crazy about me."

"Don't count on it."

"I have to. It's really all I've got."

Where there had been mostly softness a moment before, a ridgeline of hardness moved in, as Molly began to formulate a plan. "You just keep your mind open, Michael. Give me a chance. And I have a theory." She cleared her throat and began. "What if this John Grimm guy has been following me all these months, obsessed with me... you know what that's like, and you just met me." Molly's face lit up, but Lair remained stoic. "What if he stalks me everywhere I go? He's got the perfect cover for it, because he's a hog man. He can show up, say, looking for work on any farm I visit, wait till no one's around, and whack some poor guy simply because he perceives me as having something sordid going on." Molly had a thought, one that hadn't been there originally, but now blended naturally into her thesis. She jumped on it. "That makes perfect sense with the dog breeder. I get out of my car while Grimm is watching me from a distance… he sees me being attacked by the dog, and it incenses him. Maybe when he's not obsessed with raping me he feels some sort of perverted need to protect me. That would make sense, yes?" Molly reached out a hand, smacking Michael on the shoulder, demanding his attention. "So I drive out of there mauled to hell, and he moves in to avenge me. He bludgeons the poor bastard who owns the place, somehow avoids a confrontation with Cujo, and in his mind he's my savior." Molly nodded expectantly. "Well, what do you think?"

Michael thought. Then he nodded back at her, mumbled something unintelligible and thought some more. Finally he turned and looked at Molly squarely. She knew immediately his response was not going to be a positive one. "So you know what I do, right?" Without waiting for her to respond he continued. "People come at me all the time with their stories, their dilemmas, their alibis, and it's my job to wade through all the crap and seek out a reasonable conclusion of the truth, or a damn close facsimile of it. I'm very good at what I do. And here's what I'm seeing right here, right now. You've got a man, a crazy bastard, and I'll agree there is every indication that he is obsessed. So one night this guy comes after you in a parking lot, and you throw down against him. You stab him with a knife, you smack him over the head a few times with a pistol, and in general, you just beat the living crap out of him. Hell, you had enough of his blood on your knife to donate." Lair broke out a smile then, but it was more a companion for his logic than a reflection of his feelings. "So now it's a week later and you're thinking maybe this guy is so appreciative of the way you manhandled him that he's going to face a potential dog attack so he can kill somebody he's never even met, and who, by all accounts, you've never met either. Because the dog bit you and he's feeling bad about it." Reaching out his hand, Michael placed it on Molly's knee. He did so with affection, and as a kind of offering. "No, Miss Bishop. As hard as we'd like to believe it, it just ain't so. In fact, as weird as this sunuvabitch is, if he was still carrying around any amount of affection towards you, he would have whacked the dog."

CHAPTER TWENTY SEVEN

There is a small, isolated encampment just outside of Omaha called The Diggs. It is located in a desolate place, at the end of a canyon, and not far from where city workers come to dump the city's garbage. As if desolation weren't enough of a punishment, The Diggs is also situated just to the east of the dump, where afternoon winds blow through, carrying with them the acrid scent of rotting refuse. Over the years, men down on their luck or hiding out from a society too regimented for them would set up crude camps, some pressed right up against the walls of the canyon itself. They would build shelters, using a tarp or a sheet or a matting of thick cardboard, or if one was especially industrious, perhaps a slab or two of pre-used plywood pilfered and hauled over from the dump. No one bothered them much, these lost men, and they seldom ventured out to bother back.

John Grimm had just moved into The Diggs. The night before he had crept around the back of a strip mall, found a white pickup with the keys still inside, and drove until he stumbled onto this place. It was still dark when he arrived, but he found himself a site right about in the middle of the camp, and planned to stay for a day or two mending his wounds and thinking about the future. Life had been kicking hard at Johnny lately. A woman and a man had come at him from out of nowhere, guns blazing as he sat innocently on the side of a hill. It made no sense. He tried to picture them. The woman had been tall, he thought, and plainly dressed, maybe in tan pants, and a tan blouse. Nothing really memorable about her. All he clearly remembered was the gun, and looking down the barrel as she pointed it deliberately at him. Behind her came a man, also with a gun. Not a policeman or a lawman, just a man. Most likely they hadn't even been aware of his presence, or else they would have been better prepared for him. It must have been a mistake. Maybe even drug dealers or smugglers or land owners with a wicked sense of the trespassing laws. In any event, he would not be returning there. It would be much too dangerous to even consider. He thought about Molly Bishop. The woman was clearly not worthy of the amount of effort he had poured into her. She was a temptress, a seductress who would tease a man, flaunt herself at him and then, when he was at his most vulnerable, gut him like a hog. Johnny's hand went to his side, his fingers stroking away at the site of the wound. Something deep inside told him he should hate her, but Johnny had never been very good at holding on to hate. Life for him was more a series of docudramas, and when a particular episode ended it was pushed aside and forgotten to make room for something new. At the first light of the new day, he told himself, he would leave Omaha, leave all of Nebraska, in fact. Maybe head out west to Colorado. He could find work there and start a new life with a new woman who would be more appreciative of what he had to offer.

While he sat there mending and pondering, two men approached. One of them was large, with soft, kind features, the other smaller and tougher looking. "Hey," spoke the smaller man. "You're new here."

Grimm eyed both men suspiciously. "Yup," is all he said. Johnny's camp was a simple one. A sleeping bag, a tarp, and a few cans of tuna and some bread lined up neatly in the middle of the tarp.

The man who had spoken looked down at Grimm, who dismissed both men by turning his head away. "Nice truck." He spoke again, this time his eyes shifting over to the stolen pickup which was parked close by.

Johnny's head swung back around. He looked up at the man squarely, his senses now on alert. "Yup," he said again.

"Yours?"

Without seeming to move, Johnny's hand slid into the fold of the sleeping bag, his fingers curling around the handle of the revolver. "What's that supposed to mean?"

The man raised a hand in friendly fashion and grinned. "Nuthin'. Just sayin' it's a good lookin' truck. Usually when somebody drives down here he don't plan on drivin' much further." The man pointed across the canyon to several other pickups and an old Ford wagon. Most of them were covered with thick coats of rust, had no tires, and one, the wagon, had been tipped over onto its side. "Just not used to seein' a good lookin' truck is all."

Johnny relaxed. "Well it's damn sure mine. I just come here for a little rest. I ain't no bum."

The bigger man, who had not spoken till now, winced, and tapped at his companion's arm. "Hey, we ain't no bums," he said quietly.

"Look, friend," the first man spoke again, "we're just down on our luck a bit. Everyone down here is. We just thought we'd come over and invite you to supper. Andy…" The man turned sideways and pointed at a group of tents some distance away, "is makin' stew. He makes about the best stew you ever et'."

Once again, Johnny turned away. "I got my own food," he said. "I'm doin' just fine on my own."

The two men stood there for a moment longer as Grimm continued to ignore them. Finally they both looked at each other, shrugged and walked away. "What a asshole," the bigger man said, just loud enough for Johnny to hear.

Early the next morning, Johnny drove away from the camp and headed back into Omaha. After some hunting around, he turned into a paved lot at the very end of an industrial zone. Hunching down in the seat to where just the top of his head would be visible, he sat there and waited. The lot stretched out in front of him for a hundred yards or so, then turned into a narrow swath of lawn, which lay like a soft, green blanket directly in front of a large commercial building. Three statues stood on the lawn. Life sized renderings of a horse and a cow and a pig, in descending order according to their size. On a wall just beyond were large, bright-white letters, stark against the stolid grey of the wall. The letters formed the words *McMillan Pharmaceuticals*. Johnny looked at the statues. He looked at the building, and he looked at the letters. His face was expressionless. In his mind he was already driving towards Colorado. In fact, if asked what he was doing there in the lot, he would have had no answer. So he just sat there and waited.

CHAPTER TWENTY EIGHT

Sometime around nine that morning a car drove into the lot and pulled up close to the building. A young woman got out, and as she did so John Grimm raised his head slightly, a brief spark flashing across his eyes. Then he realized this woman was short and big-boned, and the spark died. The woman walked over to the building, opened the front door, and disappeared inside. Johnny continued his wait. A few minutes later a Jeep pulled up and parked next to the car. This time a man exited, a smallish man with a Stetson adorning his head. Because the man was small and the hat garishly large, he looked something like a cartoon character, especially with the distance dulling individual characteristics. Johnny's mouth twitched, the first reflex to show itself for many minutes. A slight smile formed on his lips, not created by the comic nature of this new arrival, but because he knew he could easily handle the man. He closed his eyes then, and pictured himself driving away. It was time, he told himself over and over. Time to head out for the mountain country. It was just a few short hours away. Drive out of this lot, turn west onto Highway 80, and he would be in Colorado by nightfall.

A white Camry drove into the lot. Johnny's hands moved to the wheel, his fingers curling around the worn leather grip, squeezing away at it. The fingers turned white from the squeezing. A moment later Molly Bishop stepped out from the car. Her hair shined brilliantly in the morning sunlight, and as if to showcase it further, she threw her head back, causing a golden cascade of long, curling tresses to sweep down across her shoulders. Molly paused for a moment, still standing beside the car. Her head turned and her eyes scanned the lot, coming to rest on the white pickup parked at some distance away. She seemed to stare at it. Johnny trembled. "She's a goddam witch," he said to himself. Instinct told him to duck, to pull his head down beneath the dash of the truck so he could not be seen, but he sat there, frozen. After what seemed an interminably long time Molly turned away, moving across the drive where she followed the others into the building. Grimm let out an audible sigh. But still he wondered. Stepping out from the truck, he walked around to its front, to a point where he directly aligned himself with the Camry. He turned and looked at the windshield of the pickup. A splash of sunlight concentrated directly on the glass caused a glare that would inhibit anyone from seeing the interior of the cab. He sighed again, but then considered the odds that the woman might actually be a witch, and any relief he felt washed away.

The nurse moved diligently down the corridor, poking her head into this room and that. "I'll have your medication in just a moment," she spoke through one of the doorways. "Sit tight and I'll be right back with a pan," she laughed through another. Arriving at the last doorway in the hall, she poked her head around a corner, singing out cheerfully, "Good morning, Agent Lair. How's my favorite…" The nurse stopped suddenly, mid-sentence. She backed away, looking at the wall to reaffirm the number affixed there. Then she leaned in once again, wondering at the ruffled, empty bed.

Michael Lair was gone.

CHAPTER TWENTY NINE

Observation presupposes a mathematical solution for pretty much everything that moves about in the universe. There are even laws which govern such movements. But there is one set of circumstances for which no algorithm applies. When a hunter hunts a hunter who is hunting him back there is no equation to predict, with any degree of certainty, the outcome. Simple perception suggests that when one hunter pursues another who is also in pursuit, the engagement becomes a circular one, but one where, uncharacteristically, no rules of movement apply. They follow each other in an orbit of perpetual motion, in defiance of the physical laws, and if their speeds are similar, and one's course is always set on the tracks of the other, there can be no outcome. To conclude such a hunt, one of them must deviate. One must break off the pursuit and lie in wait until the other comes around again, still locked into the parameters of the chase. The hunter who breaks form and chooses patience instead of perseverance is almost always the most successful, for he or she transforms into a most deadly kind of killer. The ambush hunter. Crocodiles, snakes, spiders, are all masters of lying in wait, and the most cunning of hominids also utilize this technique, this lethal ability to wait.

Johnny Grimm was a chaser. His very nature demanded that he select his quarry, then follow it until an opportune time when he could strike, usually from behind. That way his victim was most easily subdued, and he suffered very little risk in the encounter. It's true he could lie in wait as an observer, studying the habits and consistencies of his prey, but when it came time for the actual hunt, the takedown, he was a reactionary, moving in and striking quickly. All in all it was an efficient way to hunt, but had one serious debilitation of which Grimm had only recently become aware. If the quarry also turned out to be a hunter, he could easily be lured into a trap. That had only happened once, in his encounter with Molly Bishop, but it had happened hard and brought with it a hard lesson. This time he would use caution, and a more impressive array of weaponry. Johnny carried in one pocket a length of wire, enough to wrap several times around a woman's neck, and in another, a pair of knives, sheathed but unfastened, so they could be drawn instantly. Shoved down into his waistband, with its handle protruding enough to make it easily accessible, was the stolen pistol. The same one he had used to escape his attackers on the hill. He would still pursue and strike, but this time he was more dangerously attired.

As a hunter, Molly Bishop was the antithesis of Johnny Grimm, believing that patience was a much more faithful tool than mad pursuit. She knew the intricacies of the stalk, how to move and when to move, but most important, that successful conclusions were usually obtained by lying in wait and using no movement at all. Two years earlier, in the wilds of Wyoming, she had come across a cougar that seemed to be stalking her. She had first noticed it when crossing a meadow, for as Molly finished the crossing and moved into concealment on the other side, the cougar entered the meadow at the exact point she had, and began to follow in her tracks. Not wishing a confrontation with the big cat, Molly had turned, whistling out a warning. The cougar froze, then slipped down into tall grass where it became invisible. This brought a curiosity, and an amusing conundrum. If Molly lay stilled in the trees and the cougar lay stilled in the meadow, there could be no conclusion. One of them would eventually have to break cover. It became a game, a great game of patience, and Molly calculated that if she sat long enough the outcome would predictably tilt in her favor. After a few moments she noticed some bending grass, and a soft, moving blur slightly different in color from the golden wisps which lay in waves across the meadow. The cougar was coming. The whistle had aroused, but not frightened it. It was still hunting her. Slowly and deliberately it moved through the open field, sometimes only visible by a tiny patch of fur or the tiniest specks of black as the tips of its ears slipped along the upper edges of the grass. Finally it arrived at the edge of the meadow and just a few yards from where Molly lay hidden behind a clump of cedar. The cat paused, its ears bending back, while its whiskers twitched nervously. The ears swung forward then, reaching into the thickness of the forest to pick up any sounds its intended prey might make as it retreated. But there were no sounds, and that's what made the cougar nervous.

Molly's rifle had been raised for some time, resting atop a branch at a point level with her eyes. The sight was fast set on the cat's head, while Molly's finger was fast set on the trigger. The cougar lifted one of its paws, still nervously, with claws raking out against the bark of the one cedar that protruded partway into the meadow. It did this several times, then moved on, drifting past Molly along the same trail she would have taken had she chosen a pathway of escape. She had learned a valuable lesson. Lying in wait worked splendidly, and if the prey had any badass in it, could skew the results of a hunt entirely.

CHAPTER THIRTY

Michael Lair slid along the side of a cargo container parked behind an industrial building directly adjacent to McMillan. His ribcage hurt terribly, as the bullet that had taken him down had shattered one rib, causing a collateral echo to resonate to other nearby ribs, and a shooting pain accompanied every step. All his years of training told him that soon John Grimm would be coming for the girl. Maybe not this day, but soon. It was inevitable, and even if the killer were to wish it otherwise, he would be drawn to seek her out for a final resolution. Psychopaths aren't all wedged together into the same tiny niche where they can be neatly categorized. There are degrees of psychopathy, fraught with nuances which vary greatly from one to the next. Lair thought he had a good enough read on Grimm to consider him at the most dangerous end of the scale, by whatever means he was being measured. There was the murder of the young woman outside of Omaha. She had been bound, taped, raped and strangled. But her killer had done a curious thing. After the attack he had posed her in a position of gentle sleep. Laid out on her side with legs slightly bent, and one arm tucked beneath her head as a pillow. While it had come off as grotesque, what Lair garnered from the scene was the profile of a man who cared about his victim, or thought he did. Maybe even had a fondness for her that went well beyond the bounds of an ordinary attacker. Grimm was a fantasy killer. His encounters with Molly Bishop only reaffirmed this diagnosis. Workers at the farm where they first met reported Johnny not only lusted after the girl, but had conjured up in his imagination some sort of romantic connection between the two. He was even laughed at for it. His showing up at the nightclub further proved his devotion. He wanted desperately to insert himself into her world, become her partner and her lover. It is quite possible that if Molly had been receptive to his advances, they would be dating, still by Grimm's warped fantasy standards, but Lair was willing to bet that Johnny Grimm's final solution contained a sick relationship of some sort, one where Grimm and his victim played out a twisted relationship of bondage and love.

There was an even greater danger in the man. It lay in the fact that he could not quit. Even if he wanted to. Molly had worked him over in the parking lot, and still, on Grimm came, like a fighter who has been clubbed so many times he is effectively brain dead, yet continues to flail away at his opponent. So he had continued to stalk her again and again. There was only one way to stop such a man. Kill him.

Johnny sat in the pickup for a long time, his mind working him over. Ordinarily, only one voice poured out of him, and like most people, he responded well to it and functioned rationally. Then there were the times another voice would intervene, and the two would argue before agreeing on a prospective course, this second voice almost always dominant in the debate. On this day the second voice was especially vocal. He raised both his hands, covering his face with tortured fingers as the two separate components of his psyche hammered away at him. "Run, Johnny. Let's get the hell out of here." "Get the girl, Johnny. You have to take care of the girl." "Colorado, Johnny. A fresh start. A new life." "The bitch hurt us, man. Nobody hurts us." "No, John, it's time to run."

Grimm hollered out suddenly, ripping his hands from his face and slamming them against the dash. "It's time to drive outta here," he said aloud, his voice shaking. "A new life. That's the answer. A new life." Even as the words spilled out, Johnny opened the door of the pickup, stepped down and began to work his way behind the truck, and then along a row of trees that bordered the edge of the lot. "I'm goin' to Colorado," he said as he moved into the trees. "I'm done with this place."

At this same time, Michael Lair, moving out from the concealment of the cargo container, thought he detected movement from among the trees at the other end of the lot. He stopped and studied the grounds and as far into the trees as he could see. But there was nothing there.

Molly looked over at Carl, trying to appear as nonchalantly as she could. "So, I just got off the phone with Michael Lair. He thinks Grimm may be paying us a visit today, and he wants us all out of here." She paused. "Well, he needs you out of here now, so they can set things up. I'll be following in a little while."

Carl looked back at her suspiciously. "He's in the hospital."

"I know where he is, Carl. But he's still in charge of the investigation, and he's the one setting this up." Molly tapped at her boss's desk. "You need to go. Like now."

Carl wasn't buying it. He knew Molly too well. "Why can't I just wait then, and go with you?"

"Because you're not part of this. They need me to stay behind because, obviously, I'm the one he's interested in."

"But then you're going to leave, right?" Carl began setting a trap.

"Yes, I'm going to leave. I just told you I'm going to leave. As soon as everything gets set up. I'll be right behind you."

"No way." He shook a finger at her. "That makes no sense. Why would you help set up and then just leave if it's you the guy is coming for? It makes no sense. Your leaving would defeat the whole purpose of having you here in the first place."

"I don't even know what the hell you're talking about." Molly was growing frustrated. "You just have to go, and I have to stay."

Carl's finger continued to wave, but now more aggressively. "You're not coming. I can tell you're not coming. And where are the police, if they're supposed to be here?"

"It's a clandestine operation. Do you even know what that means? They can't have policemen running all over the place and expect the guy to show up. God, you're an idiot."

Carl sat back in his chair. The finger that had been waving around now clenched in with the rest of the fingers, forming a fist which he slammed down on the desktop. "I don't believe you. I'll go when you go."

Molly raised her voice. "Carl, get out." She then raised a hand like she might strike at him, and Carl winced, pulling his head back, but refusing to turn away entirely. "Take the receptionist, and the two of you get out of here. It's not safe."

"I'm not leaving you, Molly."

"Listen, you dumbass, this isn't a game. Michael thinks he's coming and I think he's coming. You need to get the two of you out of here."

Carl folded both arms across his chest in defiance. "If it's true, then I need to be here with you. To protect you."

"Protect me?" Molly jumped around to Carl's side of the desk. Her hand whipped out, like the hand of an assassin, striking at his face. The blow caught him on the cheekbone, staggering him. Inside, her heart broke a little, for this man was probably as close to the love of her life as she would ever have. Outwardly, she stepped forward, lashing out again. This blow caught him on the other cheek, causing him to nearly fall out of the chair. "Protect me? Why, you little shit. What are you going to do? Beat the guy up for me?"

Pain streaked across Carl's face, not pain caused from being struck, but rather a more conflicted pain, a deeper pain. He tried to speak, to reason with her, but no words came out. Molly continued the assault. "You go get the girl, and you get your ass out of here." Her face contorted as she stared hard at him, shaming him. "You think I need you, you little sissy? You'd get us both killed. Just get the hell out." She clenched a fist and waved it in front of her face.

Carl winced, tears starting to well in his eyes. "You don't mean that. You don't mean it, Molly. Let me help you."

"I don't need your help. What I need is for you to leave me the hell alone. This is my problem, Carl. This is my world. I'm warning you to stay out of it." There was something sinister in the way Molly spoke. Something deep and menacing. Carl detected it and it frightened him.

His eyes widened, like someone looking at a ghost. When he spoke it was cautious, and well measured. "It's you. Isn't it?"

It took a moment for Molly to absorb the words, digest them and grasp their meaning. A fire came into her eyes. "Yes, it's me. It's always been me. But you already know that from your little green journal."

The words stabbed at him. Carl's face darkened as guilt laced across it. "You know about that?"

"Of course I know. You have enough evidence against me yet?"

"No, Molly, it's not like that. It's not like that at all."

Molly knew it was not like that. Carl had become so devoted to her that there was no possibility of betrayal. His record keeping was more of a curiosity, and a concern for her safety. At the very worst he would have used it to blackmail her into becoming a more benevolent member of society. She knew that, and inwardly it pleased her, that he cared so deeply. Outwardly, however, it only added to the agony of the situation. Reaching down into her boot, she extracted a knife, a twin to the one she had use to gut John Grimm. She waved it in Carl's face. "You're a traitor, Carl. I've known it for some time, and I've just been waiting for the right time to slice you up."

She waved the knife at him, hoping her agony would appear as rage, but then realized it was rage. Real rage. At herself.

Carl looked at the knife in disbelief. He looked at Molly with the same disbelief. Then he rose from the chair and backed away to the door, tears streaming down his face. "I would never hurt you. Never. I love you, Molly."

"You sicken me." She snarled out the most hurtful words she could conjure up. Inside she was dying. Not the kind of death where one lays there all warm and fuzzy as the world says goodbye. This was the kind of death that straps you down, shrieks at you, and decimates your heart. Molly turned her back then. It's all she could think to do. When she turned around again, Carl was gone.

From outside, and hidden away in the trees at one end of the lot, John Grimm watched as two cars drove away. Only Molly Bishop's Camry remained. At the other end of the lot Michael Lair watched as the same two cars departed, leaving only that same Camry.

"I'm coming for you, bitch," said Grimm, a sneer spread across his face.

"Oh, god, Molly," said Michael Lair, a look of anguish spread across his.

Molly walked down the corridor leading from Carl's office to the front lobby. It was eerily quiet. She looked up at the clock mounted high on the wall over the receptionist's desk. It was a few minutes past nine. She would have guessed it was much later. Moving over to the front doors, she looked out into the lot. The pickup was still there, parked out far enough that it made no real sense. Who would park a truck in the middle of nowhere? The only practical answer was someone who had been picked up for some reason, and who would be returning. But who would ask to be picked up at the end of a dead end road in an industrial park? That struck her as inconvenient, and impractical. Any reasonable person would ask to be picked up at the beginning of the park, where the participants could then easily transition into street traffic. Here at the end, they would have to retrace a route already driven. Goosebumps prickled along her arm, working their way up past her elbow. She brushed a hand against them and the bumps retreated.

Molly couldn't have known that if she had only looked out the doors five minutes earlier, she would have seen the creeping figure of John Grimm exit the truck and make his way into the trees. She reached down to throw the latch on the master door, the one that would lock the two doors together. It clicked closed, and she paused there, contemplating. Locking them could be a mistake. If Grimm was coming, he would come, and a pair of glass doors would never deflect from his mission. But it might dissuade him from using them, breaking into them, and he would then seek out another, less predictable entry point, of which there were several. With her hand still on the latch, she unbolted it, pushing outward slightly on the door to make sure it was unlocked. Then she had an idea, one imprinted in her mind from years of hustling men, and years of hunting them. She would unlock every door leading into the warehouse, so that Grimm, when he arrived, could bask in the simple victory every burglar feels when the door he first tries yields to his touch. That would allow him to relax, turning his first major obstacle into a nonexistent one, and slip him into a state of complacency at the very moment he should be at his most diligent. Glancing once more outside, and seeing nothing there, she moved again down the corridor leading to the rear of the building, to where a pair of massive cargo doors and a side door waited. She flipped the latch on the side door, then smiled maliciously as she looked at the cargo doors. "Let's make this really easy, you sick bastard." She hit a button on the wall, and one of the doors screeched upwards, creating a mammoth square of open space. Sunlight splashed in, lighting the room, and creating what Molly thought to herself was a magnificent target zone.

She then retreated to Carl's office, opening a closet there and extracting one of her favorite weapons, a .223 caliber semi-automatic rifle, which sent forth a small but hellishly fast projectile, one that would slice through a man like a knife cutting cake. Molly knew of a place there in the warehouse, high up, a place even Carl didn't know existed. She had found it about a year earlier, when the receptionist had complained that someone had gotten into her lunch, ate her apple, ate her cookie, and took a bite out of her tuna sandwich before scattering the remains on the floor and absconding. Molly had studied the scene, then on a hunch began to follow, Hansel and Gretel-like, a trail of crumbs which led to a steel ladder, which led further to a small alcove perched some twenty feet above the floor of the warehouse. It was just a niche, actually, placed there during the construction of the building to house internal wiring and tie several of the larger ceiling beams together. A raccoon had waited for her at the top, hissing out at the intrusion. Molly had retreated then, and not wishing to cause undue stress to the raccoon, never reported it to anyone. But it was a handy place, just large enough for an enterprising person to squeeze her way into, and it offered a field of vision that encompassed the entire building.

Molly grabbed the rifle, some cupcakes, a bottle of water, and climbed the ladder. The space was vacant now, the raccoon having long since moved along, so Molly crammed herself into place and settled down to wait.

CHAPTER THIRTY ONE

Johnny Grimm approached the warehouse from the east, along the line of trees, until they ended abruptly. As he looked out from behind the last tree in the line, his eyes widened slightly. A huge door lay open before him. He licked his lips in anticipation, but then a flicker of caution caused him to pause. Surely the woman had no idea of his intention. After what had transpired between them, any reasonable person would assume he would be long gone. In fact, any reasonable person *would* be long gone. It was crazy to think otherwise. Something else nagged at him. Always in the past, he had been an attack hunter, keeping in visual contact with his intended target until the moment of the strike. It removed many of the intangibles, and completely eliminated the need to seek a victim out, for she was always right there in front of him. There was a certain comfort in that, and standing here now, still safely imbedded behind the tree, he shuddered suddenly, both from the excitement of the moment, and this new component brought about by the need to further stalk instead of attack.

Lair moved cautiously across the lot, headed for the pickup. There was no cover available to him, just an expanse of concrete, but still he moved like a man seeking concealment, shifting his body almost sideways as he walked along, his pistol drawn and ready. Like Molly, the truck had also aroused suspicion in him. There was simply no reason for it to be there. He moved around to the back of the truck, noting the license plate. Pulling out his cell phone, he punched in a number. He then moved alongside the truck on the side nearest the trees, the side that would make him the least detectable. His hand tried the handle on the passenger side door. The door swung open.

Agent Warman answered the phone. "Michael," she said, her voice surprisingly cheerful. "How are you feeling?"

"Good. Listen, I need you to run a plate for me. Nebraska plate on a pickup."

"What? Where are you? Aren't you still in the hospital?"

"Yes, yes, of course." Michael stumbled through the words. "Look, I don't have a lot of time here. I just to need to know the story on this vehicle."

"Where are you, Michael?" Warman's voice rose in pitch. "What's going on?"

"Dammit, Warman, will you just run the plate?" As he spoke, he glanced into the open door of the pickup. A roll of duct tape lay on the seat, together with an old canvas covered jacket. Lair reached in to inspect the jacket, and was immediately met with the unmistakable aroma of pigs. When he'd first arrived in Omaha, he wasn't even aware that pigs had their own smell, but since then had become very familiar with it. Pungent, musty, even somewhat offensive to a delicate city palate, it was now forever implanted in his brain. The truck fairly reeked with the scent.

"Michael," Warman demanded a response. "What's going on?"

He hung up on her. Slamming shut the side door of the pickup, Lair began to run. His ribcage cried out in agony as stitches began to pop open and blood began to flow, saturating his shirt, blood-red on the inside, but blackening as it seeped its way through the fabric. The whole time he ran, his mind was on Molly Bishop. Gorgeous, wonderfully tempting, beguiling Molly. Crazy, deceptive, most likely a serial-killer, Molly. God, he thought, it would be so fun to hate her.

CHAPTER THIRTY TWO

Molly sat and waited. From her perch high above the warehouse floor, almost the entire interior of the building lay in her field of vision. None of the walls extended all the way to the ceiling, so it was like looking down at a maze, and waiting for the rat to appear. She had just begun to pick away at a cupcake when a shadow crept its way through the open doorway. Because it was still morning and the doorway faced east, the shadow was long and gave no indication of how far away its creator might be standing. Molly tensed. Her fingers flexed open, the remains of the cake tumbling down her blouse where they landed on one of the beams. Raising the rifle, she rested it on another beam. The safety had been switched off long ago to eliminate the possibility that any clicking sound could warn her target. Her face lowered then, naturally and easily onto the stock of the rifle, bonding wood with flesh in perfect harmony. Her index finger tapped at the trigger guard before moving in to wrap itself around the trigger. The shadow remained frozen, as if the intruder had not yet chosen a course of action.

Grimm stood outside the doorway for several long minutes, trying to decide on his method of attack. He could sneak in, using stealth, which suited his nature, and try to take her by surprise. Or he could boldly race through the doorway, a pistol in one hand and a knife in the other, using more the elements of shock and awe. That way she would have no opportunity to prepare for him, no chance to evade him. But mostly Grimm stood there out of fear. This would be his first hunt of an unseen target, and he knew well the capabilities of his intended prey. He shook his head, trying to clear it, and thought once again of Colorado, and how nice life in the mountains would be. He could find a cabin, a woman, and a job as a sticker on one of the hog farms there. No more herding pigs, no more shoveling shit. He would, instead, slaughter the hell out of them, until he became a legend to the other workers. This new thought brought a look of contentment to his face, and filled him with resolve. "I'm goin' to Colorado," he said aloud. Then he walked boldly through the open door.

Molly watched as the shadow suddenly shifted. It began to flow its way towards her like moving magma, then fatted out, as boots appeared, and the building began to compress the shadow inward. Then a man stepped through the doorway, into the interior of the warehouse, and the shadow disappeared completely. It was Johnny Grimm. Raising up slightly, she tilted the barrel of the rifle downward, still using the beam to steady it, until the sights centered on the man's chest. Drawing in a deep breath, she exhaled, and began that slow, steady, practiced compression of the trigger, already picturing Grimm flopping fish-like on the floor.

At precisely that instant, Michael Lair burst through the front door and into the lobby. Fearing the attack on Molly was imminent, he ran down the hallway screaming as he made his way toward the warehouse. "Molly, he's here. Molly!" Grimm reacted instantly to the sound, dipping his head, while his body turned, seeking an avenue of escape. The booming crack of the rifle exploded outward, a bullet searing its way across the side of Grimm's face, nearly tearing off one of his ears. He shrieked out in shock and pain, diving to one side and rolling up against a wall. Lair burst into the room then, and he and Johnny began firing nearly point blank at each other. The room was filled with one blast after another, rapid, deadly fire, ripping into the metal of the walls and the flesh of the men. Molly tried to rise up further, but there was a beam blocking the way. Grimm's dive had taken him to the one place on the floor where her line of fire was obstructed. All she could see were his legs, so she began to shoot at them, the whole time knowing that Michael Lair was down there on the floor, completely vulnerable. Suddenly, an incredibly loud explosion rocked the entire building. A massive piece of sheet metal, very close to where Grimm lay, splintered into fragments, torn apart by the blast. He screamed as hot bits of metal ripped into his back, and rolled away from the wall. That brought him back into Molly's view. Before he could even consider firing his weapon again, she squeezed off three quick rounds, the last ones in her clip. The first one tore through Grimm's neck, the second caught him on the chin, with the third burrowing its way into his right temple. It was over in an instant. There was not much left of Johnny Grimm.

Molly scrambled down the ladder and rushed to Michael's side, where she collapsed to her knees. There was blood everywhere. They both started to cry. "You're okay," he cried out. "I thought the bastard got you."

"No, no, I'm fine." Cradling his head in her arms, she began to examine him. "Where are you hit?"

"I don't know." Raising an arm, he winced, rolling over onto his side. "This arm for sure, but I don't think I'm hurt anywhere else." Ripping off her belt, Molly began to apply a tourniquet to the wound on Lair's arm, just beneath a shoulder. She worked deftly at it, wrapping and cinching it off neatly as Michael laid back and rested his head in her lap. When finished, she pressed her hands against him, coursing them over his upper torso, seeking further damage. She noticed his shirt, down low near his stomach, was soaked in red.

"Oh, god, you're hurt bad." Her crying intensified as Michael reached up with his good arm to comfort her.

"No, baby. That's from my previous encounter with the bastard." Stroking her face with his hand, he began to laugh. "I'm glad you put him out of his misery. I don't think I could take much more of this running into him."

Molly began to laugh then, but because her crying hadn't yet abated, it became a soggy mixture of the two. "You really suck at this, Michael."

Lair reached out to wipe away her tears. "It would be pretty hard to argue with that right now." Pausing, he had a thought. "Hey, what the hell was that explosion? It scared the shit out of him, and probably saved my life. The whole goddam wall blew up. Did you fire a cannon at the guy?"

Molly shook her head. "No, I don't know what it was. It scared the hell out of me, too."

A voice called out. A timid, familiar voice. "Molly, are you okay?" They both looked up, and there, standing in the doorway, was Carl. He had a double-barreled 10 gauge shotgun clutched in his hands, appropriated from Molly's collection, and suitable for elephants or wall-busting. The massive weapon completely dwarfed him.

"Carl, what did you do?" Molly's mouth fell open.

Carl looked back at her, somewhat stunned. His mind was just beginning to rebound from shock, and his whole body was shaking. Leaning down, he placed the gun on the floor. He looked over at the body of Johnny Grimm, sprawled out in macabre fashion against the wall. "I thought I missed him."

Patting Michael on the chest, Molly rose and ran to Carl. His eyes widened as she closed in, fearing for a moment that she might be commencing her attack on him again. Then she was on him, grabbing and hugging him mightily. "I love you, Carl." Molly began to twirl, dragging Carl with her. "I love you so fucking much."

Carl squealed out joyously. "I thought I missed him."

Molly and Michael were both laughing now. Still crying somewhat, but mostly laughing. "Hell yes, you missed. Molly's the one who put the bastard down." Lair pointed at the gaping hole in the sheet metal. It was big enough to drive through. "You blew the hell out of the wall, though. It was the greatest miss in history."

Carl had no idea how his missing a target could be the subject of such frivolity, but since Molly was hugging and not beating him, and Michael Lair lay on the floor cheering, he figured it had been a fairly worthy accomplishment.

Molly paused then, and stepped away from Carl. Her face

tightened as she remembered something. "Carl," she said author-itatively, "call 911. Michael needs an ambulance and the cops are going to need to see this." She nodded at Lair and walked out of the room, heading out through the doorway that led to Carl's office. A moment later she returned. In her hand was a towel, and it seemed to be wrapped around something. Moving over to the body, she knelt there beside it, fumbling with the towel. Both men looked at her curiously.

"Molly, what are you doing?" It was Lair who spoke.

Turning her head to face him, Molly held up in her hand a short length of pipe. She waved it at both men. "This is your hammer," she said, her voice flat and void of emotion. "The one you've been looking so diligently for. The one that took down Lester Macon, the dog breeder." Carl's face showed confusion, but Michael's eyes lit up, and his lips curled downward in agony

"Oh, no, Molly." His voice died. Any hope of resurrecting this woman as an innocent died right along with it. It was her. He had known it was her, been convinced it was her, but deep inside had kept alive the slight possibility of an alternative. An alternative that had just met a swift death with the presentation of a two foot piece of pipe.

Molly turned away from the men and spent the next few moments working on Grimm's body. When she finally rose, he lay there on his back, his arms sprawled out to either side, one hand still grasping the pistol, but the other now had a firm grip on the pipe. Turning to face the two men, Molly lowered herself to the floor, pulling her knees up high where she could rest her chin on them. Her face softened, and she took on the countenance of a child. A beautiful, fragile, innocent child. Carl thought she had never looked more lovely, and his heart cried out for her. Michael's thoughts ran deeper and darker. He tried to speak, but the only words he could come up with were, "Oh, Molly."

Molly spoke. "This is your guy, Michael. I've told you that before. Let him be your guy." Her head raised up from her knees as hope flooded into her eyes. "This will tie everything up, all neat and tidy. All the forensics you need, right there in the bastard's hand."

Michael's Lair's face continued its journey into agony. He was a lawman. His whole life devoted to tracking down criminals, and bringing them to justice. There were no exceptions, no exclusions in his world. Inwardly, he wondered if he might be in love with this girl. He supposed he was, for at this very moment he could feel his heart breaking. But he was a lawman, and when he spoke, it was with a lawman's voice, in a lawman's tone. "Miss Bishop," he said, pointing at John Grimm, "that doesn't change anything. The forensics point to you, not him. Especially now. I don't see any way out of it. No matter how much we'd like it to be otherwise, that's just the way it is."

Carl couldn't contain himself. It had taken him this long just to understand the significance of what Molly had done. "You idiot," he cried out, staring down venomously at Lair. He also pointed at the body. "She's just given you a way out. It's right there on the goddam floor. For god's sake, man. She saved your life." Moving closer to Lair, Carl dropped to his knees. He waved a finger in the agent's face. "That's gotta mean something." His face saddened then, as he glanced over at Molly, who smiled adoringly back at him.

"Listen, both of you, that's enough." Molly spoke firmly, like a teacher about to lecture an unruly class. "Carl, you shut up, and Michael, you listen. You might have something here, and you might not. Carl and I will both swear that Grimm arrived carrying that pipe, and no matter how loudly you shout out otherwise, that's what we're going to say." She glanced at Carl, who nodded his head vigorously. "I think maybe you're delirious from your wounds, and you're just not seeing straight." She shook her head, then placed her elbows on her knees, dropping her face down to rest on them. "I still don't think you can win, Michael, but that's not really the point. I'm asking you not to even try. You're convinced that you're a righteous man on a righteous path. I wouldn't wish anything less for you, and I would be the last person to ever want you to compromise yourself. But you're wrong about me. Terribly wrong." Molly lifted her head and waved a hand at the body. "You're probably comparing me to him right now, and finding us very similar." She paused to give Lair time to absorb what she was telling him. Then her eyes shifted away from the body, turning back to bore into his. There was a fire in them. "Every day in this goddam country a hundred Johnny Grimms are caught and convicted. Some of them have committed the most heinous acts, maybe grabbing a little girl, beating her, raping her, scarring her for life. Maybe the bastard gets ten years, and we both know he'll be out in five. And he'll rape again, won't he? He'll never quit till he's dead. Or at least ninety percent of them won't. So where's the crime now? With the man who's just been turned loose to ravage society, or with a system that says— with undeniable certainty— go forth and rape. Destroy another life, and in five or six years you can do it all over again. The truth is, they make perfect partners, one just as guilty as the other." Molly raised a finger, pointing it at Lair. "You're the one who brings them in, Michael. If you were really the man you claim to be, the one who cares so deeply about justice, they would all be laying out in a ditch somewhere, with a bullet in their heads. And somewhere out there, in a bedroom filled with teddy bears and lace, a little girl would sleep safely through the night. Because you cared enough to destroy the man who would one day come to ruin her."

"I get it, Molly." Michael fought back. "And I hear what you're saying. But we're not gods. We have no right to decide who lives or dies. That's what the law is for. I'm just doing my job."

Molly laughed aloud, a sick, tortured laugh. "That's the stupidest thing I've ever heard. It's the same defense every Nazi soldier used as he herded the Jews off to the ovens." She stood then, pushing herself up off the floor. Moving very close to Lair, she towered over him. "You probably think I'm one sick bitch, without considering the possibility that I may be the least contaminated person you know. When I take someone down, you better damn well believe they deserve it. I'm extremely selective, which is exactly why you and others like you have had so much trouble trying to profile me. Those I decide to eliminate are well covered with accolades. Just ask the pigs they slaughter."

Michael tried to sit up, but the pain dragged him back down. Molly noticed the pain and wanted desperately to run to him. She took a tentative step but then froze as he shouted out, "Your thinking is crazy. If everyone did what you do we'd have complete chaos. There has to be a system of rules, of laws. No one has the right to just arbitrarily take a life. To decide on someone's life. The whole idea is insane."

"No, you're wrong. I remove a stench, a stink that fouls up everything it touches. There is nothing arbitrary about it. If I punish someone it's because they've earned it." Molly's eyes pleaded with his. "I know you feel it, too. I saw you, Michael. That day at the auction, when the pigs were being brought out into the arena for the last time. I saw pain in your eyes. Real pain. You can't possibly feel that sort of pain without also feeling the injustice. They're companions, and they don't separate from one another easily."

"Those were pigs, Molly."

"God, I hate you right now."

Sirens could be heard, still well in the distance, but growing louder. Carl, who had been sitting there the whole time, mouth hanging open and eyes transfixed on the combatants, now said the only thing he could think to say. "I love you, Molly." He then shifted his attention to Michael, deciding to plead with the man. "For god's sake, Lair. She saved your life." Turning his head, he pointed in the direction of the body. "She took his, and saved yours. You've gotta see the difference in that. You just gotta."

Michael Lair lowered his head. He had nothing more to say. The sirens were very close now, the sound rising enough in pitch to shut down the communications among the three. Molly stood there, above the two men, her arms now folded across her chest. She turned away, surrendering herself to whatever was about to happen, and stared out the open cargo door. Carl sat a few feet away, his body slumped forward, with the posture of a man defeated. The fire had gone out of him as the sirens closed in, and all that could be said, had been said. Despite the pain, Lair forced himself into a more upright position. His body ached terribly, and he had a bemusing thought that the only place free of pain was the arm that had been shot. The tourniquet, placed between the wound and his shoulder, had caused the whole arm to grow numb.

An ambulance pulled in, very nearly colliding with the one cargo door that had remained closed. Behind the ambulance came a sheriff's car, then a police car, as the jurisdiction of the industrial park, which lay at the edge of the city limits, was called into question. Paramedics and uniformed officers soon swarmed the place. A sheriff's deputy recognized Michael. "Agent Lair, you're hurt." He rushed to Michael's side. Two paramedics also rushed in. One glanced at Molly. She nodded at the man, shook her head and pointed away.

Lair spoke, wincing as one of the medics prodded at him. "God, what took you so long? I think I'm bleeding out here." He tried to be humorous about it.

"What happened?" asked the deputy. Turning his head, he addressed the body laying out on the floor some distance away. "Who's that?"

Michael shook his head, as if trying to clear it. He might have been feigning weakness, or might have actually felt weakness. Even he wasn't certain. But when he spoke, his words slurred slightly. "That's John Grimm," he said. "We've been after him for a while." He looked over at Carl, then up at Molly. Neither one of them showed the slightest signs of expectation. They just looked back at him numbly. "Look," Lair mumbled finally, "I'm beat to hell here. Let's just get me to the hospital." Raising his good arm, he pointed. "This is Molly Bishop. She's been assisting me on this, and can answer any of your questions till I'm in better shape."

The medics lifted Michael then, placing him on a gurney. As they carried him outside to the ambulance, he turned his head to search for Molly. She had also turned, to watch him leave, and she stood there near the doorway with both arms hanging loosely from her sides. There were streaks of blood on her face, blood on her blouse, and blood on her arms. His blood. Her hair, usually a perfect cascade of curls, now hung from her head in a disheveled mess. He had hoped she would be smiling at him, and was somewhat disappointed to find that she wasn't. But then he noticed why, and his heart fluttered a little. She had traded in the smile for something eminently better.

Molly was crying again.

EPILOGUE

As Carl stood there watching Molly watch the ambulance drive away, his eyes narrowed and his head nodded slightly. There was still a certain amount of confusion about what had just transpired, but it was slowly being eroded away by a quiet understanding.

"It's not over, is it?" he asked, his tone probing, but gently so. Molly turned to face him.

"I don't think he can let it be over."

"I'm not talking about him. I'm talking about you. It's not over for you." Molly had no answer. The tears had stopped, but not the sadness that now washed over her. She stepped toward Carl until she was able to reach out her hand to grasp his. "You can stop, Molly." Carl's voice started out pleading, then turned resolute. "Just stop. There's still time."

An officer who had been studying John Grimm's body moved in their direction. Carl waved him away. "Not now. Please. She's had enough. We'll come in later." As the words tumbled out he could feel Molly's fingers tighten around his, and in a kind of secret solidarity his tightened back. "Well let's just go home," he said. "We can deal with tomorrow tomorrow."

They stood there for another long moment. Finally Molly loosened her grip on Carl's hand and pulled away. She leaned in to kiss him on the cheek as her fingers reached up to caress his hair. She turned then, alone, and moved towards the opening left by the great cargo door. Just before leaving his sight, Molly swung her head around and their eyes met one last time.

Then she was gone.

BURN HOUSE PUBLISHING

We proudly support authors and artists who inspire discourse,
shine light in the darkest corners of society and tell stories that
offer reflection on what it means to be human.

You can learn more about our efforts on social media
and at www.burnhousepublishing.com.

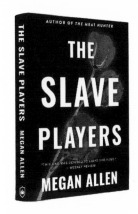

THE SLAVE PLAYERS

CHAPTER ONE
THE INCIDENT

The yellow bus wound its way for an hour or so along the Chattahoochee River, on the Georgia side of the Georgia-Alabama border. The writing on the side of the bus proclaimed in bold, black script, *Freedom Church*, and somewhat less boldly, *Blue Ash, Ohio*. It was a hot day, hot like it gets in July in the south, with that clingy, damp heat that really isn't damp at all, but life-sucking and desperate. A young girl seated near the back tried to slide open a window, hoping the rush of air from outside would offer at least some degree of relief from the heat.

"Tiffney." A large woman, with teeth that flashed bright-white against the black of her skin, spoke sharply. "Enough with the windows. It's ten times hotter out there than it is in here. Everyone just sit back and relax." She smiled then, an old, patient smile, and where her cheeks cracked into deep age lines, sweat flowed down her face, with one or two drops managing to make it onto the collar of her blouse. "Just another few hours and we'll be at camp. There's a pool there with water so cold you'll wish you were back on this bus."

"That's right girls." The man who drove the bus turned his shoulders slightly, and allowed his head to swing even further. He was a young man, with soft, kind features. "Miss Marcy speaks the

Lord's truth. I been there before when I was a boy. I seen it. That water pours straight outta the mountain. It's so cold it's gonna hit your skin and you'll be screamin' like babies. You just wait." Aside from the lady and the driver a dozen young girls sat or lay in scattered heaps all around the bus.

"Ezekiel five-twelve," one of the girls hollered out. "The Lord brought the cooling rains and Satan brought the fire. Choose one but not both to provide for your soul. And choose the one that most pleaseth the Lord." Several of the girls scrambled for their bibles.

"Ezekiel what-what?" they cried out. "That's not Ezekiel. That's not anything. You just totally made that up."

"Did not," called out the girl defensively. "Look it up. Just 'cause you don't know about it doesn't mean it isn't there."

One of the other girls thumbed furiously through the pages of her bible. "As usual, you're just nuts. There's nuthin' like that in here." She paused and raised one of her hands. "Or anywhere else, for that matter."

"Oh, sure, like you'd know," the scripture quoter shouted. "Well it's right here in mine. Maybe you just have a dumber version," she laughed. "Or maybe you're just dumb."

"Miss Marcy?" Several voices rang out as the old lady lifted herself and turned to face the girls.

"Enough," she said. "You girls settle down." She stared sternly at one of them. "And you, Elizabeth. You keep making up scripture and the Lord's going to send you a very special message. The Book is the Book. It says all that needs to be said without any help from you."

"Yes, ma'am." The girl called Elizabeth smiled obediently and waited until Miss Marcy had reseated herself and her eyes moved away from the girls. Then she lifted both hands high over her head, her middle fingers extended straight up.

"Miss Marcy!" cried out eleven voices.

An hour or so later the bus swung hard right, and moved out onto a bridge spanning the river. They had now crossed into Alabama. Evening came, and with it twilight, then darkness, and the bus rolled on. There were no lights turned on inside the bus, and so it grew as dark as the night outside. The girls slept. Sometime later, around midnight, the bus slowed.

"I think we're here." The driver spoke as Miss Marcy lifted her head and looked through the blackness.

"What do you mean, *think*, Tommy? We're either here or we're not. And *here* is not subjective. It's an absolute."

"What?" Tommy looked out through the windshield and then through the front side windows. "I dunno. I mean, I haven't been here in twenty years. I just saw a sign that said *Camp*, and I'm pretty sure this is it."

"Then why isn't it lit up? And where is everybody? They're supposed to be waiting for us."

"I dunno. But I'm pretty sure this is it. You want me to turn in?"

Miss Marcy continued to stare off to the right side. The headlights illuminating the highway ahead allowed little residual light to escape to the sides, and all either of them could make out was a patch of dirt roadway leading through an open gate and into the woods. "Well, I guess this could be it. But there's supposed to be lights." She paused. "I suppose everyone could have gotten tired of waiting and gone off to bed. Maybe they think we're coming in the morning."

Tommy clicked on his phone, which flashed *No Signal*, as it had for the past several hours. They were deep in the Alabama countryside. He turned the bus then, without waiting for further instruction or resolution, and they moved away from the main highway into the thickness of a forest. The road was narrow and winding, and seemed to go on and on. Only a moment or two passed before he spoke. "Well this sure as hell isn't it."

"Tommy!"

"Sorry, ma'am. I mean this can't be it. The camp house should be just off the highway. I remember it was right next to the highway."

The bus inched forward as they searched for a place to turn around. Finally a light shined through the blackness and they drove into a sort of yard, a small, open field with a single lamp at one end. The lamp was as confusing as the dark, as it cast its light directly at them and everything beyond was blocked out by the brightness. Tommy eased his foot down on the brake, and with a slight squeal the bus stopped. "Well I sure as heck don't know where this is," he said. A light spray of dust from the braking wheels swirled up around them.

Miss Marcy turned her face away from the glaring light, trying to reason out what sort of place they had encountered. "I think we should just turn around," she said in a whisper. "This place gives me the creeps." Tommy looked over at her.

"I hear that." He revved the engine slightly as he turned to drive. Then he screamed, "Shit!" Miss Marcy's admonishment froze in her throat as her eyes swung toward Tommy, but they never made it past the windshield. Her mouth flapped open and stayed that way. For there in front of the bus, and so close they could almost touch him, stood a man with a rifle. A grinning man. He stepped forward slightly, rapping on the hood with the barrel of his gun. His lips moved as though he spoke, but they could hear no sound. Suddenly the glass on the door just to their right shattered. Tommy screamed again. Another man stood there, and this one they could hear.

"Open the goddam door," he said.

One of the girls stirred awake. "What's going on?" Other girls were also stirring.

"Quiet girls. Not a sound." Miss Marcy turned her attention to the man standing just outside the shattered door. "There's been a mistake," she said, her voice shaking. "We're going to go now."

The man punched hard at the remaining glass. It exploded in a shower of shards. His hand gripped at the frame of the door and yanked on it. It refused to yield. The hand dripped blood but he appeared not to notice. "I said open the goddam door." His other hand came up and pointed a massive pistol at Tommy. "Now, Nigger!"

Tommy's eyes widened. His hand went to a lever at his side. He pulled on it and the remains of the door flapped open. "We don't want no trouble," he stammered. "We was just lookin' for our camp, that's all." The man stepped up the two steps to the platform of the bus. Reaching over he gently plucked a shard of glass from Tommy's hair.

"You gotta be careful," he said, wiping his bloody hand on the front of Tommy's shirt. "That shit will cut the crap outta you." Smiling, he patted Tommy on the head. "You got lights in here? It's darker than hell."

"Yes, sir." Tommy flicked a switch on the dash and lights flooded down the aisle of the bus, showing a dozen very awake and very frightened young girls.

"Toby. Get your ass in here. You gotta see this." The man slowly worked his way between the rows of seats, inspecting each of the girls as he passed. The man called Toby came from his position outside, climbing up to where he could press the barrel of his rifle hard against Tommy's chest.

Miss Marcy cleared her throat to speak. "Listen, we're very sorry if we have inconvenienced you. We'd really just like to be on our way. Please."

"Inconvenienced?" The man inspecting the girls turned and moved back to the front of the bus. He stopped only when his crotch moved right up against Miss Marcy's head. "What kinda shit talk is that? You be one of those trained up intellectualized darkies." He stuck his still bleeding hand in her face, wiping it against her cheek. "You see this? Your bus did this to me." He turned to address the girls. "Let's put it to a vote. How many of you all think I should be paid for my injuries here?" He held up the hand. "You can't just come onto a man's property and bloody him up like this without payin'." He grinned wickedly. "How many think I should be paid?" No one spoke and no one moved. But a dozen pairs of wide eyes were trained on his. The man's grin lessened somewhat. "Well I'll be goddammed."

Tommy spoke. "We'll pay you." Toby lowered the butt of the

rifle and the barrel swung upward slightly until it just nudged into the flesh of Tommy's neck.

"You goddam right you'll pay."

The man with the bloody hand began to move again down the aisle among the girls. Mostly he found them much the same. Dark, plain, and too young to have developed much in the way of womanly features. But one was different. With long legs and long, raven hair. A lighter complexion than the others, and certainly the beginnings of curves in all the right places. "What's your name, darlin'?" he asked her.

The girl looked up at him defiantly. "Elizabeth," she said. "Why don't you just take what you want and go?" The man laughed, deep and guttural.

"That's exactly what I intend to do, baby." He grabbed Elizabeth by the hair suddenly and yanked her upwards, nearly ripping her off her feet. She screamed as he dragged her to the front of the bus. Miss Marcy came up out of her seat and tried to yell something, but the man shook a hand free from the girl and smashed a fist hard against the front of her face. There was an audible crunching sound as the bones in her nose exploded and she was flung back into the space between the front seat and the railing. She lay there moaning for a moment, half on the seat and half on the floor, and then went still. Tommy tried to move, but the rifle barrel pressed deeply into his neck. "You stay here, Toby," said the man, dragging the still screaming girl. "Keep an eye on things till I get back. Me and the missy here got business."

A few hours later, just after dawn, a young couple driving down from Montgomery to visit friends in Jacksonville came across the twisted wreck of an old yellow bus. It seemed as though the driver had failed to navigate a turn and the bus had crashed through a barrier, careening into a couple of black oaks before winding up on its side in a patch of marshy grass just off the roadway. There were a few bodies scattered outside the bus, young girls mostly, with even more inside. By the time authorities arrived spectators were already gathering up and down the road.

CHAPTER TWO

THE RESPONSE

Colby County is about as far down south and east as you can go and still be in Alabama. In fact, it almost wound up as part of Florida when the lines were drawn, but the Colby clan, rich in numbers acquired by a massive breeding program, put up such a squawk that the lines were drawn a bit more to the south. Patriarch Nathan Colby was often heard to say, "There is nuthin' close to Redskin about this family and we ain't gonna be part of any damn Seneca nation." The statement was as close to racism as it got in those early days, and only pertained to Indians. As far as blacks went, you either owned them or you didn't. And Colby owned a few. So the county lines were drawn just south of the main hub at Dolan City, and continued south another thirty miles to the border, with two minor highways running through, one running a trade route into Georgia, and the other slashing downward into Indian Territory.

Onto this southward highway, some two hundred years later, a sheriff's car moved methodically toward a call. The radio inside the car crackled to life. "Sheriff, you coming?"

A uniformed man inside the car responded. "I'm comin', Larry. About ten minutes out. You have the place secured?"

"Yes, sir," came the response. "Folks are out here already, but I've got 'em pretty well backed off. You're not gonna believe this shit."

"I heard." The sheriff smacked his lips. "It's bad, huh?"

"Bad." Larry's voice was shaking. "Man, I've never seen anything like it. There's gotta be a dozen or more. Laying out all over the place. And everyone's dead. Deader than hell."

John Parrish had been sheriff of Colby County for over twenty-five years. He'd run and won the first time on a platform of firm and fair justice, citing the completely fabricated fact that a distant step-cousin was a man of color who'd married a white woman, which seemed to make him a bit more palatable to half the county's inhabitants about whom he and his cronies would whisper were racially impaired. And he'd stayed in office through four more elections by being a most intimidating man with a cunning ability to discourage possible opponents. Now he lowered his voice. "All darkies, right?"

"Yes, sir," came the quick response. "More than a dozen, I think. And all dead."

When Parrish arrived a few minutes later, the first thing he did was walk along the roadway above the crash site. He bellowed at the onlookers to move along, and out of respect or fear everyone complied. Cars scattered up and down the highway, and as they departed an ambulance and a couple of tow trucks arrived. The ambulance driver looked at him hopefully, but the sheriff shook his head. "Bodies only," he said. "A bunch of them." He pointed at the driver. "You wait here till I call. Gonna be a while." He then moved down a sort of pathway cut into a slope marking where the bus had slid along on its side. He studied the bus first, then motioned to one of the truck drivers. "You guys might as well go back into town. Come back this afternoon and you can haul this baby outta here." The drivers looked like they wanted to stick around, out of morbid curiosity, but a look from the sheriff and they started up their trucks and drove away. A deputy emerged from behind the bus.

"Hey, Chief. Told you it wasn't pretty. I spent the first ten minutes puking my guts out." They walked together over to a body. A young girl, around fourteen. One arm had a deep gash and her neck was slashed so deeply that her head tilted back, away from her body, like a hand puppet with no hand inside.

"You see anythin' wrong with this, Larry?" The sheriff prodded at the girl with his foot, turning her slightly.

"No. What do you mean? She's dead."

"I mean there's no blood. At least not here there isn't." Looking up, the sheriff paused until his eyes rested upon another body. "Don't you think with a cut like that there oughta be a little blood?"

Larry tipped a visor back on his head and scratched at his ear. "Well, yeah, I guess. But maybe the blood is in the bus."

Sheriff Parrish spoke even as he began to move to the next body. "So she bled to death in the bus and then threw herself out here as an afterthought?"

"What are you saying?"

"Nuthin'," said the sheriff. "Just thinkin'."

They moved to the bus then, and had to crawl up onto one of the wheel wells before climbing down through the shattered door and into the bus's interior. And here they found the blood. Lots of it. Together with lots of torn bodies and caved-in heads, and the driver, whose face was smashed beyond recognition, lay in a near fetal position with one arm still locked around the steering wheel. A slight smile played at the sheriff's lips. "You know, we could have just walked in through the windshield," he said.

Sometime later a coroner's van arrived and the bodies were stuffed into the van and the ambulance. All together there appeared to be one large male, one equally large adult female and eleven young girls. While the bodies were being loaded the tow trucks reappeared. With the two drivers jockeying a hoist and a pair of winches they soon righted the bus. And what at first had seemed a horrific crash brought something of a surprise. The bus had suffered very little. The front windshield and door had been shattered, and some of the side windows had broken out, but there didn't seem to be much major damage. It was as if the bus had merely slid off the incline, impacted a couple of minor trees and tipped. The sheriff mumbled something to himself and then joined the coroner in a caravan back to town.

The town was Harbor Springs, Alabama, about twenty miles southeast of Dolan City, though strangely there was no harbor and no springs. The town's name might have originated as a sort of joke. No one ever really knew. But it was a tidy place, with clean streets, lazy dogs and a kind of southern charm if one didn't probe too deeply. Shawn Briggs served as coroner here, coroner for the whole county, in fact. He had come down from St. Louis a year earlier with his daughter, Olivia, to start a new life. In St. Louis he had been accused of tampering with evidence in a poisoning case involving one of the richest families in the state. He hadn't tampered, of course. He hadn't done anything but reveal evidence that would have put a very important man into a most unpleasant circumstance. And so he had fallen, from the big city to the most remote of places.

A couple of older black men who were always about town seeking odd jobs had heard about the crash and stopped by as the van and ambulance pulled in. "You need some help, Mister Briggs?" one asked. The back door of the van swung open just then. "Jeezus," gasped both men. "There's a whole bloody pile of 'em. Jeezus." Sheriff Parrish walked over to the van and the coroner signaled him.

"Look, I don't have room for all this. I've got six lockers and some table space. And it's going to be hotter than heck today." Briggs raised his hands helplessly.

The sheriff nodded. "We can take some of them down to the butcher shop. George has a big ice room. That should do it." He smiled sheepishly. "His customers are gonna love the hell outta seein' all these little darkies hangin' up there with the beef. But it's the best we can do." The two black men looked sharply at the sheriff, but then quickly lowered their eyes as he looked back. "You know I don't mean nuthin' by that boys. Hell, it coulda happened to anyone, white or black. And we'd still have to ice them down. That's just the way it is." He clapped one of the men on the back, then turned dismissively back to Briggs. The coroner caught the downcast eyes of the men, and his own eyes dimmed in shame.

"Look, Sheriff. It will take a few days to get the autopsies done. And we'll have to bring the bodies back and forth." He raised his hands. "Is that going to work?"

"Autopsies?" Parrish reached out, placing a firm hand on the coroner's shoulder. "Look, man. This is a bad situation for everyone. We're gonna go to work identifyin' everybody and gettin' the next of kin down here to claim the bodies. From what we found I think they're all down from Ohio. It was an accident, for god's sake. We all saw that. Let's get them the hell outta here and save ourselves a whole kettle full of grief. The last thing we need is a bunch of autopsies slowin' things down."

By the time the sheriff returned to his office in the middle of the township of Harbor Springs, throngs of people were waiting. Most were from the church camp a few miles outside of town. He patiently stood there on the steps with them, listened to them wail and cry and scream out in despair even as he wondered what in the hell he was having for dinner and why in the hell he couldn't have been out fishing when this whole thing occurred. Maybe with a little luck it would all just blow over.

That night, to his own personal consternation, nearly every television station, local or national, led with the story:

Thirteen African Americans Lose Lives in Fiery Bus Crash
Most Are Teenage Girls.

"Fiery, my ass," he thought to himself. "A little wax on, wax off and that bus would look like new."

The next morning crept in with ominous signs. A thunderstorm struck as a deluge of rain pounded down over much of the county. People poured in from all over, soaked from the rains and drained of spirit. There was a meeting hall set up at the Baptist church on the outskirts of town. Families were arriving all the way from Ohio, having driven through a long night of agony. And sometime before noon it was discovered that a girl, on the original roster of bus passengers and presumed present with the others, had not been found. Sheriff Parrish returned to the crash site with a group of townsmen, but a thorough search of the site turned up nothing of substance. The missing girl was just that. Missing. Her name was Elizabeth Courtier, and the one thing the sheriff noted when comparing her photo to that of the other girls was her beauty. It was remarkable. She would stand out in any crowd.

"Strange," he said to his deputy. "She's gorgeous."

"Yeah, she is. But what's strange about it?"

"I don't know." He pursed his lips together, making a smacking sound. "But if someone was to pop in and pluck one of these girls away, she'd be the one."

The phone rang then. It was the coroner, and he needed to see Parrish right away. When the sheriff arrived at the mortuary, Shawn Briggs met him even before he could exit his car.

"I have something to show you," he said. He led the way into a small alcove, and then down a flight of steps beneath the mortuary wherein the coroner had his office and laboratory. "I've been working all night on the bodies." He turned and looked directly into the sheriff's eyes. "This was no accident." He pointed to one of the tables. A large black man lay there, cut deeply open in a variety of places.

"What the hell." The sheriff spoke sharply. "I told you no autopsies. Just let this thing go so we can get these people outta here. We're gonna have a goddam circus on our hands."

"I didn't cut the man. I just laid him out there." Briggs spoke softly, but a firmness gripped his voice. "I didn't like it yesterday and I like it even less today. You know as well as I do that crash couldn't have done all this damage. These people were cut to bits, and not by a damn bus tipping over on its side."

The sheriff's face reddened. He stepped towards the coroner.

"Listen to me, you dumb sunovabitch. This was an accident. Just an accident. Do you know what could happen if folks, especially black folks, got wind that this was anythin' else? We'll have a goddam riot down here. A goddam riot. Is that what you want? No matter how it happened, it was a goddam accident. You come down here from St. Lou thinkin' you're all kinds of big shit. I've seen the report on you. You were a dumb sunovabitch up there and you're a dumb sunovabitch down here." He moved even closer to Briggs, until they almost touched. Turning his head the sheriff looked around the room. Several battered bodies lay about on the tables in varying degrees of undress and mutilation. "Now what's to say you didn't do all this crap yourself? You're a cutter, right?" He moved away to one of the tables, allowing a very intimidated Briggs to draw a breath. Reaching onto a tray he picked up a long, narrow scalpel. Bits of cloth and tissue still stuck to the blade. "So we say you did this. During your autopsy. Hell, man…" Parrish brought his hand down hard, implanting the blade deeply into the belly of a young girl. Briggs gasped, mouth open wide, as the sheriff continued. "Anybody asks and we just say you're a lousy cutter. Or that you're overly enthusiastic. And we say nuthin' else."

The coroner gathered himself and slipped a hand into the pocket of his waistcoat. "And what about this?" he said. He opened his hand, palm upward to display a small, shiny chunk of metal. Stepping over to the table where the body of Tommy, the driver, lay, Briggs slipped a hand gently under the man's head, tilting it to one side. And there, just above an ear, matted with a mass of dried blood and hair, was a hole. A small, precise, penetrating hole. Sheriff Parrish stared hard at the hole for a long time, speechless. Finally, he reached out a hand in a silent request for the lump of metal. "A rifle, I think," said the coroner softly. "Fired at very close range." He pointed across the room to where Miss Marcy lay, her face badly bludgeoned and her body rife with bruises. "She has one, too. In her back."

CHAPTER THREE

THE COVER UP

The sheriff looked deeply into the eyes of Shawn Briggs, probing at the depths of this man. There were several ways he could handle the coroner, and his mind raced through a variety of scenarios trying to figure out which one suited him best. That the man feared him he had little doubt. He had seen the fear cloud Briggs' face during their confrontation. But fear as a binding tool is usually only temporary, and with time and circumstance can be overcome. In his mind the sheriff sought out a more permanent solution. Finally he spoke. "Listen, we need to be very careful about this." His face softened. "I've seen what can happen when folks get the wrong idea about somethin'. When they see hate instead of tragedy. If we lead people to believe this was anythin' more than an accident all hell is gonna break loose. And if you haven't seen hell in the south, then you don't know hell. I've lived it. Seen it. Down here everythin' boils down to race. It's a sad fact but it's a fact." The sheriff held out his hand, exposing the torn bullet between his fingers. "And it doesn't matter who the hell did this. If it's blacks that are killed it's gonna be blamed on whites. It's always been that way. Hell, for all we know it was their own kind done this, but that's not the way it's gonna come out if we're not smart. I remember way back to the eighties, when I was a boy. Every black man down here was screamin' about his new-found rights. Seems every other day my daddy would come home and tell us about some darkie who'd been strung up or beaten and there would always be this rush to judgement. Hell, feds would pour down from the north, pointin' fingers and blamin' all the whites. You'd be hard-pressed to find a case of a nigger killin' another nigger, even if the nigger done it." The sheriff reached out —not aggressively, but purposefully— and tapped at the coroner's chest with the bullet. "We gotta be careful, is all."

Shawn Briggs tried to meet the sheriff's eyes, but the eyes held too much strength and he was forced to look away. He stood there, about as frail as a man could stand, still shaking slightly as his glasses slipped down his nose, stopping abruptly at its very tip. He tried to refocus on the sheriff without being too obvious about it. Sheriff Parish was undeniably a big man. A big man with a strong face and a strong jaw that appeared unbreakable. Adding to this look of invincibility, a long, jagged scar slashed downward from beneath one ear, running its way down the neck until it disappeared into the collar of the man's shirt. Briggs considered for a moment whether it might be the one who handed out the scar who was the invincible, but quickly realized it didn't matter. The sheriff was there, standing over him, and the scar-giver was not. So he continued to tremble, his eyes finally moving away to focus on one of the bodies lying nearby. He lifted a weak hand and pointed. "What are you saying? These folks are dead. And it wasn't the bus that killed them. What are we supposed to do about that?"

The sheriff's voice lowered and became friendlier, and pointedly conspiratorial. "Look, all I'm sayin' is we don't wanna start somethin' that'll be bad for everybody." His mouth twitched as an idea came to him. "I saw your daughter the other day. Down to the market. Sweet young thing. Her momma musta been somethin'. This is a good place you've brought her to. A fine place to raise a youngster. But we've gotta be smart and keep it that way. And this ain't St. Lou. Things are different here. Folks down here don't reason as much as they do up north. Everybody's a goddam reactionary. They're not like you and me. You know, sensible. And sometimes the best of us or the ones we love wind up hurt for no other reason than we weren't smart enough to keep our mouths shut and do what's best."

The coroner looked up, trying to read the meaning in the sheriff's words. "Are you telling me not to report this? To just let it go?"

Parrish nodded, smiling warmly. "Hell, boy. I'm just sayin' let's wait a bit, that's all. I've got somethin' to do this afternoon that can't wait. But later on I'll be back and we can work it out. We can work out what's best for all of us." The sheriff extended his hand as a bond, and waited a long moment before Briggs reached out to take it.

The sheriff had a problem. A big one. The bullet that now resided in his pocket was familiar to him. The lower most portion of the metal, the part last to enter a body and the least likely to be damaged, had a system of rings molded into its sides. Three of them. They were unusual and easily recognizable to even a casual eye. In addition, the caliber was also familiar, and quite rare. A Thirty-Forty Krag. First cast for the early army Springfields, the round had not been particularly popular and over the succeeding hundred or so years had just about died out. Few people owned a Krag, and fewer still used one in any regular fashion. But the most amazing thing about this particular bullet was its composition. It shined more than a normal casting would, and upon impact had cracked apart a bit instead of just mushrooming out in the way one would expect of lead. This bullet was made from pewter, a sort of lead-base with a portion of tin melded in. He recognized it immediately for a very special reason. He had cast it. Together with his son Toby, to whom he had presented an old vintage Krag, they had broken down and melted an old mining stanchion, feeling the pride of a pioneer using the resources at hand. It had been a bonding moment for both of them, as Parrish knew the road he had presented to his son had not always been a pleasant one. There had been years of firm discipline and punishment and beatings, not cruelly undertaken, but in the same way his father had raised him. Still the boy seemed to persevere, and even prosper. So when his son finally arrived at manhood, a great change came over their relationship. Parish had begun to treat the boy as an equal, for they had both survived a trial by fire, and from this pride emerged the exchange of the rifle as a sort of rite of passage, with a touch of penance.

The sheriff drove now, east on the highway to Georgia. He passed by the church, and rolled on into the countryside. Soon he passed the sign for the Freedom Camp, and a few miles further along came to the crash site. He slowed to survey the trees and the meadow, and then drove even slower for a few hundred yards as his eyes probed the roadside and every clump of brush that might have helped camouflage the body of a girl. He suspected there would be nothing to see and he was right. Finally, after a time, he came upon a narrow drive, cutting off to his left. A broken sign near an open gate read, *Camp*, and propped up against a post on the ground nearby was another portion of the sign, mostly covered by weeds, which read simply, *Dixie*. Turning left he drove down a winding country road. It was not well tended, and clumps of swamp sage growing from its center where tires were seldom felt brushed roughly against the bottom of the car. Finally he emerged into an open field. Off to one side, and mixed into the brush, were several old cars, and parts of cars. On the opposite side were a series of pens built up close to the trees. In better days they might have held goats or sheep or hogs, but not anymore. Torn boards and busted wire would have had a hard time holding back anything that wanted to escape. Straight ahead, and tucked back in a cluster of oaks, stood a house, or shack, dismal and worn from many years of harsh southern weather. He drove further across the field, pulling up close to the shack. A man moved out from the trees and approached as the sheriff stepped from the vehicle.

"Hey, John," said the man. He was tall and rangy, with unkempt clothes and a hand bandaged by a bit of white cloth.

"Vern." Parrish moved to one side, ignoring the man, while his eyes inspected the house. "I guess you heard about the crash."

"Yeah. Heard about it this mornin'. From the trash boys. Terrible thing." The sheriff turned to face the man, who began to fidget uncomfortably. "All darkies though, right?"

The sheriff nodded. "What did you do to your hand?"

Vern looked down at the bandage. "Ah, shit. You know me. Bustin' up some wood for a fire. Hit the shit out of it."

The sheriff smiled. "A fire? In July? What the hell you got goin' on, Vern? A still?"

Vern laughed, but nervously. "Hell no. You know me better than that, John. I'm long done with that shit. Hell, last time you put me away for six months."

Parrish began to move around to one side of the house. "My son around?" he asked.

"He's out back, I think. I'll get him for you."

"I can do it." The sheriff continued alongside the house until he came to the backyard. An attempt at growing a lawn had taken place there, a long time ago, and a few yards further back was a pen and an old shed. Suddenly Vern hollered out loudly from behind.

"Toby. Your dad's here. Toby!" John Parrish turned his head and stared hard.

"Some reason you're announcin' my presence, Vern?"

"No, sir." Vern looked down. "Just wantin' to let him know you're here."

As the sheriff turned back, his son Toby climbed out and over a wide board bracing the bottom of the shed. "Hey, Dad. What's up?" The boy walked quickly away from the shed, distancing himself, and approached his father. At the same time, Vern turned and retreated just as quickly back around to the front of the house and disappeared from sight.

The sheriff's eyes seemed to lose some of their brightness as he looked at his son. His voice was almost sad. "You still got the Krag?"

Toby looked at his father curiously. "Yeah, I think so. Up to the house. Why?"

"Use it lately?"

"Nope." The boy paused, scratching his head. "I mean, I shot a pig a while back." He tried to smile. "Big sunovabitch. He about took my foot off. Had to stick the barrel in his ear to get him off me." The sheriff pawed at the ground with the toe of his boot. His eyes now bore deeply into the eyes of his son.

"I'm lookin' for a girl. I'm thinkin' she's there in the shed." He continued to stare at his son. "What do you think?"

Toby began to visibly shake. His hands grabbed at his pockets and the color flushed from his face. "I don't know, Dad," he stammered. "I don't know."

"You don't know what?" Anger began to rise in the sheriff's voice. It danced there like a living thing. "You don't know if there's a girl in the shed? Or you don't know about a girl?" He moved menacingly toward his son. Reaching out a hand he grabbed a fistful of hair, twisting it as he forced Toby to his knees. The boy cried out.

"We found her, Dad. I swear we found her. We didn't do nuthin'." A foot swung up and crashed into the boy's stomach. He retched and rolled onto the ground as his father released his grip. For a long moment Parrish stood there, looking down.

"You damn, miserable fool," he said. Then he turned and walked to the shed.

The door to the shed swung inward, which was not usual, as it was more likely to allow wind and weather access that way. But it had been broken and mended and broken again until the door just didn't care anymore which way it swung. As the sheriff's eyes grew accustomed to the dim light filtering in, he noticed an old, worn mattress lay off to one side. Just beyond the mattress, where the light was even dimmer, sat the huddled mass of a young girl. She sat in a corner with her head bowed, pressed right up against a wall, with a length of burlap pulled up loosely around her. Her face came up as the sheriff spoke. "It's alright darlin'. Everythin's gonna be alright." For a moment her eyes nearly closed as they struggled with the light to make sense of his shape. Then she saw the uniform and the badge, and the broad, smiling face, and she rose swiftly and ran to him. "There, there, little one," cooed the sheriff. "It's over now. It's all over." The girl sobbed openly and uncontrollably as she clasped her arms tightly around his waist, with great tremors of anguish racking her body. He bent down, stroking her hair gently with both hands. "I know," he whispered softly. "I know." His hands moved down from her hair, stroking her face, then moved even further down until they found her neck. They stroked there gently for a moment, and then her eyes told the story. They went efficiently through phases of relief, then confusion, then terror as his fingers began to squeeze away at her throat. She clawed at him then, but not much. Mostly, she just yielded herself up to him. As if even she knew this was the best possible conclusion.

When Parrish came from the shed a bit later he looked blankly at his son, still lying there in the grass. "You clean this shit up," is all he said. Then he walked back alongside the house to his car, and drove back to town.

WE HOPE YOU'VE ENJOYED THIS BONUS READING.

THE SLAVE PLAYERS IS AVAILABLE AT

WWW.BURNHOUSEPUBLISHING.COM